THE RED DAUGHTER

THE RED DAUGHTER

JOHN BURNHAM SCHWARTZ

corsair

CORSAIR

First published in the US in 2019 by Random House
First published in Great Britain in 2019 by Corsair

1 3 5 7 9 10 8 6 4 2

A CIP catalogue record for this book
is available from the British Library.

HB ISBN: 978-1-4721-5508-5
TPB ISBN: 978-1-4721-5509-2

Printed and bound in Great Britain by Clays Ltd, Elcograf S.p.A.

Papers used by Corsair are from well-managed forests
and other responsible sources.

Corsair
An imprint of
Little, Brown Book Group
Carmelite House
50 Victoria Embankment
London EC4Y 0DZ

An Hachette UK Company
www.hachette.co.uk

www.littlebrown.co.uk

FOR MY FATHER

IN MEMORIAM
SVETLANA IOSIFOVNA ALLILUYEVA
1926-2011

Stalin was the father of Russia.
All children adored him.

PART ONE

EDITOR'S FOREWORD

Her face was staring up at me from the front page of *The New York Times*. On the right edge of the grainy black-and-white photograph taken at Kennedy Airport that day forty-four years earlier, I could just make out the crescent-shaped smudge that had been the tip of my elbow, before I'd been digitally amputated from the frame. For years a copy of the original picture, with me still included, had hung on the wall of my law office, signed "To Peter with love." Clients would frequently remark on it, such was her fame in those days.

"She's really the daughter of Joseph Stalin?"

"Yep, she really is."

"Jesus. Can you imagine what that must've been like?"

No, actually. The Great Famine, the Great Purge, the Great Terror . . . Stalin guilty of the murder—it's clear now, if it wasn't fully so at the time—of more than twenty million of his people through mass political executions, Gulag labor camps, enforced starvation, deportations, and other means. Of course, through much of this his daughter, Svetlana, had been just a girl—Daddy's *Little Housekeeper*, as the dictator used to call her with tender affection. Many of her own family members had disappeared with the others.

She'd first defected while on a Kremlin-sponsored trip to India. From there, with covert American assistance, she'd managed to get to Switzerland, where she was forced to wait for months while the United States decided whether we would accept her. In 1967, at the height of the Cold War, Stalin's daughter was seen by many in the CIA and State Department as too radioactive to handle, likely to upset the fragile balance of nuclear forces thought to be keeping the world, if only barely, from self-annihilation.

Meanwhile, one evening in Princeton, New Jersey, George Kennan, the greatest diplomat and Russia analyst of his era, was playing bridge with his neighbor Lucas Wardlow, Senior Partner of the Manhattan law firm Wardlow Jenks & Hayes and, as it happened, my employer and mentor. Which was how I came to be witness when, in the middle of a three no-trump bid, Kennan let Wardlow in on a secret then known to only a handful of people in the world: Svetlana Alliluyeva (she'd taken her mother's family name after her father's death in 1953) was in possession of the only manuscript of her unpublished "memoir." Kennan asked Wardlow, with the State Department's blessing, to look into arranging for possible publication of the book.

First, however, the U.S. government would have to agree to admit the author to our country. That very evening Kennan phoned the Attorney General's office in Washington and requested that a meeting of the various "interested parties," as he called them, be scheduled for the end of the week. Wardlow was to be there. Seeing my chance, I suggested to my boss that having me at the meeting as his assistant could be of practical benefit. To my surprise, he agreed.

As it turned out, on the day of the meeting I was not the only "young" man in the AG's office. A CIA officer named Dick Thompson, a Yale grad about my own age with an affable but obscure manner and a noticeable limp, nodded to me as his superior from Langley launched into a speech about how the Soviets were likely to react if we took in Stalin's daughter and then published her memoir on the eve of the fiftieth anniversary of the October Revolution. "Brezhnev will blow his fucking top. As a matter of fact, Langley's already picking up serious chatter about Russian plans to assassinate Svetlana while she's still on Swiss soil."

"Hold on a second," Kennan broke in impatiently. "Don't tell me we're going to turn away the single most important Soviet defector in our country's history?"

"Not our business," the AG replied. "The United States government cannot officially be seen to be involved in this matter in any way."

"*Officially?*" Kennan repeated, nailing home his point.

There was a knowing pause, an understanding in the room; then the renowned Russia expert shot a glance at Wardlow, who demanded a phone and placed a call. Within the hour a deal had been struck with Harper & Row for world publishing rights to the first memoir by the only daughter of Joseph Stalin for one and a half million U.S. dollars. This was the offer of welcome that would be presented to Svetlana Alliluyeva in return for her promise not to actively engage with her former nation while living in this one. Her father might be officially discredited in the Soviet Union, but never in the history of the world had there been a ghost with such stubborn and malevolent power over his traumatized people. No, she must not needlessly antagonize. Her presence would be enough. Her presence and her voice, captured in a book read and analyzed by millions of Americans and, eventually, by free people everywhere. Besides which, the woman would be rich. If that didn't make her feel American, the men in Washington believed, nothing would.

However, it was not Lucas Wardlow who clandestinely traveled to Switzerland to smuggle the Cold War's most famous defector out of that country and into ours. The eminent attorney was feeling his age; these days he preferred golfing at the Princeton Country Club to the cloak-and-dagger stuff. I, on the other hand, was thirty-four, married and with a young daughter, and—perhaps most relevant—

considerably closer to the subject-in-question's own age of forty-one.

Wardlow phoned me at home during dinner to check that my passport was up to date. I confirmed that it was. "Good," he said, "because you're leaving tomorrow afternoon. Keep your eyes open. You'll be flying home under a different name."

The next day, still as Peter Horvath, I flew to Frankfurt and took a taxi to the rail station, where I boarded a train to Basel. In Basel, I was met by a Swiss Italian gentleman, distinctly courteous, who I was to understand was head of the "Eastern Section of the Swiss Intelligence Facility." Over coffee, he calmly made the observation that the Soviets would rather kill Svetlana on Swiss soil than see her handed over to the Americans; kill me too, was the implication. He then put me on the train to Zurich and waited patiently on the platform, a faint half smile on his very correct face, until he was sure the train had left the station with me still aboard.

In Zurich, a discreet Swiss lawyer picked me up at the station and drove me to a "motel" (I seemed to be the only guest) near the airport. It was almost midnight. He advised me in his clipped German-English to get some sleep as "they" would be coming for me at half past five. With these words of good night he left me and, after locking my flimsy door and securing it with a tipped desk chair (I too had seen *The Third Man* and read *The Spy Who Came In from the Cold*), I collapsed on my bed with my eyes wide open.

Six hours later, wearing a clean shirt but the same suit and tie, I was led by an armed guard into a small windowless room in the departures terminal at Zurich Airport. Seated at a table were yet another Swiss "lawyer" (likely a secret service agent of some kind) and a pretty woman roughly my own age with pink cheeks and a head of thick red hair worn in a short, full style that, while feminine and attractive on her, nonetheless—to my mind, anyway—suggested an upper-echelon Eastern Bloc aesthetic.

"Mr. Staehelin?" Svetlana Alliluyeva said to me in a strong Russian accent, a lively smile on her face.

I stared dumbly at her.

"Our passports," she explained in clear, excellent English. "We are the happy couple?"

"Yes!" I blurted out, suddenly remembering the names on our false documents. "Right. Sorry. I'm Mr. Staehelin. And you must be Mrs. Staehelin?"

By now I was smiling too, unable to help myself. Her Russian-accented English was rich and charming. Her blue, brown-streaked eyes radiated intelligence and an unfiltered vivacity that hit me where I stood. Her figure—in a gray skirt-suit that flattered without trying—was athletic, full-breasted but trim.

"I've come a long way to find you," I heard myself saying.

"Yes," she confirmed, "it is the same for me."

Her smile retreated then, and I could only wonder at the life, and the woman, behind it.

We were the last people to board the plane. At my request, the Swiss stewardess brought us each a vodka martini almost as soon as we took our seats in the first-class cabin.

"Cheers, Mr. Staehelin." Svetlana winked at me, raising her glass, her smile now willfully brave.

"Cheers, Mrs. Staehelin." My own attempt at a wink felt more like a grimace.

Then we clinked glasses like astonished, intimate strangers who have just robbed a bank together and are escaping with the loot in broad daylight. But what sort of loot was this?

Too late to ask the question: we were already in the air.

An hour into the journey, the stewardess murmured in my ear that the pilot would like a word. I followed her to the cockpit—and there was accosted by a grim-faced aeronaut in a crisply pressed uniform who, for a Swiss, appeared apoplectic. No one had warned him of the dangerous, incendiary cargo he was carrying—he'd only just now learned the news from the control tower in New York. The daughter of *Joseph Stalin*? Had he known, he would have refused to fly and faced the professional consequences. But now, obviously, this was no longer possible. We would have to hope that we were not all blown out of the sky by the fucking Soviets. And then on landing—*if* we landed—there would be the press to deal with. But that would no longer be his or his country's problem—no, from then on it would be America's problem. Good day to you, sir.

On my way back to my seat, even more rattled, I ordered second martinis for Mrs. Staehelin and myself. Having some inkling now of the historic madhouse awaiting us at Kennedy (more people to greet her, it would turn out, than were there for the Beatles in '64), I offered to help her write out a simple public statement. But with a firm, confident set to her expression that, like the sadness buried in even her most winning smile, I would come to know better, Svetlana assured me that when the moment arrived she would feel most comfortable speaking her own words.

We finished our second round of drinks. Then she turned to me, hand warm on my arm and tears in her eyes, and confessed that at this moment she was missing her dear brother Yakov terribly. Yakov, captured by the Germans during the war, whose father, the Supreme Commander of the Soviet Republic, had refused to exchange him for a captured Nazi general, leaving him to die in a concentration camp. She never saw him again, the one brother she truly loved.

"You are like him," Svetlana insisted. "You are like my Yakov."

I could only shake my head. Because though I never knew this dead brother of hers and in fact hardly knew her yet, I believe I already understood that it was not her brother I hoped one day to be.

It was three weeks after I'd seen Svetlana's obituary in *The New York Times*—mid-December, 2011, now, the early-darkening air just above freezing—when the UPS man rang my bell.

"Got two boxes for you today, Mr. Horvath—good-size." He checked the return labels before handing them over. "Looks like somebody in Spring Green's wishing you happy holidays."

I stared at him: I had been to Spring Green, Wisconsin, only once in my life, for a wedding in the spring of 1970.

"Thanks, Mario. Happy holidays."

I closed the door. My breath was starting to come shallow and quick. I half-carried, half-dragged the boxes into my living room one at a time, then cut the first open with a pocketknife. My hands were trembling.

A thick layer of bubble wrap obscured the weighty contents of the box. On top of the bubble wrap was a letter.

Dear Mr. Horvath,

Following instructions from my mother's lawyer in Spring Green (a man she contacted through the yellow pages, apparently), I'm sending you all the papers and notebooks that were found in her apartment after her passing last month. In her will—copy attached to this note—you are listed as her literary executor. As you know, my mother and I had a pretty complicated relationship. I doubt there was any other sort of relationship to have with her, frankly. I'm sure you know what I'm talking about.

I've chosen not to read these journals of hers. That might strike you as weird or coldhearted, but I have a son of my own now, with his own name, and I don't want him tainted by association with that monster, the grandfather I never met. I never read her memoir for the same reason. It's not my son's fault who his relatives are. Just as it wasn't my mother's fault.

Whatever you decide to do with this material, I'd rather not know about it. I hope you can understand that this isn't personal—you were always kind to me when I was younger. If by some unfortunate turn of events you end up publishing part or all of these contents, please give any profits to a local arts organization or a charity for the homeless. I don't want the money for myself or my family.

I loved my mother very much. I know you did too, in your way. And she loved you. Even if it was never very easy, ever, for either of us. Because that's how she was.

I think it's safe to say that, except maybe for the nanny who raised her, you and I were the only two people who ever really understood her.

There were times I wanted to pity my mom, but she wouldn't let me. She had such a deep heart, and so many wounds, and this crazy courage that never gave up or let go. She could be fierce. She loved her children—all of us, however it may have looked to the outside world. She survived her life, which under the circumstances is maybe sort of heroic. And she came to know, finally, what real love was. Yes, I believe she did.

Thank you.
Yours sincerely,
Jacob "Yasha" Evans

Inside the same envelope as Jacob "Yasha" Evans's letter was the original copy of the Last Will and Testament of his mother, Lana Evans, formerly known as Svetlana Alliluyeva; formerly known, before that, as Svetlana Stalina.

The document was written in English on one of those generic forms that can be bought at certain stationery or copy stores or downloaded from the Internet for a few dollars, signed by her and witnessed by a notary public in Spring Green in the early autumn of 2011. It left Svetlana's limited possessions and all her "private journals" to her son Jacob "Yasha" Evans. These journals were to be organized and "made into catalog" by her "appointed Literary Executor Peter Horvath, Esquire, of Princeton, New Jersey." It was very like Svetlana, I thought, to consider her appointments firm and binding regardless of whether the appointee had ever been notified of his position.

That was the end of her will; but it was not the end of the document, whose final page, I realized only as I came to it, was a letter, also written in English. I recognized Svetlana's handwriting at once—the way the *P* of my name seemed to lean down over the letters that followed, as if not sure whether to scold or to embrace:

My Dearest Peter,
You will be surprised by all this. But you promised me, remember? On the plane from Zurich. You ordered vodka martinis from the stewardess for us both and I asked what is it and you said it's only the greatest drink in world. All night and into the morning we drank, I was too frightened and excited to sleep, then finally

out the blue window we saw your tiny island with its strange name: Block Island. My first sight of America. You said you had a summer house there. I must come and stay with you and your family. And I thought to myself, Americans, they are all like this? Come to my house, live with my family. Come inside, welcome. So that summer I stayed on Block Island with you. I saw your daughter, Jean, run naked on the rocks. Martha in her tennis skirt. We ate lobster over newspaper. You showed me American fishing. I took my first shower outdoors. You and I, we drank that evening on your porch. I know you remember.

But here is the thing, Peter: my father's cage turned out to be attached to me. It went where I went. Years passed and the bars turned from gold to brass, but never disappeared. I feel them still in my breast now as I write these private words that I have been writing ever since I first came to this country so many years ago—this country that you brought me to with your own hands and heart.

Here they are, Peter. My other words, for what they are worth. I hope you know what to do with them. Since I do not.

Do not regret me, Peter. You I will never regret. I would take that flight again if I could, your hand on my arm, wherever we land.

Your loving
Svetlana

In all, there were twenty-eight identical school-ruled note-books with cardboard covers. Every page of every book filled with her Russian. They sat in my study for several months—unread, obviously, since I have never learned the language.

And then one day I received a reply to an ad I'd placed at the back of Princeton's alumni magazine asking for a native-speaking Russian translator with experience. Vera Dubov is currently Visiting Lecturer in the Department of Slavic Languages and Literatures at Princeton University. She worked tirelessly on this challenging project for the better part of a year, and I am indebted to her for bringing Svetlana's private world to life with the tone, rhythms, and emotion that I recognize as true. Reading my dearest friend translated from her own Russian allowed me to realize for the first time, with a force that still takes me by surprise, that until now I had known her only in her second language, that is in English, which, while accomplished, could never possibly show the whole of her.

Now that woman has been revealed to me. What else can I be but grateful? Yes, grateful and moved.

What you are about to read, then, is a selection of Svetlana's private journals, made by me, from those twenty-eight notebooks that she put in my trust after her death.

I wish to emphasize that all "editorial notes" in this volume are mine alone. If in the end they strike the reader as more intimate and personal in nature than would be expected under such circumstances—giving my own story, as it were, mingled with hers—I make no apologies. I may call myself her editor, but that is not what I was.

There are things I'm trying to understand while there is still time. She might be gone, but I am still here. I still have my feelings. I still want to know—sometimes I think I *do* know—who she really was, and what, in the end, we were together.

PETER HORVATH
Princeton, NJ
April 2015

THE PRIVATE JOURNALS OF SVETLANA ALLILUYEVA

1967

23 April
Locust Valley, New York
3:40 A.M.

My father would have had me killed for what I've done. And then he never would have given me another thought.

People believe that because my mother died how and when she did, and because my father became what he became, that he alone must be the mountain in my life—the immovable object that I can neither climb nor see around.

Why I have made this choice to abandon my two children and my home to wake in this foreign darkness, in this strange country, in a stranger's strange house.

But people are wrong. They will always be wrong. My father is not the mountain.

My father is the shadow on the mountain that keeps me from seeing the mountain.

The mountain is my mother.

Instead of actual memories I'm left only with impressions, stolen from photographs or the odd letter, of a strong dark-haired young woman with a wide oval face, full mouth, and the saddest eyes I have ever seen. When she was angry or disappointed, it could be as if a translucent shutter had slid down over those eyes, a shutter not from outside but from within her; I remember feeling a terrible cold distance where I wished she had been. I remember her voice saying to my brother Vasily and me, *The more time you have, the lazier you are*. I remember her rapping my knuckles raw one day when she discovered that I'd cut up her new tablecloth with a pair of shears. I remember almost never being with her, yet sensing her firm committed presence everywhere I turned, an omnipresent shadow that I could see but not hold. I remember the scent of her French perfume—which my father hated, since it was a luxury, and which she wore anyway, fiercely protective of this one personal indulgence—still lingering on my pillow the mornings after those very rare nights when she would stay with me and stroke my head as I fell asleep.

Nadezhda Alliluyeva met Josef Stalin when he was twenty-five and she was a toddler of two; he was a family friend, so the story went, and saved little Nadya from drowning. She wouldn't see him again until she was sixteen; by then she was at least as devout a Communist as he was, as well as beautiful and fearless. And he was a hero to many. Yes, in those days of Civil War following the Bolshevik victory, when the fate of the Great Revolution was still uncertain, my father was in the throes of establishing himself as Lenin's Man of Steel. He asked Nadya to accompany him to Tsaritsyn (soon to be Stalingrad) as his personal secretary, an offer she accepted without hesitation, since she was probably already in love with him.

Two years later, in the thick of the growing cult of violence of which my father was the unquestioned conductor, they were married.

I was six months old when she first tried to leave him. This was in 1926, and her disillusionment over what he was then becoming must have been profound. She and my nurse packed up five-year-old Vasily and me and piled us all onto a train to Leningrad, where we moved in with my grandparents. We would start new lives, free of his tyranny! Yet several days later, when my father telephoned, beside himself, enraged, beseeching, threatening to come fetch us himself, my mother quickly relented, all the while insisting that we would return by ourselves, without his bloody help, so as to save the cost to the State.

Until I was sixteen, I was led to believe that her sudden death on the night of 8 November 1932, was caused by a ruptured appendix. I was not alone: the entire nation believed this.

Then one day, ten years after the fact, I happened across an article in a British magazine that referred to my mother's death as a suicide. Joseph Stalin's second wife, I read, had *shot herself in the heart* in her bedroom, where she had gone after my father publicly humiliated her at a state dinner. And this had always been known by certain people in my father's inner circle, it was reported, including my dear nurse, Alexandra Andreevna, who had raised me from the moment I was born.

I went straight to my nurse and demanded that she tell me everything she knew about my mother's death. Weeping from shame and grief, Alexandra Andreevna did as I asked. And so I learned not only that the magazine article was true but that my mother had left behind a suicide note for my father in which she called him a monster and a murderer. Those had been her exact words. She had cursed him and declared that she would never forgive him for destroying the soul of the Party and, with it, her hope for a better world for her and her children. Then she had shot herself and left her dead body for him to find.

I am playing outside by myself one morning when my nurse approaches, kisses my forehead, says, *Come, we must put on different clothes now*. And in these different clothes I am driven in a state car to an official building in Moscow, a large hall with a ceiling like a reaper's blade overhead, where many adults, some of them acquaintances and relatives I recognize, stand in hushed black poses.

I am taken by the hand, led through ghoulish, whispering silhouettes to a long black box the length and width of a grown-up person. The box has a carved lid on hinges, propped open. I see blood-red silk, unfamiliar clothing, and my mother's ghost-white face—

I step back and begin to scream.

Returning with my nurse to Zubalovo (our dacha in Usovo, less than thirty kilometers outside Moscow, which all my life had been the happiest of places), I discovered that my father had ordered the tree house that Mother designed for Vasily and me in the woods by the playground dismantled. The playground itself was gone too, nothing left but a patch of sand on the ground to suggest it ever existed.

Within weeks men in Party work clothes were completely rebuilding parts of the house, painting and reconfiguring, one by one stripping the rooms she'd inhabited of their memories. It was all *state property* now, maintained at government expense; and the people who worked in our households were all employees of the secret police.

The systematic process of my mother's erasure had begun.

It was the same in Moscow, where my father exchanged our former apartment for a new one on the first floor of the Senate building in the Kremlin. Not a true residence but a cold formal office structure posing as a dwelling for warm-blooded humans, the walls so thick that small voices attempting to reach from one room to the next often died before arriving. Other than a single large photograph of my mother in the dining room, the only mementos of her that remained were relegated to my bedroom. I spent much of my time reading and drawing in the company of these silent friends, while my nurse did her sewing in her room next door. My schoolwork I did at the dining table under the lonely gaze of the woman whose living face was already becoming, to my confused recollection, a kind of shade of itself.

Beneath that same heartbroken stare my father and his regular group of wine-swilling underlings dined most evenings, the meals always beginning at six or seven and lasting till midnight. At which point without fail the *vozhd* was driven—in one of three cars whose routes changed nightly for security reasons—to the new dacha he was having built, just for himself, in Kuntsevo, twenty minutes away.

But merely a new residence could never be enough for a man seeking to dig the deepest possible moat between himself and the past. What was required was a house cleansed of all personal history. To this end he would have Kuntsevo rebuilt every summer for the rest of his life, keeping only one constant: the single large room on the ground level where he lived and worked. The dining table heaped with books, newspapers, documents was long enough to fit the entire Politburo, with a small clearing at one end for eating when alone. The large sofa doubled as his bed, with telephones on either side. The china cabinet was always stuffed with his various medications, which he insisted on picking out himself every morning and evening, because there was no doctor in all of Russia he believed he could trust . . .

This was the room in which—perhaps he already knew—one day he would die.

My father lived apart from us. That was his choice. By now in his fifties, his working hours increasingly strange and relentless. He could be remote, issuing detailed written instructions to his faithful bodyguard, Vlasik, on how not to spoil me.

But he was not invisible. Sundays when the weather was good he would still come to Zubalovo. On his shoulders he would carry me off the walking paths, away from the shrouded yes-men who followed everywhere, and into the forest of tall ghostly birch trees that he preferred to most human company. Hidden there like two castaways, we would sit on the leaves and enjoy a picnic lunch together.

At such times I noticed a change in him: his shoulders relaxed; his smile came more freely. Of course, I had known him to laugh once in a while when dining with his coterie of ministers—he was not without a sense of humor of his own kind, I suppose. But even as a little girl I would notice a jagged edge buried just beneath the surface of his public laughter, and how the sound of it put all those men in his presence on edge too. Alone with me, however, he seemed free of any need to prove or challenge, and consequently our infrequent visits together in those early years after my mother's death always seemed to pass more quickly than I wanted.

He still called me his *Housekeeper* then.

And how is my Housekeeper? Is Housekeeper getting enough sleep and minding her nurse? Housekeeper, would you agree to pass your poor papa another piece of that good brown bread? Your poor tired papa is very hungry today, practically starving, don't you see? Because he doesn't have his little Housekeeper to take care of him nearly enough.

Then he might be gone again for long stretches, sometimes whole summers, during which we communicated only by letter:

Hello, Little Sparrow Hostess!
I'm sending you pomegranates, tangerines, and some candied fruit. Eat and enjoy them! I report to you, Comrade Hostess, that I was in Tiflis for one day. I was at my mother's and I gave her regards from you. She gives you a big kiss. Well, that's all right now. I give you a kiss.
From Svetanka-Sparrow-Hostess's wretched Secretary, the poor peasant J. Stalin.

Hello, my dear Papochka,
How do you live and how is your health? I arrived well except that my nanny got really sick on the road. But everything is well now. Papochka, don't miss me but get some rest and I will try to study excellently for your happiness.
Your Svetanka

He created an imaginary friend for me named Lyolka. Or at least he insisted that she was my friend. Why wouldn't she be? Lyolka was perfect in every way. She was always doing the most extraordinary things—things, my father advised, that I would do well to imitate.

Once he added a little drawing of my doppelgänger, saying it was amazing how alike we were. The girl in the drawing had braids and a snub nose and a large smiling mouth and freckles. She looked nothing like me.

Lyolka became my secret enemy.

To My Hostess Svetanka:
You don't write to your little papa. I think you've forgotten him.
How is your health? You're not sick, are you? What are you up
to? Have you seen Lyolka? How are your dolls? I thought I'd be
getting an order from you soon, but no. Too bad. You're hurting
your little papa's feelings. Never mind. I kiss you. I am waiting to
hear from you.
Little Papa

It is summer. Another letter: an invitation, finally, to join him in Sochi for a couple of weeks. Will Lyolka be there?

Down by the barnacled rocks where the Black Sea never stops pounding, Papa plucks a sea urchin out of a tidal pool and turns it over to show me its gummy, feminine mouth. He says to be careful of the sharp spines but not to fear them. *Remember, Little Sparrow,* he instructs me, *there is always a part of every creature that Nature fails to protect.* To show what he means, hardly moving his arm, he grinds his thumb into the soft exposed flesh with such pressure that it breaches the glistening buttery muscle and, with a sickening crack, splits the spined shell on the other side.

Papa, you're bleeding! I cry out.

He drops the ruined creature on the rocks, crushing and smearing it under his boot. Sucking blood from his fingers, he turns and walks away, knowing I will follow.

Perched like a squat little doll on the lap of Lavrentiy Beria, newly elected member of the Central Committee of the Communist Party of the Soviet Union and known to be the *vozhd*'s most trusted subordinate, I watch my father swallow an oyster with one deft scoop of his strong blunt hand. How like a shark he feeds himself carelessly, never tasting the food, his attention darkly riveted by papers and charts spread over the round stone table on the terrace outside his summer dacha. Of course, it doesn't occur to me that these must be food production numbers: thousands, millions, starving to death in the countryside, though no one dares speak or write of it.

My father's face is a fist. Without looking, he tosses the empty shell back on the ice-covered tray.

And now, from behind me, Beria's hand emerges: the lithe manicured fingers of a knife artist. His arm brushes my ribs, then retracts holding a plump, glistening oyster on its shell—someone's stolen gray tongue. I listen to it being slurped down inches from my ear, smelling the seawater in which it lived, mixed now with the sickening taint of Beria's breath. The sunlight reflecting off his pince-nez. The cunning smack of his lips practically inside my head.

A starving man is no threat, he observes to the *vozhd*, the oysters already decomposing in their stomachs. And my father in his simple peasant tunic doesn't bother to contradict him, says nothing. Closed for business. With a twitch of nervous satisfaction, Beria lights a cigarette.

I am being taught to swim by a military instructor. My father observing me from the rocky beach, Beria a human tuning fork beside him. Out in the water the instructor's strong hands let me go: I begin to sink, mouth and throat filling with liquid salt, which is the drowning taste—I know this even then—of the black sea of my mother's absence.

Swim, Housekeeper, swim! That's an order! My father walks away, not waiting to see whether or not I will obey him and live. It's half-amusing to him, this idea of his giving me, his bossy little Housekeeper, an order. Beria, meanwhile, round lenses of his pince-nez silvered like coins in the sunlight, never cracks a smile. He lingers behind a few moments, hoping to see my arms flail and my legs thrash and my head go under once more. But I refuse to give him that pleasure. I will swim, or I will die.

Bravo, calls the snake in his snake's voice when I finally crawl and gasp my way onto the shore.

He makes sure to say it loud enough for the *vozhd* to hear. Unfortunately for him, no one is listening.

As the *vozhd*'s only daughter and Little Hostess, she who (at that time, anyway, and aided by that doll-master of perfection Lyolka) could do no wrong, I was to a large extent removed from direct experience of my father's increasingly vindictive temper. My brothers, however, were not so fortunate; you might say that our father's nose for human frailty was not mere sport, but a form of insatiable hunger. It could hardly be coincidence that Vasily began drinking heavily at the age of thirteen; or that by the age of twenty, in 1941, good-looking, arrogant, thin-skinned, and hysterically insecure, he had become both a raging alcoholic and a colonel in the Red Air Force. I tried never to be alone with him.

But it was Yakov, my Georgian half brother, nineteen years older, gentle and shy, from the first marriage to Kato Svanidze (a dark beauty who died of typhus six months after giving birth), who paid the steepest price. My father would not agree to even meet his firstborn until Yakov was sixteen—and then only because my mother threatened to leave him if he did not exhibit, at minimum, this basic sense of decency. So they brought him into their sphere, if not exactly their home. My mother grew to love her stepson, I believe, and worried about him. But my father would not relent. He bullied the young man with the quiet nature who looked, everyone said, so much like his mother; no opportunity was missed to remark on some perceived failing, some weakness or slowness. When Yakov's first daughter died in infancy, our father's silence rang like a personal indictment. And sometime afterward, when Yakov's despair led him to attempt suicide with one of his father's pistols, only to flinch at the last moment so that the bullet missed its intended target, that great deep heart, and passed straight through to his other side, leaving him badly wounded but still alive, my father's contempt knew no bounds. *Weakling!* he snarled. *Look at you! You can't even shoot like a man!*

But eventually Yakov did learn how to shoot, oh yes: he became a soldier. And when war with Germany was declared, he chose to prove himself by volunteering for the front the very next day. Our father's parting message to him was to publicly declare that his son was to be shown no special treatment of any kind—not on the battlefield or anywhere else.

A month later, Yakov and his unit were captured by the Germans. During the next four years, the enemy made numerous attempts to engage the Supreme Commander of the Soviet Republic in a prisoner-of-war exchange for his son, but Josef Stalin refused every offer.

Reports on the death of Yakov Iosifovich Dzhugashvili (our father's birth surname, before he began to call himself Stalin) are now, as they were then, impossible to verify. Some vow that he was shot by German camp guards as he attempted to escape from the concentration camp in which he'd spent the last four years. Others swear that one frigid, endless night, mustering whatever reserves of strength he had left, he threw himself against the electrified razor wire surrounding the camp and, hanging there as if crucified, was electrocuted to death before his captors' bullets could touch him.

The only thing that is absolutely certain is that he never returned.

I once overheard my aunt Anna, my mother's sister, saying to my uncle Stanislav, through a closed door that I should never have been anywhere near, *What about exile?*

And he replied, *We don't have exile. We just disappear.*

Stanislav was executed in 1940. Eight years later, Anna was arrested. The only thing my father mistrusted more than strangers was family.

The *vozhd's* death, in 1953, finally liberated my aunt, but she was never the same. More and more over the years, she found it threatening to leave her little apartment. Every day she sat in the same chair in the same room and said the same things, her thoughts magnetically sealed inside her imprisonment, which had grown more real to her than her life. It was as if she too had never returned.

But I can't know any of this yet. It is August 1942, I am sixteen, and my head is filled with my own concerns.

Word comes: I am summoned to dinner at Kuntsevo, the rarest of invitations. Why this evening in particular? I am not told. My nurse, Alexandra Andreevna, insists I wear the longer skirt, the one that falls well below my knee. I am still a schoolgirl, reading all the time, half in love with Mayakovsky and Dostoyevsky and Chekhov. Yet when the summons from my father comes, without so much as a whiff of irony, I put on the longer dress and go.

I enter the room and there is a bald man, round and full-fleshed, wearing formal clothes and smoking a preposterously large cigar, which he holds between the thick second and third fingers of his right hand. The room pungent with his cultured, foreign smoke. And because of the nature of that smoke, though I am still ignorant of the identity of the man producing it, I become aware that for the first time my father has invited me to witness a meeting of the highest diplomatic importance.

Prime Minister, my father announces in his gruff voice nonetheless warmed by a certain strategic pride in showing off his domestic qualities for his visitor, *this is my only daughter, Svetlana, the youngest and bossiest of my children. Quite bright and opinionated she is. Always telling me what to do and not do with myself. And most of the time I listen—isn't that so, Svetlana? Now give greetings to Mr. Winston Churchill, Prime Minister of our ally Great Britain.*

Mr. Winston Churchill smiles at my father, his manner at once perfectly jolly and perfectly grim. *Allow me to say, Mr. Stalin, that you are a most fortunate man to have such a charming, sharp-minded adviser at your constant disposal. And redheaded. My dear*—he turns to me, gesturing with the glowing eye-tip of his cigar about his hairless round skull—*I was a redhead too, you know. But look what the war has done to me.*

Moments later, I am ushered out of the room.

It is years hence, of course, that I come to understand the reason for Churchill's unexpected visit to Kuntsevo that night, and why my father might have wanted to present me to him. The

Prime Minister had come in person to discuss strategy, but really to deliver the unwelcome news that the Allies were delaying still further any attempt to establish a second front in the war in Western Europe—meaning there would be no immediate relief for the USSR in our bloody struggle against Hitler in the Eastern campaign, which was on the verge of annihilating our country. Even now, I confess I am rather moved by the thought that my father could have been desperate enough to imagine that trotting out his redheaded *Housekeeper* (who in truth was no longer that girl) before Democracy's great aristocratic orator might have been enough to tilt history's compass in his favor. In any event, I was quickly dismissed from the room, and then from Kuntsevo altogether, and many more thousands, indeed millions, of human beings would go on to lose their lives in the carnage presided the world over by men who smoked cigars.

Three months later, I again find myself at Kuntsevo, this time at a party thrown by Vasily. The evening has grown late. Wearing my first real dressmaker's dress, low-heeled shoes, a garnet brooch of my mother's, I am being guided in the fox-trot by Alexsei Kapler, a handsome and well-known Jewish filmmaker more than twice my age, with a reputation for enjoying the company of beautiful women wherever he goes.

He is just back from filming guerrilla fighters in Belorussia, he tells me. He adds that he keeps an unheated room in the Moscow Savoy, where he greets friends and colleagues with black-market coffee. Do I like coffee? In a few days, he will be leaving for Stalingrad. Who can say how long he will be gone?

My close friends call me Lyusia, he says.

Last record! someone shouts down the room—it is Vasily, drunk as an entire brigade. (Where is my father? On this night at least, I have no memory of him.) I can feel Lyusia's warm hand in the small of my back, our feet somehow moving in unison.

Tell me, he murmurs in my ear, his troubled, knowing eyes on mine. *Why do you look so unhappy?*

And because I am already a little in love with him, and because no one else has thought to ask, I answer his question.

Tonight, I tell him, the eighth of November, is the tenth anniversary of my mother's death.

That night I hardly sleep for thinking about him. Waking me in the morning, my nurse calls me silly, but she is tender as she makes me breakfast; for with her animal-hearted love she understands that something important has happened to me, and that suffering and grief are the only possible end to it.

There has been no promise, of course, no plans made. To attempt such a thing with the *vozhd*'s daughter would be an act of unthinkable recklessness.

Yet next afternoon, as I emerge through the gates of my school into the November gloom, he is the first person I see, hunched in a doorway, smoke from his ration cigarette blurring the sharp lines of his face. Waiting for me. His slow smile causes my breath to freeze in my throat.

Then he notices Klimov, my official shadow, a few meters behind me, and his smile deserts him. A stocky, middle-aged fellow with a round, pushed-in face, Klimov regards me with an attitude of resolute apology. But he will not be deterred. His life depends on this, I have no doubt. Several times a day I catch him writing down his observations of my actions, acquaintances, conversations in a small leather notebook he keeps in his breast pocket.

Lyusia strides up and offers him a cigarette. Klimov appears momentarily disarmed—there is nothing about this sort of scenario in his field manual. But when the Jewish filmmaker flourishes his steel lighter, the KGB flunky sticks the cigarette between his lips, bends over the flame.

Klimov trails us to Gnezdnikovsky Street, where for six hours he waits outside the private screening room of the Ministry of Cinematography, while I am shown *Queen Christina* with Greta Garbo; then *Young Mr. Lincoln* with Henry Fonda; and finally, best of all, Walt Disney's *Snow White and the Seven Dwarfs*.

I still do not know how Lyusia got hold of those films, or how on this day he is privileged to use the theater, but it doesn't matter. There is nowhere else we can go. For these few blissful hours we are able to sit together in the darkness, alone. Ours the only eyes in the room, the only ears. At the start of the second reel, he takes my hand. I lean my head against his shoulder. His heavy tweed suit, wool cardigan sweater, his thick black hair—everything he wears or touches smells of smoke. By the end of the day, I smell of it too, it has infused me. His smoke. Not the smoke of war, incinerated villages, rationed cigarettes. But the smoke of burned love letters, shared secrets. The smoke of promise.

Klimov smells it too. I see him sniffing like a confused dog as we emerge from the theater. But he cannot identify what Lyusia and I are now, has not recorded us with his own eyes, has no Party-approved definition of us to put in his notebook for the *vozhd*. And so he can do nothing but stand there looking fidgety and downtrodden as my lover and I bid each other a polite good night on Gnezdnikovsky Street. Snow has begun to fall, large flakes sifting down through vessels of dim yellow light formed by the streetlamps, endlessly filling their emptiness.

Poor Klimov! He has not yet grasped the greatest truth about the *vozhd*, which is that smoke is the thing he fears most. The smoke of fires not his own.

And now it's March the third, 1943. Just another morning—or so I believe, rushing around the Kremlin apartment where I live with my nurse, late for school, searching for a misplaced sweater. I enter the dining room . . . and there to my surprise (he is always at Kuntsevo at this hour) stands my father. He turns on me, his face inflamed by months of pent-up rage but his voice like a cold steel blade:

You think your boyfriend wants you because you're pretty? Are you fucking joking? He's got twenty other whores besides you, this I know for a fact.

Only now do I notice the sea of confetti spilled over the dining table and the floor around my father's boots. And realize, as in a nightmare, that he has found and torn to shreds every last letter and photograph that Lyusia ever gave me.

Papa, where did you find those? What have you done?

Think you have secrets from me? he bellows, making the room quake. *From me? Are you out of your fucking mind? Do you know who I am?*

I practically spit at him. *No. But now I know what you are.*

With one quick strike of his powerful arm, he slaps me across the face.

Your boyfriend's not even Russian! You had to go and find yourself a fucking Jew to make yourself feel important. Well, there's nothing left of him. You'll never see him again—yes, I've had him arrested. Now get out of my sight before I tell them to take you too.

For many months afterward, I was banned from Kuntsevo and my father's inner circle for what he called depravity. And then, for unexplained reasons, I was reinstated into his life, though never fully: never again would my father and I be *Housekeeper* and *Secretary* to each other.

During the next ten years I was married to two men—one a Jew, one not, in the end it made no real difference to him—and with them had my two children, Josef and Katya. I can report that for the rest of his life my father showed no interest whatever in his grandchildren, and only intermittent curiosity about his daughter.

Yes, the rest of his life:

On March the second, 1953, I am at the academy as usual, pursuing my advanced studies, when I am called out of French class to find a gray-faced man I have seen before in my father's company.

Malenkov wants you to come to Blizhny, he says to me.

Surprised and unsettled—Blizhny is the code for Kuntsevo, and the only person who has ever requested my presence at the dacha is my father himself—I say nothing. The man turns on his heels, sure that I will follow him to the car outside.

The short ride through the Moscow suburb passes in total silence. Of course, it occurs to me that my father is dead. Why else would this be happening? And yet my thoughts during the silent trip are tinged with banal recriminations. It has been a long time since I've seen him. He is an iceberg glimpsed from a distant ship, perhaps a mirage. From the usual sources I know that on the eve of my birthday the previous week he was at the Bolshoi seeing *Swan Lake*, though he did not think to ask me to join him. My last visit to Kuntsevo was many months earlier, when I could not help noticing the large color photographs of children on the walls of every room—not pictures of Josef or Katya or his other grandchildren, but enlarged images of *vital young comrades of the Motherland*, as he proudly referred to them. Who were these young heroes? I asked. Had he ever met any of them? Some boy expertly skiing, another sitting handsomely, *bravely*, in a blooming cherry tree, and so on. But he had not met any of those young comrades. No, he had no idea who any of them were.

We pass through the gates of Kuntsevo. Khruschev and Bulganin, both in tears, are waiting outside to intercept me the moment I step from the car. Each takes one of my elbows, ushering me inside the house, murmuring only that Beria and Malenkov will tell me everything I need to know.

The scene inside, however, in the place my father always kept so controlled, is a study in human panic. There are no familiar faces. I am led through the front hall and down the corridor, through a shifting maze of obscure medical personnel (his longtime personal doctor is in prison) and weeping apparatchiks, to my father's quarters. His once-spacious room so packed with people that I can't see to the back, where a still denser knot of human obsequiousness—I can hear Beria's constipated voice above the rest—has gathered around the sofa where he always slept. Near this cultish scrum looms a large machine with oxygen tanks, which must be an artificial respirator, though it's obvious that none of the men tentatively pawing at its tubes and switches has the slightest idea how to make it, or my father, breathe.

It is then that I see Beria, his entire body vibrating with the kind of rage only terror can bring, berating a professor from the medical academy.

You call yourself a doctor! You idiot! Now get over there and do something!

The singled-out victim steps forward with utmost reluctance—one almost pities him, forced to walk the fatal gangplank leading to the *vozhd*, which he has no doubt spent his entire professional life desperately trying to avoid—and I follow in his wake, the crowd briefly parting around us. Passing Beria, I note his round lenses streaked with the sweat that drips from him like madness. His drawn-out half bow in my direction is cynical in the extreme.

A body lies prone on the sofa. My father. Eyes open—but staring, dulled, nothing like the eyes I remember. His gaze a cruel illusion, the medical professor assures me, meaning to be kind, I suppose: the hemorrhage that erupted in my father's brain in the middle of the night has left him in a profound state of unconsciousness. It is clear to me already that none of them knows how to wake him, and even if they did, are too terrified of failure to succeed.

As I stand watching, an injection is given into his limp arm. Then leeches are applied to his neck and the back of his head. It is medieval even by Soviet standards, and I turn away. *Forgive me*, sighs the medical professor under his breath—to me possibly, or to the *vozhd* himself, unlikely though he is to hear, or perhaps to the *vozhd*'s son Vasily, who at this moment comes storming into the room like a vengeful prince from the wrong fairy tale, shoving men out of his path and shouting, *You've killed him! You'll pay for this! All of you! Poisoned him! I'll see to it myself!* Just a few seconds, too drunk to recognize me or his own truncated future—or perhaps this is exactly what he recognizes—and then, as if struck by lightning, he turns on his heels and bolts from the room.

Over the next three days, while Josef Stalin, trapped in that unwaking body, suffocates and withers, my perpetually drunk brother will return and replay his histrionics twice more, each time looking no one in the eye, each time running from the room as fast as his legs will carry him.

Meanwhile, I sit down. And take my father's lifeless hand. And wait.

With the exception of my brother's hysterical apparitions, I will be the only member of our family, distinct among the Berias and Malenkovs and the entire unimaginable apparatus of state power now witnessing its own demolishment in the dying body of a single man, to sit vigil over my father to the end. The rest of our people are either in prison or exiled from Kuntsevo by my father's own decree. When I want company, which occasionally I do, I venture to the kitchen and sit quietly among the servants.

And Beria? He is a spider, spinning his web around the *vozhd's* body while the blood is still warm. He wants to wrap up something that never existed and hold it for himself alone. He thought he understood its nature, but he was wrong: they will kill him anyway.

By the third day, my father's lips, cheeks, throat, the tips of his fingers and toes have turned a necrotic black, as his lungs fill with fluid and slowly, ceaselessly his own biological system strangles the life from him. He is rotting from the inside. I refuse to leave my place beside him. It is strange and awful how, now that it is too late, compassion for him riddles my perception. In every one of his struggling breaths I imagine a fatherly tenderness from a lost childhood which contradicts all that has transpired between us since. The more ravaged his face grows, the more beautiful I find it.

And then, as the death rattle grows imminent, just when it seems the final exhalation of his power has gone forever, something happens that I will never be able to unremember. His eyes, closed these last hours, open, his head turns to the side, and he looks out over the room, over every single face, his anger dissolving into a small child's lonely fear of the dark—when suddenly he raises his hand and jabs a blackened finger at us all, one last wordless curse over those who would watch him die.

Within weeks of the *vozhd's* death, those multitudes who somehow had managed to survive the Gulag and the prisons began returning to the strange ruins of their existence. Some of them were walking ghosts, but not all.

It's been said that Saint George's Hall is painted with more gold than exists in certain countries. Perhaps. All I know is that the light that evening in 1953 at the Congress of Soviet Writers was radiant in a way I can't recall seeing anywhere else before or since. As if the sun had entered the night, and the night had entered the hall. I had arrived only a few minutes before, had just excused myself from a conversation with a former professor of mine, when, walking past a group of garrulous, good-looking filmmakers—garrulousness, or the Soviet version of it, was then only just coming back, at least among writers and artists—I noticed the cluster of male bodies shift ever so slightly, revealing a face whose every line (deeper now, but topographically exact) was known to me.

Alexsei Kapler saw me too—I'm certain he did—and for a moment my insides shuddered at the prospect that he was about to ignore me. Instead, he stepped away from his coterie, walked directly over to where I stood, and, without a word of greeting, took my hand. Then he laughed. Heads all around turning to observe this sudden, unforeseen meeting: my hand in his, my face looking up into his, after all that had happened and not happened between us.

We leave Saint George's Hall together, then the Kremlin, walking arm in arm to the little café on the far side of Sokolniki Park. The maître d' with the sallow face and silver walrus mustaches (how in the name of Saint Peter did he manage to survive this long?) seats us at the precise table we occupied eleven years earlier. I know Lyusia is thinking the same thing because he murmurs, *Remember old Klimov?* and laughs again. It is his way, his remarkable ability, or agility, to laugh in the face of whatever is thrown at him. I remark as much, but he shakes his head. A silence follows, horrible to me, broken only by the waiter bringing vodka. This fellow wears a broken watch chain—just filigreed links dangling pointlessly from his vest pocket. I drink my vodka and confess to my former lover what is, now that I am with him again, my greatest fear.

I am afraid, Lyusia, that you hold me responsible for what . . . was done to you. I hope you understand that the only reason I never tried to write was that I assumed it would make your situation worse.

This time he does not laugh. He looks at me a long time. Rather than absolve me, he removes a hand-rolled cigarette from a dented tin case—a memento, obviously—and lights it. He offers it to me first, but I decline. He inhales deeply, the smoke entering and stirring him, darkening his eyes. The smoke alone—his scent, the scent of his hair and clothes—makes me nearly insane with longing.

Do you know what happened to me, Svetlana?

I shake my head.

They took me off the street. March the second. I was on my way into a film meeting. The car was a Packard—black, too clean—and sitting up front was none other than General Vlasik. You remember him: chief of your father's personal security. Never far away, even in one's sleep. When I saw him was when I began to have an inkling of what they were going to do to me. And then at Lubyanka, what an honor to have Deputy Minister Kabulov himself read out my arrest: "By Article Fifty-eight of our law . . ." The man was a terrible actor. Can you believe they accused me of being a British spy? Among many other made-up charges. Of course, the real reason was never spoken. I had crossed a personal line, I don't deny it. And the fact that I'm a Jew . . . and your father . . . Well. I was allowed no possessions, no communications with my wife. Do you know how it is to make a film, Svetlana? On set, I mean. The people, actors, actresses, production designers. The community. The human community of it all. Where silence exists only in relation to the talk. In Lubyanka, you see, they kept me in isolation for a year. Nothing but silence. And to think that now I have outlived Vlasik, and Kabulov too. Well, as they say, life is just one long, very interesting movie, no?

He laughs, more quietly than before, and lights another cigarette.

After a year, without explanation he was put on a Black Crow prison truck and sent with other *deviationists, Trotskyites, and terrorists* to Vorkuta, one of the most brutal Gulags in the coal-mining area of Siberia. But Lyusia was not everyone; he was famous and charming, and lucky too, and he was named the camp's official photographer. As a *zazonniki*, he was allowed to live and work outside the prison zone, where he joined a prisoners' collective theater. One of the actresses he met there became his lover.

His sentence was five years. Upon his release, he was told he could travel anywhere he wanted except Moscow. His parents were in Kiev, so that's where he decided to go. But first he stopped in Moscow to visit the woman who was still his wife. Though he had never been literally faithful to her, he loved her, and his love and his hubris in the face of danger were inextricably bound, they were what made him who he was. Any woman who'd ever loved him knew this. My father, who could smell weakness at the very point where it began to corrode iron, also knew this. Two days later, his plainclothes security men pulled Kapler off the train before it could leave Moscow station for Kiev.

Our waiter brings more vodka. Lyusia lights a third cigarette.

Following his second arrest, he tells me, he was sent directly to Inta, another Gulag in Siberian coal-mining territory. This time he had less luck, none, and only one thing allowed him to survive with his mind intact. The actress who'd been his lover in Vorkuta would come to see him, bringing food and tenderness. There was nothing else. (By then, his first wife had divorced him.) Another five years passed in this way. Then the *vozhd* died and Lyusia's case was reviewed, by whom he never knew. One day he was summoned and told he'd been rehabilitated and could go home. A telephone was handed to him. *One call.* For the first time in ten years, he began to weep.

He returned to Moscow and married the actress who'd been so devoted to him, and they moved into the city flat which their marriage now entitled them to.

I'm going to Crimea on a photo assignment, he tells me now. *My wife is staying behind. Why don't you come?*

The café will close soon. Our waiter with the broken watch chain leans against an unoccupied banquette, watching us out of the corner of his eye: he will have stories to tell, this one, oh yes. But Lyusia doesn't give a damn. He has lived nine lives to my one. He is made of smoke and mirrors and more smoke. He opens his cigarette case and, finding it empty, gives a faint smile of unsurprise.

So you'll come?

I have Josef with me. My son.

How old is he?

Nine.

Bring him. He will enjoy the sea.

Where would we stay?

With me, of course.

All right, Lyusia.

There is just one thing you need to understand.

What is it?

Whatever we have, whatever we do, I will never leave my wife.

I went on that trip, and one or two others. But Lyusia was as good as his word and remained married to his wife, the actress.

One winter night, I found myself in the bitter snow-dripping cold outside the theater where she was appearing in a play, I can't remember what play it was, waiting for her to come out. There were only two of us there by the stage door: a few feet away from me stood a man in a trooper hat and faded military parka smoking a state cigarette beneath a lamp and a poster that said ANSWER THE CALL OF THE COMMUNIST PARTY. Was he there to spy on me? It crossed my mind. Or perhaps waiting for a different actress? Clouds of smoke rose from his face and mingled with the falling snow. After ten minutes of this, I could no longer feel my toes. Then the door opened and she emerged, bundled in her coat, her theatrical face under her *shapka* wiped clean of makeup as only a tired professional would do. She stopped when she recognized me, then turned her face away to show that she could not stand the sight of me.

You may choose not to look at me, I said. *But I have loved Lyusia since I was sixteen years old.*

Slowly the actress turned her head until our eyes met. Her gaze that was trained to penetrate hearts at the very back of the theater; up close, she possessed a force I was not prepared for.

Did your husbands know?

I'm trying to make you understand.

I understand I never saw you at Vorkuta. Or at Inta. Because you were never there, were you? You never visited him. Never wrote him. Not once in ten long years. Tucked away in your perfect complacency. Nice and protected. Celebrated, even. So tell me, Princess: Who are you now that your daddy's just a fucking ghost? You're nobody and nothing. Isn't that right? You pathetic, poisoned bitch. You can't touch what Lyusia and I have, and you know it. Don't come near either of us ever again.

She walked away then—made her exit through falling snow. As I said, she was a professional. And of course she was right.

A minute passed, possibly more. I stood there unable to move, as if my feet were literally frozen to the ground.

Then a noise: the man under the Party sign, crushing the last centimeter of cigarette beneath his boot.

He raised his head and looked me square in the face. My shame between us.

You should go home, he said.

I returned to my life: Josef, Katya, my nurse, the four of us living together in our simple apartment on the Embankment. With my ability in English and my degrees, I was able to teach and translate. I took my mother's name. It was Khrushchev's country now: my father's image began to disappear from the walls, if not the memories, of our people.

In 1962, my brother Vasily, after being released from prison, where over the previous years his mania and chronic inebriation had landed him repeatedly, died of heart failure. I wanted to mourn him, or at least to pity him, so cruelly distorted had he been by our father, but at this I cannot honestly say I ever succeeded.

In truth, however, in those grim days of drifting, it was not the state of my late brother's orphaned soul that concerned me most, but my own.

One evening, under cover of darkness, I rode a bus out to the Moscow suburbs, to a little church next to the Donskoy Cathedral called Deposition of the Shroud. Father Nikolai Alexandrovich was waiting for me there.

In the USSR, of course, then as now, to convert to Christianity was an offense punishable by prison for all involved. And so on the night of my secret baptism Father Nikolai never recorded my name in the church registry. I can only assume that he took this risk because of who he knew I was. Yet he assured me—I hear his voice as I write this—Father Nikolai did, oh, he promised, that God loved me, even if I was the daughter of Josef Stalin.

———

Already in my thirties, I did not expect to fall in love again. But one day in the hallway of a state hospital, of all places, to which I'd been admitted for an emergency appendectomy, I met an Indian man nearly twice my age. Brajesh Singh was a Communist intellectual who had come to the Soviet Union to study our political system firsthand. Though not young or especially handsome or in good health—his heart and lungs were failing—Brajesh was a thoughtful, kind man who radiated an Eastern respect for all he encountered. We spent the long days of our convalescence together, discussing literature and old movies and the spiritual aspects of life (in this department, as in so many others, he would always be far wiser than I), and when the time came for my release, I realized that I did not want to part from him. I told him so, and we agreed that when he was well enough to leave the hospital he would move in with my family and me.

As it turned out, Brajesh would never be well enough again; he required an oxygen mask to breathe at night. But he moved in with us anyway, and they were happy months for our little family. In his very being, Brajesh brought a dignity and patience to our existence that I was incapable of producing on my own.

I had no idea how First Deputy Premier Kosygin got wind of our domestic arrangement, but one day I was summoned to the Kremlin. Kosygin's office I knew well enough, because it had been my father's; with that familiar portrait hanging there (one of the few places where one could reliably find his image still publicly displayed), our meeting had an ironic quality that was not lost on either the First Deputy Premier or myself. He immediately came to the point, which was to inform me that while the Party might tolerate my living with this *Indian*, as he put it, I must be aware that under no circumstance would I be allowed to marry him.

He is dying, I said.

Kosygin shrugged; of course he knew. *The law is the law.*

He has asked me to take his ashes back to his family in India when he dies. I've promised him I will.

We have your passport, Kosygin pointed out.

But the State is the State and its contradictions are its own. A few months later, after Brajesh had taken his last breath in our bed and his ashes had been returned to me in a small plastic container, there came a knock on the door of my apartment. It was Kosygin's special courier, hand-delivering my passport so that I might personally return the *distinguished foreigner*'s remains to his family in India—and thus remove his foreign presence, once and for all, from the Soviet Union.

One afternoon shortly before my departure—it would be my first trip outside the USSR, two weeks carefully stage-managed by the Kremlin—I was emerging from the GUM department store with my arms full of gifts for Brajesh's family when I encountered Lyusia, whom I had not seen in over a decade.

We stared at each other in shocked, wary silence.

You're looking well, he remarked, finally.

And you.

It was true. Like a beautifully carved, much handled pipe of burled wood, he had grown only more burnished and interesting with age.

My husband . . . I said.

I had no idea what led me to begin this embarrassing sentence, but once begun it was too late to stop.

Well, we were not allowed to marry. In any event, he died from an illness not long ago.

I'm sorry.

And you? Are you still married?

A nod, his expression fatalistic, raising his hands as though they belonged to someone else and so could not be judged any fault of his own.

What can I say? You know me.

Yes, I knew him.

A sudden wind gusted along the wide expanse of sidewalk then, forcing us to duck away to catch our breaths. Turning back, I was shocked and moved to see tears in his eyes.

Just the wind, he said quickly, dabbing at his eyes with the corner of his coat sleeve.

Lyusia . . .

He cut me off. *Good to see you, Svetlana. I wish you happiness. Goodbye.*

On the day I was to leave for India, a blizzard swept over Moscow. All afternoon and evening the snow continued to fall over the city, as I waited in our apartment with Josef and Katya, calling the airport every half hour to try to learn whether my 1:00 A.M. flight for Delhi would be allowed to take off. The news was shifting and contradictory, and I found the tension hard to manage. At one point Josef picked up my heavy suitcase to move it by the door, and I snapped at him to put it down. I apologized immediately for my harsh tone, explaining that unbeknownst to him, I had put the urn containing Brajesh's ashes into the suitcase. But the damage had been done. On the eve of my departure, when we all would have wished to feel closest together as a family, my son turned remote from me. It was my fault.

Josef, I'm sorry.

He looked at me, but his heart was somewhere else.

Please forgive me?

My son's nod suggested acquiescence at my request, rather than the sentiment itself.

If you're still angry when Mama gets back, Katya remarked to her brother from the table where she was studying, *you can tell her so then. But right now, if you ask me, you should just get over it.*

Josef glared at her. After a moment, he went into the kitchen. I heard him filling a glass with water from the tap.

Mama?

Yes, my Katya.

Will you bring me back one of those colored cloth skirts?

A sari?

Yes.

With pleasure.

Something with some red in it, please. I have nowhere to wear it, but I can at least hang it on the wall.

Just then there came a knock on the door of our apartment. It was Mrs. Kassirova from the Ministry of Foreign Affairs, who would be accompanying me all the way to Delhi to make sure there were no *surprises* on my journey.

The snow has stopped, Mrs. Kassirova informed us.

And so it had.

Outside the foreign departures lounge I embraced Josef, who had driven us to the airport. He could come no further with me.

I'll be home soon, I said, believing my own words.

We'll be here, Mother, he replied solemnly. *Have a good trip*.

I kissed and hugged my son, my firstborn, and then I turned away from him toward the plane.

The Singh family lived along the bank of the Ganges, six hundred miles from Delhi. There were many of them, and though their son and I had never married, they welcomed me into their house like a newfound relative.

The day after my arrival, I watched wooden boats carry Brajesh's ashes out into the river. After the ashes we tossed flower petals, which remained floating on the water's surface long into the falling dusk.

The following morning, I was taken by an old woman to bathe in the same part of the river. Climbing out of the water, cleansed though not clean, I discovered flower petals stuck to my skin.

One day after another passed in that place, with those good people who were so kind to me. Each morning began with a bath in the Ganges in my sari, accompanied by the same old woman—one of Brajesh's many aunts, whose name was Maya. The river was always crowded with people likewise bathing; one was never alone. It was a village, a community, an ongoing narrative in which I, a foreigner in every sense of the word, had no part, yet which absorbed me all the same. Each morning came to feel like a reenactment of that first morning after Brajesh's funeral, when Maya had led me into the river the color of milky, oversteeped English tea so filled with the runoff of human life and death that, wading into it, one hand holding the hem of my borrowed sari and the other a small clay pitcher, it was as if the cool viscous weight climbing my legs, steadily rising, emanating an acrid bovine stink, was the hand and breath of all those who could not bring themselves to let go or give up. Here was a way station of some kind, I'd only half-understood, a hallowed, ever-flowing bridge between worlds: where our ghosts had not quite left us yet, were still with us, grasping on, and for these last minutes we might bathe in their ashes and shit with a sadness so keen it was almost like joy.

After bathing, Maya would sit with me on the riverbank as we dried ourselves under the rising sun. We communicated in the most basic English, though mostly we were silent. To her, I believe, I was simply a woman her nephew had loved, and who had loved him. That was enough. My Russianness, let alone the details of my personal history, any notions of status or legacy, power or shame that so completely defined me in my own world and determined who I was and would always be in the eyes of my own people, anything to do with Josef Stalin or the murder of countless millions—such biographical information was to her irrelevant, or perhaps even nonexistent. What she wished to know—all she wished to know—was about my children.

On our eleventh morning together, she asked me their names.

Josef and Katya, I told her.

Their ages?

Twenty-one and sixteen.

Were they healthy?

Yes, thank God.

And happy?

When instead of answering this last question I began to cry, Maya appeared unsurprised. Her smile was calm and knowing as she stroked my hair with her small wrinkled hand, her long fingernails pleasantly scratching my scalp, until my tears stopped.

That afternoon in my bedroom, which was decorated with only a few colored cloths, I fell into a sleep that overtook me like a sickness. I traveled so far down the tunnel of mental exhaustion that my dreams floated above me like clouds I could see but not touch. Within these ethereal masses, I somehow understood, were narratives of my past I had forgotten or never known; truths I must discover if ever I was to wake up. And I longed, as I slept, to know what these truths were.

I came awake two hours later, painfully clearheaded. The dream-clouds were gone. In their place, I sensed Josef and Katya close but not reachable, their loving, troubled spirits floating above me like airborne kites tied to a tree.

While I'd slept without dreaming under the spell of that old Indian woman's touch, some space in my mind had cleared, and a realization had entered. I could not say how this had happened, but it had; nor could I honestly say that it was knowledge I'd been waiting for or wanted. But it had come just the same. And now I was awake.

Josef and Katya were trapped. They could not fly away because they were kites tied to a tree.

The tree was me. And it was my father. And like my father—like me, who every second of my life in the country of my birth had always been, and would always be, Josef Stalin's daughter, a character written in blood in the ledger of his atrocities—the tree that was holding back my children was dead but still standing. It would always be standing in Russia, no matter the future. And it would always be dead.

So long as my children remained tied to that tree, I now understood, they would never be free.

Which left only one thing for me to do, if I truly loved them.

I had to cut the strings that held them.

And I must do it now, without thinking anymore, while I had the chance.

26 April

It is hard to know what time it is in the ballroom of the Plaza hotel, whether day or night. Ornate crystal chandeliers spread every couple of meters across the wood-paneled ceiling shine like unblinking stars. I am seated beside my handsome young lawyer, Peter Horvath, and his senior partner, Mr. Lucas Wardlow, Esquire—an elegant and distinguished older man of precious few words who, it

41

is said, regularly beats the crafty Mr. George Kennan at cards—on a raised stage in the center of the massive room. The hundreds of reporters and photographers from newspapers around the world who have gathered to hear me answer questions appear as little more than faceless presences, mere reflections of the light shining from above.

Peter is wearing a different suit from our first day together, of brown wool carefully pressed, and a boyishly striped necktie. His short dark hair neatly parted to the side. Today for the first time I am aware that his eyes are an unusual shade of light brown, hon-eyed like walnuts.

One by one in a steady, slightly hoarse voice, Peter reads out the questions that we have agreed on in advance, and waits for my answers with a patient but curious leaning-in of his shoulders that reminds me once again of my brother Yakov. This, and the trem-bling edges of the sheet of typed questions in his hands, is the only sign of what must be a considerable case of nerves. Every so often, he casts a sideways glance at his boss, Wardlow, as if trying to gauge how things are really going.

Miss Alliluyeva, can you tell us something about the actual mo-ment of your decision to defect from the Soviet Union, the United States's avowed Communist enemy, the country that, from 1922 until his death in 1953, your father Joseph Stalin ruled with one of the bloodiest, most paranoid, and most ruthless hands in history?

This last is a bit of dramatic flourish on Peter's part. I am not saying that it isn't accurate, in its way. I am saying that until now I have not recognized my new lawyer's quiet, well-mannered wish to have some of history's spotlight fall on himself.

I turn to him and smile. *Have you ever been to India, Peter?* I begin. And then I turn my face and smile directly into the blinding lights:

Have any of you ever been to India? Have you ever bathed in the Ganges?

After the final question and answer, Peter guides me through ex-ploding camera flashes to the elevator. The Plaza hotel elevator is a beautiful creation, fitted out like a small mobile salon. Peter and

Lucas Wardlow lead me into it, with a few of the more senior newsmen insinuating themselves inside just before the door closes. Male eyes stare uncomfortably at empty space as we begin to descend. We are between the third and fourth floors when the car comes to a sudden, grinding halt. Tense silence, then one of the newsmen lets out a crude curse. I glance at Peter and am surprised to find his brow glistening with sweat.

It is Lucas Wardlow, the former Navy admiral, who manages to save the situation. *Don't take this personally, my dear,* he says to me with his gentleman's small dry smile. *Khrushchev got stuck in here too. It was nearly World War Three.*

Now some relieved chuckles, followed by general chatter about Khrushchev's shoe-banging incident at the United Nations. This is still going on a couple of minutes later, when the elevator suddenly begins to descend again. Before we know it, Peter and I are out on the street and inside a waiting car. Wardlow has gone off in a separate limousine. Peter gives our driver his office address and falls back on the seat beside me, silent and pale, dabbing at his shining face with a handkerchief.

The limousine begins to move. I ask Peter if he is all right.

The elevator, he confesses. *I'm not crazy about confined spaces.*

I stare at him awhile. *Confined* is the word that interests me, here in this country. My lawyer looks quite young now, American young, still not wholly made.

You don't like to feel trapped?

He nods.

I take the handkerchief from his hand. In the backseat of the car, I press the damp square of cotton to his brow to calm him. He lets me do this like a dog that expects to be petted.

I say, *Maybe this is why you and I, we get along so well.*

Maybe, he acknowledges, with a quick inquisitive glance at me that I find charming. *You could be right.*

4 May

Katya's birthday: she is seventeen today.

Weighing less than two kilos, she arrived weeks early into this world. The nurse whisked my baby away to the heating unit before I could properly welcome her. I was terrified—was there something seriously wrong with her? But as it turned out, my daughter was just anxious to get going with her life. Even in the incubator, where most of the premature infants slept from morning till night, my Katya would not rest. A stubborn scientist even then, gathering data with her tiny fists, probing silent questions with her miniature wrinkled feet. As if she already knew how she must strengthen and prepare herself for the day, so many years in the future, when her mother, the one person who should never do such a thing, might fly away to the other side of the world and not return.

From the convent in Fribourg, Switzerland, where this winter and early spring I was forced to wait to learn whether or when the U.S. government would take me, it was arranged for me to place a single telephone call home.

It was evening in Moscow when I heard the double click of the line being connected, and Josef's manly voice saying hello. His tone changed the instant he understood it was me.

Oh, dear God . . .

And then, with a sharp intake of breath, he fell silent.

At the same time, in the background, I could hear the unmistakable groan of the oven door being opened; and with a feeling like being scalded, I saw my son standing at the three-legged phone table in the corner of our kitchen and my Katya opening the oven door to put in or take out whatever it was she was making for their dinner. That kitchen that had been our family's home for fifteen years, where, on my own, with my dear nurse departed to the grave (her heart finally exhausted from giving so much for so long), I learned to cook on a gas stove, sew basic clothes, do the washing up—to become a mother. That kitchen where now my children would be standing with only themselves for company, as over the crackling, infiltrated line their mother kept repeating in a voice of barely contained panic, *I am not a tourist . . . Josef, do you understand? I am not a tourist . . . I will not return.*

My son asked me no questions that day. All he would reply, like a bank teller speaking through a grated window as you try to explain the problem you are having with your account, was *I hear you.*

Then the line went dead.

17 May

My host, Mr. Gus Seward, a kind widowed gentleman of Locust Valley, New York, knocks carefully on the door to my room. This was his daughter's bedroom—she whom I scarcely have met but who supposedly is going to translate my book, though I must say I have serious doubts about her Russian credentials—and so he must know it well. How many times during his daughter's adolescence might he have heard coming from here similar sounds of wretchedness and anguished confusion?

Svetlana? Are you all right?

I can't help it—I begin to cry all over again. He enters then, a gallant fireman in baggy tennis whites, yellowed faintly at the hems from age. His legs practically hairless, pale as fish bones. His hair reduced to a white horseshoe that sits atop a nicely shaped head. He has a regular game of doubles tennis that he never misses, I've learned, with three other widowers like himself at the country club.

Gus stops short, perhaps taken aback by the trail of used tissues running from his feet to the dressing table, where I sit hunched, my face averted from him.

Are you feeling sick?

Still sniveling, I translate aloud for him my son's Russian message, delivered to me this morning by Peter's office:

You may rest assured that your words on tourism were fully understood, and I have no intention of inducing you to return, especially after our talk. I consider that by your action you have cut yourself off from us and, therefore, please allow Katya and me to live as we see fit. I want to emphasize that I do not take it upon

*myself to judge your actions; but since we have endured fairly
stoically what you have done, I hope that from now on we shall
be allowed to arrange our own lives ourselves.*

Oh dear, murmurs Gus.

I glance up and see compassion in his faded blue eyes.

*I don't suppose you'd like to come with me to the club? It really is
a very nice place to relax.*

No, thank you.

*No, of course not, why would you? Well, we'll meet for dinner
then, as usual? I have a new Brahms record I think you might like.*

I nod and blow my nose, adding another balled tissue to the
pile, and he backs gently out of the room, shutting the door softly.
A minute or so later, I hear his car—a magnificent Buick convertible about six meters long—roar to life in the driveway, then move
slowly out into the quiet street and away.

I rest my cheek against my son's letter. Fearing that this, right
now, might be the closest I will ever come to my children again.

7 June

Egypt and Israel are now at war, joining America and Vietnam.
Meanwhile, here in Locust Valley, we have our own little United
Nations.

I am informed that the bus that has been parked near the
house all this past week belongs to an Italian television company.
Who knew Italians could be so patient and watchful? The best
they could manage thus far, Gus tells me with a glint of victory in
his eye, was an interview with the Polish gardener. As the gardener
speaks very little English and no Italian, I'm not sure what news he
was able to provide, save for the fact that I seem to be especially
fond of azaleas.

The two private security men who have taken up virtual residence in the kitchen downstairs are brothers from Budapest. Together they must weigh three hundred kilos. They take turns eating

vast quantities of the stews and chops prepared by Gus's German housekeeper, who grumbles about the added work but cannot help looking pleased at the reception her food is getting. The brothers are unfailingly courteous to me, despite the fact that it was the Soviet Army's invasion that forced them to flee their country. It is their job to scare away the newsmen who come every day to photograph the house and the windows of my borrowed room, my one haven in this place, which more and more I am reluctant to leave.

The other day, however, my translator, Marina, came for a visit ("consultation with the author," she called it), and she and her father coaxed me out for a shopping expedition in town. We were accompanied on our walk by Gus's Irish setter Geronimo, whose nervous and overbred disposition was not helped by the noise from the news helicopters following us everywhere we went. No surprise then that by the time we reached Main Street, there were gawkers and photographers everywhere we turned.

My translator desires me to buy new shoes. On this point she is strangely insistent. Her intimation, not in so many words, is that the shoes I have brought with me to this country are representative of a discredited, evil time in history. Actually, I want to tell her, they are just shoes, and French. Marina herself, I observe, has large American feet. Blond and rangy and long of limb, she is a woman who clearly spent much of her childhood playing tennis and riding horses; *stallion* is a favorite word. Her Russian she learned at college under scholars of varying quality, I would say.

She desires me to buy several pairs of shoes at once. Apparently what one does in America, as soon as one can, is buy as many of everything as possible. Without asking me what catches my fancy, she takes the store manager over to the window and points out several pairs of the latest styles for me to try on. All have substantial heels to improve my meager height. When after ten minutes I agree to buy only one pair of low-heeled walking shoes, and insist on paying for them with my own money, I can see the disappointment in her face, much as she tries to hide it. Perhaps my stubbornness and lack of appreciation for commercial opportunity and high fashion are traits associated in her mind with the world I come from, the anticulture of Soviet Russia. At any rate, the shoes I buy with my own money are shoes that I can see myself walking in anywhere in the world, not just in Locust Valley, New York.

Because—I want to grab her and say—*anywhere in the world* is a place I might still go. And so I must be ready, in case that happens.

25 June

Today at a UN press conference, Kosygin delivered Moscow's first public remarks about me since my defection:

Alliluyeva is a morally unstable person and she's a sick person and we can only pity those who wish to use her for any political aims or to discredit the Soviet country.

26 June

Tonight Gus takes me in his Buick convertible, the top pushed down, to his favorite restaurant on the Long Island seashore for a farewell dinner. Though no longer young, he drives rapidly but with ease, a look of quiet refreshment on his face, dipping the steering wheel this way and that with the first two fingers of his right hand.

We come to the coast road and there is the moon, full and fat, suspended above the silver-streaked ocean, brackish wind in our faces. And I cannot explain it: suddenly each breath I take, braced with salt and memory, strikes my heart like a blow.

The restaurant is a *steak house*, that temple of carnivore abundance that Americans must be dreaming of when they exclaim to each other, with genial innocence and a boundless smile, *You know, I think I could eat a horse!* The *Stars and Stripes* flaps and snaps in the ocean breeze atop a tall metal pole beside the parking lot. The other cars filling the area are as long as Gus's, some even more

48

handsome. The dear man looks faintly crestfallen when I don't wait for him to open my door.

We are seated at a table near a potted tree. In Russia, the grim half joke goes, even the potted trees have been cut down. Vodka martinis are brought. A few stares from other customers, but for once no reporters. Gus is charming in his boyish enthusiasm at having eluded them. *I've always wanted to drive at Le Mans,* he says with a wink. I have no idea what he's talking about. *The shrimp cocktail is very fresh here,* he adds with gallant sincerity. *And then I'd recommend the sirloin, medium rare. It's the house specialty.* Declaiming his best intentions thus, his voice is suddenly more than it was a minute ago—deeper, more confident—and I feel myself happy to be under his care for the evening.

Is the steak cooked enough for you?
    Oh, yes.
    Would you like some more creamed corn?
    No, thank you, Gus. Too rich.
    A waiter in a tuxedo pours us more wine.
    Is Russian food anything like this? asks Gus.
    I pretend to think for a moment, already knowing my answer: *Not really.*

Apple pie à la mode follows. Then we drive home under stars, moon, moist air, salt wind. Gus turns on the radio, twists the dial. It is not classical music or American jazz that he chooses but Elvis Presley singing "Long Legged Girl." To my astonishment Gus begins whistling along with Elvis, his left hand playing rhythm on the outside of the car, his self-made notes dry but on key, quickly swept away by the onrushing wind.

The light on his front porch must have been on all the time we were at dinner: shining, it welcomes us back now. The car doors open and close like steel wings. Gus pours us a *nightcap.* We sit on the porch with our drinks, gently swinging and creaking on a wooden bench hung from the beams by chains.

4 July

I have been now for a week on Block Island with Peter and his wife, Martha, and their young daughter, Jean. From their rented cottage, covered like so many others here with wooden shingles, you can't see the ocean, but you can smell it, and at certain times hear it. My hair and skin have grown soft from the salt in the moist island air. Even the tap water has a faint briny flavor, reminding one that this is but a tiny outcrop of rock where no one is ever very far from the sea; or from the cliffs that have been a hazard to ships and submarines for two hundred years, frequently sinking them; or from the graves of the Native Indians who were the original settlers here, and who, when they were not slaughtering each other, were massacred by the white islanders without a thought. Or so I have heard.

But America's birthday is perhaps not the day for such histories. The main town is awash in red, white, and blue. I have never seen so many stars and so many stripes, to say nothing of watermelons, hot dogs, corn *on the cob*. Members of the local fire department shoot a cannon out into the bay—no bullets, only water, powerful and oddly thrilling. I am with Peter among the crowd at Old Harbor. (Martha has taken Jean off to meet a group of young mothers and their children.) Like the other men, he wears a white tennis shirt, khaki short trousers, and sunglasses like the ones Vasily and his pilot friends used to wear after a night of drinking. Smelling of a suntan lotion called *Coppertone*, his jaw darkened by a scrim of unshaven beard, my lawyer looks rather reborn in this place, his own master finally, no longer the young legal apprentice. Of course, I do not tell him this because I do not think he would consider it a compliment.

What do I know about Peter? Only what he has told me in fits and starts. He grew up on the outskirts of a small Pennsylvania city—a *depressed* place, they say here, as though describing a person. His father had some permanent illness or disability that affected his fitness to work; there was never quite enough money. Peter was an only child. He sat alone on the school bus, at the front, staring each day at the same wheat fields and dying factories, dreaming of escape to a bigger and better city. They were Jews, and on Friday evenings, whether his father was well or not, Peter accompanied his parents to the city's only synagogue for services. The intensity of his prayers exhausted him. And then his father died, and he never prayed again.

It is late afternoon. The fire truck with the water cannon has driven away. The crowd is starting to thin. I try to remember whether from the Swiss Air plane that brought me to this country these dozens of sailboats and motor yachts anchored here, with their white hulls gleaming of money and privilege, were part of the island I saw, my first sight of America.

You must come and stay with me and my family.

But of course, I realize, we would have been too high up. Only the crude shape of the island would have been discernible, not its details.

There will be fireworks on the public beach tonight, I have been told, of a kind that will amaze the young and the old alike.

I think of Josef and Katya, alone without their mother.

9 July

It rains today, all day, rain tapping ceaselessly on the shingled cottage roof and falling in slower fatter drops, like little wet deaths, from the eaves and gutters onto the wooden boards of the back porch. One of those days where you wake to rain and go to sleep to rain. The sheets and towels damp from the rain in the air accumulated over so many hours and days. The pages of this notebook damp, absorbing too much ink. The air cool and not like summer.

Peter lays a fire first thing in the morning. He crumples pages from a recent *New York Times*—one containing an item about me—into a pile on the andirons (each in the shape of an owl) inside the brick fireplace, and then stacks several sticks crosswise over this messy bed, followed by two split logs. As the paper flickers into flame and smoke begins curling up into his face, he steps back, his expression anxious. *Damp*, he mutters.

We are drinking mugs of hot coffee in the living room. Mingled with the woodsmoke is the smell of the bacon Martha is frying in the kitchen. Martha, I have noticed, keeps to herself in the morning. She is awake and functional when I come down at around eight, the coffee made, the cereal box and milk set out at the kitchen table for Jean. (She is a very conscientious mother.) Something is always on the stove. Her clothes and hair are casual but neat. She is polite and considerate to me. But to draw anything richer or more spontaneous from her in the first half of the day is to fish for foxes, as my dear nurse used to say. And the rest of the day is not much more fruitful.

And yet, from the evidence, Martha Horvath would not seem to be a woman without strong currents. A few times since my arrival, as I was getting dressed for dinner, I thought I overheard the whispered edge of a private quarrel she was having with Peter in their bedroom; once, I was quite certain I heard her say my name. But in my presence her mood and demeanor are admirably placid. A certain rote quality almost, something learned rather than felt. Which jam do I prefer, strawberry or raspberry? Which meat for dinner, pork chop or hamburger? Do we use suntan lotion in the Soviet Union? Do we eat spaghetti? Does Block Island remind me of any place from home? She is careful, determined even, not to initiate any more complex connection between us, anything that might spill into unwanted intimacy—in case, I half-suspect, I were to seize on a loose thread of feminine warmth as a pretext for extending my visit beyond the month already planned. It is also possible that she resents me for my blood. Not once during my stay, for example—though her cottage has frequently been filled with curious guests and journalists doing just this—has she mentioned or asked me about my father.

The wood catches. The flames rise and fill, and the glass eyes of the iron owls glow amber. Wherever you sit, the owl's gaze will find you, as though seeking you alone. But to exert his haunting power—you realize only later—he must have a fire always lit behind him; or else his eyes are dead.

Peter, not believing in the fire that burns before his eyes, pokes at it anxiously with an iron tool.

And staring at his long back, I ask myself: if Martha Horvath is a person of some control, her most unruly feelings held in check behind a façade of polite gesture, then what of her husband? What is a lawyer, after all, but one who has strategically guaranteed his own place in society as the asker of questions and the giver of wise counsel? For such a man, the mirror only ever points outward, to the safety of another's distress. His role requires no real personal exposure on his part.

So why does it sometimes feel as if I were the one who carried Peter to freedom in the middle of the night, and not the other way around? And that he, in his private heart, believes the same?

18 July

I am taken to a dinner party in town. A babysitter arrives for Jean, and I ride with Peter and Martha in their Chevrolet across the island to one of the houses that line the road from the harbor. According to Martha, the Penshaws are among the original Block Island families, *very old New England.* (Is this not a contradiction in terms?)

Blue bloods, Peter mutters.

I am confused. What blue?

Yes, well, responds Martha, a sudden edge to her voice. *Be that as it may, the current Penshaws, Jasper and Raisa—*

She is Russian?

Yes. Peter didn't tell you?

No, Peter did not. An apologetic wave from the driver's seat. *Raisa Malinov, Jasper's wife, has translated Akhmatova and Voznesensky,* he says. *Very plugged into the émigré literary scene in New York. She was determined to meet you.*

The house is impressive, *Federal style.* (Martha is a fount of such terms.) Warm light from high front windows turns the sidewalk bricks to bronze. Panes of old fine glass. A brass knocker, and a brass bell too.

Our host, Jasper Penshaw, opens the door, extends a hand. A voice not so much restrained as never let out of its throne room: his jaw remains almost still, his lips do not move. His hair is gray with touches of copper. His posture in a navy blue sport coat is erect but with the conscious addition of a very slight stoop, as if to stand any taller would be in bad taste. The end of his necktie disappears into the opening between two of the horn buttons of his light blue shirt. What could this mean? Not a moment to ponder, however, for now his Russian lady is upon me with magnificent cleavage and a flounce of mahogany curls, brushing my cheeks with her own, leaving traces of rouge and French rose.

How pleased I am to meet you! I am Raisa Malinov. Come, come and meet our distinguished guests.

And I see at once what sort of evening this is going to be. Her voice that melodious stage whisper that we Russians created: she is speaking not to me but to the balconies of history in her own heroic émigré narrative. Very well. If this is the price of hearing my own language for a couple of hours, I accept, even if listening to her is like having an overstewed fruit preserve fed into one's mouth a silver spoonful at a time. What one needs is the tannic corrective of a strong cup of black tea—or some vodka.

An eminent literary publisher; an Associated Press journalist recently returned from Vietnam; a director of a New York bank; a female novelist of some repute; a slim woman with a man's haircut wearing clothes of her own design; and several more *blue bloods*—these are my fellow dinner guests. The journalist approaches first, hands me a large glass of vodka to match his own. *I thought you might appreciate one of these,* he says.

I accept, thank you.

He raises his glass to my eye level and drinks. *Budem zdorovy.*

I smile. *You speak Russian?*

No. But I can say Cheers *in twelve languages.*

That is clever.

Useful at dinner parties, anyway. Tell me something. How does it feel to defect to America only to realize that this government is run by fucking liars too?

I am not surprised, I reply. *Governments will always lie. It is the job of artists and intellectuals to tell the truth.*

All right. But when a government's lies are criminal and go unpunished, they make liars out of everyone.

I refuse to accept responsibility for other people's lies. Only my own.

Again he raises his glass at me, but this time I sense something ironic in the gesture.

You are mocking me.

Not at all. He is quite a lot taller than I, with a canny well-worn face, and I must crane my head to meet his steady, penetrating stare. The whites of his eyes are stippled with blood veins.

I don't believe you.

His grin disarms me. *Hey, it's a free country, right?* His impudence reminds me of Vasily: the reckless manners of a prince who has been drinking since breakfast.

Of course. Why else would I have come here?

Ever been to Vietnam?

No.

The shit going down over there is worse than anything even your old man ever cooked up. And I'm not fucking kidding.

Suddenly, Peter is at my side, a hand on my elbow. *All right?*

Our Russian friend and I were just talking about travel, the journalist says in a tone that might as easily be sincere as a savage joke. *So many places to go and so little time.*

Peter glances at me for confirmation. I allow him to guide me across the room to the female novelist, whose black hair is cut straight across her forehead like that of a schoolgirl in a provincial town. She lives in Atlanta and has written fifteen books. When I ask whether she has a particular subject that she returns to in her work, she replies, *Human beings, more or less.* We find common ground in our admiration for Chekhov, though not so for Pushkin, whom she clearly has never read.

At dinner, I am seated between our host and the bank director, who regrets to say, goddamnit, that being in a war, any war, he means to say, is simply good for business. *I'm very sorry, but it just goddamn is, Jasper. That's the way of the world and everyone knows it.*

Oh, my grandfather Lawrence certainly would've agreed with you, Jasper Penshaw replies. *He made a killing in coal during the First World War, you know. And he only had one leg.*

The bank director appears startled. *Your grandfather lost a leg in the war? Christ, I didn't know that.*

No. He lost the leg flying a kite.

There follows a brief silence. Then as the borscht is served by a waiter, our hostess rings a crystal glass with a tiny silver spoon, rises to her feet, and, with one diamond-encrusted hand placed over her significant breasts, recites:

> Everything is plundered, betrayed, sold,
> Death's great black wing scrapes the air,
> Misery gnaws to the bone.
> Why then do we not despair?

> By day, from the surrounding woods,
> cherries blow summer into town;
> at night the deep transparent skies
> glitter with new galaxies.

> And the miraculous comes so close
> to the ruined, dirty houses—
> something not known to anyone at all,
> but wild in our breast for centuries.

Staring at me across the long oval table, she then speaks the same poem in Russian. Last, comes her toast:

> Our late prophetess Akhmatova was persecuted for what she be-
> lieved and had the courage to say in her poetry and in her life. Our
> honored guest this evening has made her own poetic statement
> against the morally bankrupt Soviet system by choosing freedom of
> act and expression over the chains of her own blood. We salute her
> for her courage and welcome her to our country.

Two hours later, we embrace by the door. She calls me sister and predicts an everlasting bond between us. I profess my deepest debt of thanks for her heartfelt welcome, the poetry of the great Akhmatova, the most generous toast, the pristine Russian vodka— though in my private mind I already have doubts about my new sister. Here in this country, cut off from its roots, her abject roman- ticism for survivor-heroes strikes me as a couple of shades too bright. She is enjoying herself too much. Only in the drawing rooms of émigré nostalgics like Raisa Malinov will we go on making toasts and singing songs as though the original film were still running, over and over, the villains larger than life, the heroes ever arriving.

I did not leave my children and my homeland to traffic in such fairy tales.

19 July

Almost noon and I am still in bed. This cottage made of flimsiest wood, reverberating sound. Half an hour ago, I heard Martha say to Peter in what I am sure she believed was a low voice, *This is ridiculous. We're not waiting another minute for her.* And the family gathered itself together—towels, suntan lotion, beach umbrella, sandwiches by the sound of it—and piled itself into the car and drove off for the beach on the other side of the island, where the surf is always strong.

I have brought my notebook into bed so that I may revisit yesterday and lie here a little longer and think. The story goes on. There is more to say. And still one tries to tell the truth. Yes, one tries.

All right: I drank too much. But I wasn't the only one.

On the way home from the Penshaws', Martha sits in the shadows of the backseat with a hand covering her eyes as though a spotlight is trained on her and she is trying to disappear. Migraine. We arrive at the cottage and she goes straight upstairs, leaving Peter to pay the babysitter.

The teenager drives off, and Peter and I are alone. For a moment my lawyer stands with slack features, looking suddenly doubtful and tired and all too young. But then he seems to recognize this as a dangerous condition in himself, some weak or drifting quality that he must remain vigilant against. He puts a smile on his face and asks if I wouldn't care for one more drink for the road.

I have no idea what road he's talking about, not that it makes a difference.

I'll just go check on Jean, he says. *Be down in a minute.*

By now, I know to look for the vodka in the freezer. I pour two drinks in plastic blue glasses designed for small children and take them to the back porch, where folding chairs are set up around a small wooden table. If the crickets would be quiet, I might hear the surf breaking on the beach. But these insects are something plugged into an electric current, pulsing like stars in the black sky.

In a few minutes Peter emerges, sits down next to me, and picks up his drink.

Once in a while Jean has nightmares. He keeps his voice low, presumably to spare Martha's headache.

What do you do for her?

Nothing much. Hold her and tell her it was just a dream. Give her a back rub till she falls back to sleep.

And Martha?

He swallows more vodka. *We each have our roles*, he says finally.

I say nothing. Because when my children were small enough to have nightmares that caused them to shiver with fear, it wasn't me they called for in the middle of the night. *Nurse!* they would cry. *Nurse, come! Come now! I'm scared!* And Alexandra Andreevna would always be near; she was the one who would comfort them in their beds. As she did for me when I was a child. Yes, we may call our land *Mother Russia*; but it turns out that we are not a land of mothers after all. I cannot remember, not really, physical tenderness from my own mother. Nor, though I was unquestionably more demonstrative in my love with my children than my mother ever was with me, can I honestly claim that I ever was for them what my nurse was for all of us, which is to say a physical mother whose love daily and nightly was delivered through hands and hugs and kisses; whose body, profound in its comforting solidity, would always lean across any distance to bridge the ever-yawning gap between lonely child and all that is cold and cruel in the world.

Peter and I finish our drinks in silence. He goes inside and returns with two more. And we finish those too.

Mr. and Mrs. Staehelin.

There is a kind of drunkenness one finds only in Russia. The

Irish don't know it, the French, the Greeks. An ecstasy of melancholy. The oldest lament in the world. A sadness that has no limits and so is very close to joy, but never reaches it. Joy's dark cousin. I want Peter to know this feeling, I think. To be drunk like this, like a Russian, just once in his life. I want him to live.

I reach out and touch my hand to his cheek. His chair creaks as he leans his face toward mine. We kiss, but still he seems to be waiting for some kind of permission, a sign.

I take his hand and place it inside my blouse, on my breast. As I press against that hand, a small groan escapes him—and suddenly he grabs my hair, twists my head around, and kisses me hard on the mouth.

Then, just as suddenly, he is standing, our bodies divided; prickling, cool air where his hand was.

Sorry, he mutters.

He is careful to close the screen door softly behind him. Careful to climb with a penitent's guilty attention the stairs to the room where his wife sleeps. Yet still those stairs crack and groan beneath him. And I wish to tell him—because I want him to live, because he needs me to tell him, because if not I then who?—that he cannot spend his life sitting alone at the front of the school bus, dreaming of foreign cities he will never visit. Sometimes we must act on our truest instincts, no matter the cost to others, or we will never escape the cages our cursed histories have put us in.

PART TWO

From the moment I met Martha Lewiston, at a cocktail party thrown by a friend of a friend on East Seventy-eighth Street in the spring of 1960, when she rather fiercely explained to me the difference between a *barn* owl and a *barred* owl, I believe I recognized that she was a person who guided herself according to the stringent comforts of a few deeply held convictions. Then one evening in the third month of our relationship, following a day filled with menial frustrations at the office, I joined some young associates from Wardlow Jenks at the bar at Grand Central. One martini led to another, one bar to another, and after a few hours I was pretty well adrift and thinking, frankly, about Martha and laying my hands on her. Stopping by her apartment, however, I found her in tears, declaring that she never wanted to see me again.

What I had done was unacceptable and very threatening to her. We had not had plans for the evening, she admitted, but that wasn't the point. By gratuitously going out without her, then dropping by to rub her face in the gap between us, I had betrayed her, turned something private and beautiful into something exposed and cheap. I could never quite understand why this was so, but looking at the tears on her face, I found it impossible to doubt her certainty that it was.

Svetlana's entry into our marital orbit was something neither Martha nor I ever recovered from. Our own personal Cold War, you might say, a living embodiment of an existential security threat; to the point where, toward the end of her life, four decades later, my wife would not under any circumstance utter the other woman's name.

After my retirement from Wardlow Jenks five years ago, my study on the third floor of our Princeton house was for a time littered with towering stacks of file boxes containing material from virtually every legal matter I had ever worked on during my fifty years as a practicing attorney. Martha's cancer had by then spread to her spleen and lungs, leaving her more or less housebound. I, on the other hand, with so much time on my hands, was often out running minor errands, trying my best to remain "useful." (If lawyers are trained to successfully negotiate people's problems, then cancer, it must be said, is truly the client from hell.) Returning from the pharmacy one day, I found Martha's usual chair in the sunroom empty. The nearest bathroom too was unoccupied. I called to her but got no reply and, suddenly panicked, began climbing the stairs two at a time.

I finally found her in my study, head bent over my desk, reading something with an almost violent intensity. The most recent round of chemo had taken her hair again and this time it had not grown back, and the sight of her shiny exposed scalp filled me with dread and pity. Open before her was a legal file, perhaps the thickest of any in my possession. And trembling in her fingers, I saw, was a document—from which now, in a hoarse attenuated voice, she began to read aloud.

"'Subject is an active, alert and intense individual who probably is somewhat immature and naïve for her age and experience. Essentially a very dependent person, used perhaps to being bullied by her powerful father, she is prone to become a disciple or a follower rather than an activist in anything she undertakes. She has a discernible fear of being taken advantage of and is cautious in how she accepts authority and direction, but once committed, she will competitively strive for acceptance and is (1) jealous and disappointed when others receive the acceptance and praise she wants and feels she deserves; and (2) furious when she feels she has been misled or misdirected by someone she thought she could trust. She is particularly vulnerable to humiliation.'"

Martha glanced up sharply, her gray eyes shining with a vindictive triumph that I had never seen in her before. "Do you know what I'm reading from?"

"Yes." A lawyer's response: say as little as possible.

"What is it?" A lawyer's rejoinder, learned from me: never ask a question whose answer you do not already know.

"Right after she requested political asylum at the U.S. Embassy in New Delhi," I said, "the CIA had one of their shrinks do a clinical assessment of her."

"How long have you had this?"

"A very long time."

"Why didn't you ever tell me about it?"

"Would it have helped if I had?"

"It's *exactly* what she's like. *It's who she is*, Peter." Two pink blotches were emerging from the papery hollows of my wife's cheeks.

"Martha, you're exhausting yourself. Come downstairs. We can talk about this after you've had some rest."

"I *can't* rest! Don't you see? This is who she is. This is what she's done."

1970

9 January

I have bought a house in Princeton, my first American house. Peter is nearby; and Lucas Wardlow; and George and Annalise Kennan too. The town is neither city nor country, which suits me. Still, I was not especially looking for this particular house, but it found me anyway: a small white Cape Cod with black shutters, a brick porch in front, and a brick patio in back. A small garden with a dogwood tree.

But now that I'm physically settled in my new home, I feel as though I'm waiting for something to happen, I don't know what. So many movements over time, shiftings and haltings across continents and lives, my children left behind: and here this period of stillness, domestic but uncertain.

I refuse to let this frighten me.

12 January

Peter and I are nearly neighbors now, separated by at most a twenty-minute walk. And yet, it pains me to say, the distance between us feels greater and more awkward than that. There is no obvious problem or break—that would never be Peter's way. But we are not as close as I'd imagined we would be by now. These days I rarely see him except by happenstance; most of our communication is by letter or telephone and professional in nature—he is the lawyer and I am the client. And so it has been ever since our porch encounter on Block Island three summers ago. Perhaps I shouldn't be surprised; perhaps it's better not to mix these things. Fewer complications this way, but also fewer possibilities. Still, I can't help but feel that something precious has been carelessly misplaced, and that it was I who caused it to happen. Turning closeness into distance as I have done in this case, with a man I like, is something I regret. I have had too much distance to begin with. I live and breathe it. I, who cannot see my children even through the telescope of my longing.

23 January

She has written me again, the Widow, her third letter in as many weeks. I recognize the stationery, her cursive on the envelope, the address in Scottsdale, Arizona, the postage stamp bearing the likeness of her late husband, the famous architect Frank Lloyd Wright, with his handsome, self-regarding mien and flowing white hair. The letter, like the others before it, so full of exotic intensity it practically opens and reads itself:

> *It was clear the moment I first saw your name, then read your extraordinary book. You have been returned to me. You are the first Svetlana I have heard of in this country since my daughter's death, twenty-three years ago. A rare and luminous name. Nowhere else have I found it except in Russian fairy tales. And suddenly here you are, in this country where we have landed and reborn ourselves. Like you, my own darling Svetlana was filled with light and courage. I gave birth to her in Georgia, not far from the village outside Tiflis where your mother was born and raised. Yes, your mother. Whose own mother's name was Olga, from which my name too comes. I do not believe in coincidence.*

The world is made of interlocked layers of energy and receptivity. Only the rare few, having trained and understood, can secure the pathways through time so that their energy may reach us here unmitigated. I have long steeped myself in the study and teaching of sacred dance, so that these pathways might never be closed to me. So that I may see them where others may see only walls and dust. In this way I have kept my husband's spirit and genius alive here and throughout the world. His buildings are those very pathways I mention. His vision reaches back into the depths of time even as it grasps the energies ahead. You will see all this when you come here to visit. My daughter, you must come! You must.

It is strange and unsettling to be courted like this—made cosmic love to—by someone I have never met (at least, not in this life).

Contained in the envelope are photographs of the architectural compound in the Arizona desert where the Widow lives with her *students* and *fellows*—an entire *Fellowship* and *School* organized, as she describes it at proud and mystical length, according to the architectural principles and creative philosophy of her late husband. I study these pictures, hoping they might reveal something. He was a very famous architect—I have looked him up—though it is not greatness I think I see out there among the reptiles and cacti, but rather a claustrophobic flattening of space combined with theatrical displays of decoration. The ceilings oppressively low, the light generous, yes, but bowed down. No people in the photographs, no human faces. Standing by myself in my Princeton living room—pretty, square, with quaint details and plenty of room above my head—I try to read in these images the heart of this woman, this stranger reaching out to me across a vast, unknowable desert and the shadows of time, but all I see are empty rooms lacking comfort.

The letter continues. She wishes to tell me everything about herself, she insists, as a mother would to a daughter. At the center of her tale, a tragedy: in 1946, in Spring Green, Wisconsin, where the Fellowship has a second compound to which they all migrate for the warmer months, her daughter Svetlana was killed in a car accident along with Svetlana's four-year-old son. *As though the light of the world was stolen by a great hand and buried deep beneath the earth.* The grieving son-in-law, Sid Evans, stayed on at the Fellowship, never remarrying, eventually becoming chief architect of the practice that still bears his father-in-law's name and is faithfully sustained, I am to gather, under the Widow's vigilant guidance. *You will like Sid as much as I do. He is a man of substance, vigor, loyalty, a true man who knows true things.*

True things—this is a phrase that recurs in the letters. Put together like this the words are seductive, taking on the sound of their intention, becoming irrefutable as idea, if not as fact. Not very Russian. (The Widow claims Georgian blood in her veins, along with Montenegrin.) My father was never one to talk much about *Truth*. Of course, he had no need. Whatever he said was by definition beyond truth—instantly it became reality, as it would thereafter be understood by anyone who valued his life.

The famous Architect named both his compounds, in Wisconsin and Arizona, *Taliesin*—a Welsh word, the Widow informs me, meaning *the shining brow*. Above the stone hearths he carved more Welsh words, meaning *Truth against the world*. This is beautiful and stirring language, a battle cry etched on a battle shield, and I confess that just the thought that there could be such a place, *Truth*, set opposite this other place, *World*, and that at the center of it could be this woman who presumes, without ever having met me, to know me intimately and call me daughter tugs sharply at the thread of longing I find ever dangling from my heart.

Us and *Them*.

My real mother believed in an *Us* too. In the Party that was her life and soul, all people were equal, and all equals had to sacrifice the same, none made special, including her own children. It was when she realized that human beings by their nature could not live this way for long, that in every garden there is a serpent and in every *Us* a young man who upon robbing his first bank for the revolution and getting his first taste of righteous bloody power, decides to change his name from Dzhugashvili to Stalin, I believe it was then she understood that her beloved *Us* was actually a cancer waiting to bloom, and that sooner or later *They* would win.

Four times in my life have I known this feeling of *Us* that my mother so desperately needed to believe in. The first was during the years before the war, when my widowed father still returned home each evening, calling out *Housekeeper!* as he entered the front hall and letting me dawdle on his lap in the dining room under the large portrait of my mother; when each evening after dinner (me sitting on his right among the six other adults—always six), before leaving to spend the night at Kuntsevo, in his overcoat smelling of pipe tobacco he came to my bedside and kissed me good night as I lay suspended in the comforting wash of his tenderness, halfway between dream and waking.

The second was that single miraculous day in the privately procured cinema with Lyusia, when for once we existed happily under the illusion that there was us and no one else.

The third and fourth were the births of my children.

I will never forget the moment I first truly understood. My memoir had been published, three autumns ago now, and after weeks of traveling everywhere and saying everything to a country that was still a stranger to me, I retreated to the Rhode Island house of a kind, older widow I had met on my travels. The two of us were sitting one evening in her living room, watching the television news while eating our dinners from plastic trays (something Americans are always eager to do if given the chance). *Now to international matters,* the newsman Walter Cronkite was saying. *It turns out that, one way or another, the dead Soviet dictator Joseph Stalin is still very much on the minds of his people. What you are about to see is from a recent interview with Stalin's grandson Josef Alliluyev, whose mother, Svetlana, defected to the United States last spring.* And with that, Cronkite's trustworthy face was replaced on-screen by my son. The setting I immediately recognized as our old Moscow apartment. Seated rigidly at the desk where I used to work on my translations, he looked as though he were presenting himself for an exam he knew he would fail. In poor Russian (with English subtitles) the German correspondent asked Josef if he had anything he would like to say to the mother who had abandoned him.

Josef nodded. Taking a few moments to compose himself, he said in a flat clear voice, *If Mother should wish to return now, there would be no punishment.*

And so, through my son, the Mother State spoke, an invitation unofficially extended. And in my son's mouth, for all the world to see, *Mother* became a word interchangeable with any other term of use, preowned and easily corrupted, a means of delineating avenues of barter and politics.

Us. Them.

That was the last of the communications. For the past two years, only silence. The letters I get now are from people not my children. This is what happens to you when you become *Them*. There is no going back.

But the Architect's Widow writes me. Yes. And writes. She who does not know me calls me daughter.

27 January

Today I went into the city to lunch with Peter. I was the one who called; he sounded reluctant, but I insisted.

But first I stop by the legal office to say hello to Lucas Wardlow, Esquire, elegant silver fox of a man sitting behind his wide mahogany desk. He gets to his feet and kisses my cheeks and leads me to the leather couch at one end of his office for a little chat. Not as spry as once, perhaps, but still illustrious. An ex-president in habit and manner, used to crowds and audiences and making speeches now only when it suits him.

And how is my new home treating me? he wishes to know. Am I teaching? Working on a new book?

I tell him that my new home is treating me fine, thank you. He ought to come and visit, since he lives not far away.

Yes, yes, he answers vaguely, rubbing his callused golfer's hands together.

I tell him that I turned down the offer to lecture in the Department of Slavic Languages and Literatures because I do not wish to be pigeonholed in the typical Russian émigré bunker.

You turned Princeton down? He cannot hide his dismay. *Well, of course, I can certainly see . . .*

As for writing another book, I interrupt him, *before beginning such an endeavor I would of course demand correction of one issue that troubles me.*

What issue?

How my lawyers allowed the copyright for my memoir to be put in my translator's name instead of mine.

Ah . . . Lucas Wardlow, Esquire, reaches—energetically for a man his age—for an intercom console sitting like a nuclear trigger on his antique coffee table. Depressing a red button with his fore-finger, he talks to the machine invisibly connected to his secretary. *Margaret? Margaret?*

Does he think I intend to let him escape so easily? *Tell me, Mr. Wardlow, does this seem at all fair to you, in a country such as this? Who wrote my book—me or my translator?*

I see . . . Margaret, do I have a lunch meeting? Lucas Wardlow, Esquire, calls hopefully toward the open door, abandoning the in-tercom altogether.

It is not Margaret who walks into desperate Wardlow's office a moment later. In the months since I last saw him in person Peter has become, I am aware, a full partner at the firm—an extra inch of title that has given him a certain additional presence. The gray at his temples and sideburns makes him rather distingué, as do the tortoise reading glasses he puts on in order to study the menu at the Japanese restaurant on Lexington where he takes me to lunch.

Know what you'd like to eat? he asks politely, once we're settled at a table by the window.

Martini.

Peter glances at me over his reading spectacles, our eyes meet, and it seems to me that he almost smiles.

Two vodka martinis, he tells the Japanese waiter, just now arriv-ing. *Very dry, straight up, twist.*

Hai, domo!

And so I find, to my great relief, that we are not entirely broken.

———

Later, tongue loosened, I tell him that I am glad—no, very glad—to finally be sharing a meal again with my lawyer.

I'm glad too.

I can be difficult.

No, he demurs.

Yes.

Well—all right, maybe a little.

Sometimes, maybe it's true, I can be frustrated about the book contracts you wrote for me. I know this. But, Peter, I count on you to understand these are just minor complaints. They don't matter. I point them out because they are there and need correcting, but I don't need them to live by. More money, more things—what would I do with them for myself? I have everything I need. My simple house, my brand-new, four-door green Dodge—you have not seen my beautiful car! I tell you, Peter, I am finally in love. Like a girl. Like a brand-new American girl with her brand-new pony. Only my pony has tires!

My lawyer laughs then, heartily and with relief, and we are good again. His firm pays our lunch bill and tips like a titan. *Hai, domo!* Peter escorts me out into the blue winter sunshine on the crisp sidewalked street. A lanky man wearing long mustaches and yellow-tinted sunglasses slouches by on the arm of his skinny blond girlfriend, her bare navel and hip bones showing out between flaps of shag-rug coat. Peter and I pause to stare at them. For they are beautiful in their ugliness and unbounded in their desire, and this is not their part of town. Nor mine.

Here is my new lover, I say boldly, as we approach my new car parked on Madison and Fifty-fifth Street. *Is Mr. Dodge not handsome?*

He's the real McCoy, all right, Peter remarks—the bottled cowboy phrase so unlike him that after a moment we are both grinning.

Darn tooting? I say, teasing.

He shrugs, grin frozen, suddenly self-conscious. I reach for his hands to bring him back to life. He subtly resists.

Peter, I say.

He looks at me.

It is mood that matters most to me. The mood between us, not the words. Not papers or signatures or dollar signs. You understand? The mood and the feeling between us. This is what matters.

I feel the same way.

Good.

He leans down and kisses my cheeks, each one with emphasis, and hands me into my car. So much unsaid.

I am careful pulling out among the buses and taxicabs, well known to be aggressive lunatics. And then, too soon, Peter is just a small, shrinking figure in my looking glass.

February 17, 1970
Taliesin West

My Dearest Daughter,
It is increasingly strange to me that you are not here. I look up, expecting to embrace you, only to remember that you have not yet come. Once, I spoke your name out loud. At dinner the other evening Sid said something about Svetlana and I mistook it for you, not my own Svet, and my heart began to race not with grief, at last, but with excitement. This is good pain, and I welcome it.
Your loving Mother

March 2, 1970
Taliesin West

Dear Svetlana,
I wanted to write and join Mrs. W in saying how happy we all are here to know that you will soon be coming to visit. This is a unique place in America, as you no doubt have heard. It would be my pleasure while you are with us to take you on a tour of the historic buildings and grounds and to show you the surrounding area as well.
Yours, with my cordial regards,
Sid Evans

8 March

I am in my attic looking at suitcases when I hear a car pull up in front of my house. Quiet late-winter afternoon. Two doors opening and closing in quick succession with that chilling echo that announces, wherever you are, *We have come for you.*

Three minutes later, Dick Thompson, the CIA man, limps into my kitchen holding a bouquet of red tulips. I am almost glad to see him after more than a year.

Wasn't sure about the color, he apologizes for the flowers.

I told him yellow might be a safer choice, Peter says, entering after Dick.

I point out that they come well prepared for what is apparently a surprise visit.

That's a pretty good description of my job, Dick says with a wink.

I put the tulips in a vase with water and a touch of sugar. I make tea for my guests. Russian tea with fruit jam, and some heavy oat biscuits given me by my neighbor the Jungian psychiatrist. We sit at the table in the kitchen, Dick unconsciously rubbing his deficient leg now and again. (According to Peter, it is shorter than the good one for some unfortunate reason.) I have already noticed his eyes cataloging my shelves of plates, cups, glasses, to say nothing of my jars of flour, sugar, bread crumbs, baking soda, brown sticks of vanilla.

You see my secret? I say with a mischievous smile. *I am just another middle-aged housewife without a husband.*

Peter chews a biscuit, staring at the table, and I use the silence to ask Dick whether the American government is aware that the copyright for my books was granted to my translator, thus depriving me of financial rights and valuable income?

Not my area of expertise, I'm afraid, Dick replies with a sideways glance at Peter. *I'm sure Peter is handling that.*

Svetlana, Peter changes the subject, *I was telling Dick about the letters you've been receiving from Taliesin. That you're planning a trip there.*

I explain to Dick about the Widow of the famous Architect who believes I am a cosmic substitute for her dead daughter.

Interesting perspective, Dick remarks.

Dick thought you should be aware of the reputation the institution has in certain circles, Peter says.

My CIA man rubs his poor leg. The result of an old bullet wound? I have to wonder. *Some intelligent people consider the place something of a cult,* he observes.

What do you mean, cult?

A situation where everyone is more or less compelled to believe the same power and follow its directives, Peter says.

Russians invented this, I tell him. *More, not less.*

Dick Thompson smiles.

I ask him, *So you do not consider Frank Lloyd Wright a genius?*

No, no, he was truly brilliant. A great artist. A tax-evading spend-thrift egomaniac, but the real deal.

So I will spend a week viewing his Arizona residence, then travel out West a bit and come home. Everyone already knows I have my own mind about life and politics, government, freedom. Everybody knows this.

Very true. Using the table for support, Dick gets to his feet. *Hell, maybe I just wanted to bring you flowers.*

I smile. *Next time yellow?*

Next time it is.

I watch Dick Thompson make his way down the brick steps and out to the sidewalk and his government sedan. It is obvious that in the time since last I saw him something in his leg has grown worse.

He never complains, Peter says quietly. He has lingered behind in my kitchen, still buttoning his coat.

I touch his arm. *How is little Jean?*

He peers at me as if the question is pregnant with other questions. *Jean's decided she wants to be a writer when she grows up.*

Then you must send her over to me when I return from my trip. I will give her an interview.

I'll tell her. He opens the door. A gust of cold air makes the house shiver to its bones.

Peter, I will call you if I need anything?

When he looks back, his gaze has turned lawyerly. *Of course. Have a good trip, Svetlana.*

16 March

In the Phoenix airport, a woman I know only by hearsay steps forward and embraces me. Roughly my own age, attractive, dark curly shoulder-length hair cut straight across her forehead over painted and shaped eyebrows. Rather dramatic use of black eye shadow for a desert airport afternoon. She calls herself Vanna and declares her hope that I will be her sister. I return the hope, adding that I have never had a sister, not in Russia and not in America.

But such is the locked past and not to be spoken of in Phoenix, Arizona, where the sun shines nonstop over mountainless land. My new sister leads me by the arm through the air-conditioned terminal to the luggage. Her pretty turquoise dress ends at her thighs, muscular and shapely from daily hours of sacred dance. Her chatter as bright and unignorable as her dress, even if the rampant energy behind it feels like overflow from a dammed-up performance going on elsewhere.

Here is what I know: she is half sister of the other, previous Svetlana and the only full offspring of the famous Architect and his Widow. And here is what I learn, once we are in her cherry red sports car out on the interstate highway between Phoenix and Scottsdale: she is a casually reckless driver. At high speed, the engine of her Volkswagen Karmann Ghia produces a deep-throated German ruckus that she conducts with one hand while steering the vehicle with the other at seventy and eighty miles per hour. Hot wind buffeting us through half-open windows adding to the maelstrom. She is an anxious bossy talker, though with the noise and the wind I catch only half of what she's saying:

> . . . Mother first . . . so eager to see you . . . fairy tale . . . bigger than . . . tonight you'll meet . . . tall handsome hugely . . . sad too . . . stoical . . . gentleman . . . dinners we all . . . everyone puts a lot . . . going to wear . . . performance of the very best . . . Saturdays . . . black tie . . . evening dresses.

The Karmann Ghia swerves from one lane to another. Far out in the countryside hammered flat by sunlight, the odd cactus passes with such slowness that I wonder if they are perhaps desert mirages. I explain to my new sister that I have not brought a single evening dress to Arizona. In fact, do not own one.

No worries! she shouts back at me with happy certainty. *You'll wear one of mine! Chiffon and silk! You will be a princess!*

I am led by a handsome young man in work clothes down a tiled walkway through a gallery of bougainvillea in full pink bloom. Scents of orange blossom, lavender, sunbaked dirt. The sound of a fountain burbling somewhere nearby. The overall property far too extensive to be absorbed in a single view, even from on high. Rather, one already suspects, it is a series of heavily framed and curated tableaux that, while indicating Nature at every turn, is laid out so as to never let one forget the Genius who designed it all. Or perhaps, the woman who reigns over it now.

I climb a set of stairs to a room that is indoors but feels out, raised up yet sunk down, with walls made from native rock and sand and countless meters of window placed high on the body, where it is harder for the light to get in. Here on a deep settee with strange triangular armrests the Widow has framed herself. Her uniform is singular: artificially black straight hair, white Greek tunic of fine muslin, heavy silver and turquoise jewelry, and at her feet a black Great Dane the size of a baby horse.

She extends a thin, parchment-skinned hand in my direction. Does not speak my name but sings it: *Svetlana!*

Incanted in this voice, I feel myself a rare golden bird.

Svetlana! Come sit by me. Gideon, for God's sake, move!

The Great Dane lifts its bullock head, yawns as if to swallow me whole. On splayed coltish legs it turns twice in a tight circle and, thump, collapses again on the far side of the settee. I approach. The Widow's papery hands reach out for mine with an iron grip. *Svetlana!* An ancient singing voice that could draw tears from stone.

I am so glad to finally meet you, I say.

Mother. You must call me Mother.

Oh . . .

Tell me everything, she sings.

And I would. I swear. I might. Everything.

But there is a problem. From her letters, I only now realize, I have come expecting my mother's velvet-dark Georgian eyes. My mother's face. The Widow's eyes, however, are light brown, each with a streak of yellow. There is something feral in them. My father's eyes, not my mother's. They sparkle restlessly but do not shine with heart. They speak but do not listen. They are ready to act but not to wait. Shallows rather than depths. I can find in them none of my mother's shy humility or rigorous conviction, her fierce sense of sacrifice.

I stand before the Widow with the smile of a stunned child on my face, trying to hide my disappointment. Of course, it would be pathetic of me to believe whatever rhetoric about cosmically substituted daughters and the magic of rarely found names.

But instead of answers, I am left now with the wrong set of eyes. The wrong face. A feeling, looking into this older woman's voracious gaze, of meeting, out in a wilderness I did not realize I was wandering into, a very sophisticated predator in camouflage.

What would it mean to tell her *everything?* How would I begin?

But she is talking, not listening.

We are special here, different from others. Abiding by shared principles of aesthetics and mutual obligations. Seeing what we do and how we live as inseparable from nature. It was my husband's belief that not all nature is architecture, but all architecture should be nature. This place you have come to, this community, is the living embodiment of his vision. My role is essentially that of humble messenger, guiding protectress, spiritual den mother. I do what I can to teach our ways to those who choose to be a part of what we do, to keep energies flowing, to ensure that nothing vital gets lost.

You will meet everyone of importance at dinner this evening. I am seating you next to Sid. He was my husband's very first apprentice here. There is nothing about this place or our sister home in Wisconsin that Sid does not know. Quite simply, we are his life and family. He could not be fulfilled without his work here, nor would he wish to be. You could not be in better or more considerate hands. You may trust him completely.

So she instructs me, when I fail to attempt to tell her everything. When I smile and am silent. She takes my silence as a vessel to be filled, and fills it. And I let this be done.

17 March

A brief respite before drinks are to start again, day number two, in the main structure, past the triangular pool and the stone Buddha and the Japanese lanterns that do not feel like what I imagine Japan feels like. Everything, even recognizable objects and shapes, has an imprint upon it, bears the watermark of the Artist, who, like God, decided that all aspects of his world would be like this. And it is like this. He had this place built out of the desert rock. Tens of strapping young apprentices brought across the country from green Wisconsin, some hardly more than beautiful boys who wanted to learn from him and one day be like him, and he set them to work in the rock with shovels and pickaxes and levels.

There are other young apprentices here now. Last night at dinner they stood behind us as we ate, dressed in theatrical finery, serving us course after course of rich, spicy Mexican food prepared by yet more apprentices toiling unseen in the kitchen. A willing army of architect cooks and waiters, constantly refilling our plates and wineglasses with abundance.

Is there something wrong with your back? the Widow hisses to one handsome fellow, carrying a bowl of *mole* chicken from the kitchen.

No.

Then stand up straight.

We are eight people, including the Widow, her daughter, and Sid Evans—*the innermost circle*, it is called. Sid in his late fifties, tall and imposing, with a masculine square American face. Other tablemates hold various positions of significance within the Fellowship and architectural practice. But there is only one true authority among us, of this there can be no doubt. From her seat at the head of the table, the Widow directs all conversation. It is she who doles out topics, observes us as we speak, listens to us as in the ancient days of the gods oracles once listened to the poor, believing mortals. Will our prayers and beseechments be heard?

What will our futures be? A red cloak draped over her shoulders. The table too, red and polished, centered by an elaborate floral arrangement, gleaming with golden cutlery and crystal goblets.

Have you tasted the pico de gallo? Our cooks make their salsa the way the Mayans did, with mortar and pestle. I insist on the traditional method. I used to teach them the proper technique myself, but by now my lessons are so ingrained they are absorbed without direct intervention.

Which doesn't keep Mother from sending dishes back all the time, Vanna says.

Work must be done correctly. Standards upheld. Or the point of the labor is lost and there is no surrender and no enlightenment, the Widow says. *I am sure Svetlana knows what I'm talking about.*

My father's table was like this. He sat at the head and watched and listened. He pronounced and declared. He rarely laughed and never alone, for there were always others ready to join in at the first sign of bitter amusement in his eye.

What do you think, Sid? the Widow demands.

Seated on my other side from her, he has said almost nothing throughout the meal. Not rude, but kept within himself. Even without much conversation, however, he has managed to suggest a certain attentiveness. Several times I have found him watching me from quite close with a gentle sorrowful expression, as if regretting his laconic qualities but helpless before them. *Sid's a real westerner,* Vanna said during our wild ride from the airport. *Taller than John Wayne and better looking.* Some kind of cowboy, then? Not with his gaudy evening attire, I would say, the sand-colored tuxedo and lavender shirt ruffled down the front, which he seems to relish wearing, and the golden owl pendant with sapphire eyes hanging from a long gold chain around his neck (all the other men at the table proudly exhibiting the same ornament, like winking members of a secret guild), and the nugget-size silver-and-turquoise ring on the small finger of his left hand.

The salsa, the Widow prompts, beginning to sound put out.

Perfectly authentic, Sid assures her.

She smiles and turns to the rest of us. *I am so glad that Sid and Svetlana have finally met!*

At the end of dinner, as we are to proceed into the living room to hear a recorder concert performed by some of the same apprentices who have been serving us at table, Sid stands first and helps me from my chair. His hand on my arm surprisingly soft and smooth; I see half-moon, carefully tended fingernails and knuckles like buffed marbles. His powerful height, unfurled now, and those bereft eyes move me, I confess. The air of loneliness about him all the more acute for persisting in the midst of such communal self-regard, heightened rather than relieved by the excessive displays of costume.

Has Sid offered to give you a tour in the morning? The Widow is suddenly beside us, fingering her red cloak.

I was just about to, he says.

You'll want to show her Scottsdale too.

Yes, I'll take her shopping.

Her gaze fixes on him a moment longer, a hardening lacquer over some fluid, private dialogue between them. *As you can see, Svetlana, Sid adores beautiful things. And he loves to be generous with others, regardless of cost. He's like my husband that way.* She reaches out and firmly grasps my hand. *Come, let us hear some music. If we're lucky, perhaps Vanna will dance for us.*

21 March

Sid is silent all the twenty-minute drive to Scottsdale in his Cadillac *Eldorado*, strong hands resting lightly on the steering wheel. (I think of Gus Seward, my Don Quixote of Locust Valley, whistling Elvis Presley under moonlight. Dear old Gus: he died last year of a stroke while playing his usual doubles game of tennis at his club.) The land to both sides of the Arizona highway is flat and prickly, perfume of oranges mixed with carburetor exhaust. My guide appears relaxed and in no hurry. Trucks roar by us. A packed tour bus of men in brimmed caps (one with price tag still attached) and a sign stuck in the rear window: DREAM GOLF VACATIONS, INC. A band of motorcycle riders dressed head-to-toe in leather, women grappled to the backs of their hairy men like baby koalas to their mothers. A gas station materializes out of the desert like a Shangri-la.

There are times, still after nearly three years, when to inhabit this country's landscape is to feel myself on the distant side of the moon, the part I was raised not to see or believe in. We move through it now with impunity, in broadest daylight. Sid's automobile drinks twenty-two gallons of fuel at a meal, I am told.

The outskirts of Scottsdale are a spreading accumulation of low buildings the shade of sunset. A Mexican feeling, Spanish names on many street signs and food halls, and Native Indian people with their creased solemn faces standing like carved figurines on corners under multicolored blankets despite the dry withering heat. They seldom move, as if they have been waiting in the same spots for centuries.

It is the Indians who make the most beautiful jewelry, Sid tells me, conversational now as he maneuvers the Cadillac past *Scottsdale's oldest mall* and into the Old Town. They are artisans and connoisseurs of turquoise, coral, silver, delicate beads, and to wear the finest of their designs is to feel imbued with the spiritual powers of their ancestors who once roamed these lands on foot and horseback.

My guide is more than polite, sincere, never garrulous, tall and reassuring in his presence, handsome in some iconic American way that I have never before experienced in person. From the passenger seat I have him in profile, his high-browed head, which Vanna in histrionic tones called *Lincolnesque*, relating him to that great but brooding American murdered by his own people. With his robust hair only partially tinged with gray, Sid could be a decade younger than his fifty-seven years. I find that I'm happy just sitting and looking at him as the minutes pass.

We arrive too soon. He docks his gorgeous yacht on wheels, asks me to wait, comes around and opens my door. This sort of old-fashioned gallantry means less to me than he thinks it does, but then he is not a flirt. On the contrary, the melancholy in his eyes that I noticed the first time we met may be his permanent condition, I am beginning to sense. He has known terrible loss, and twenty-five years later the memory of it seems undiluted, giving him the stubborn myopic frankness of a boy. I want very much to put my arms around him.

He leads me across Main Street to a shop window in which a female mannequin stands in coquettish tête-à-tête with a male counterpart. We pause before this exaggerated human mock-up. Her long dress appears sewn from some native cloth, no doubt highly expensive. A hand on her hip, elbow cocked, expresses her sexual availability, while the plastic-bodied male, dressed in a wide-collared suit and lizard cowboy boots, leans toward her, a lip-less smile on his artificial face, helpless before her charms. Sid informs me that this is his favorite clothing shop in all Scottsdale. Would I care to go in and have a look?

We walk inside, setting off a light-toned Mexican bell of some kind—loud-seeming because there are no other customers. A middle-aged man in a more conservative suit than the window display would suggest steps out from a back room, hands cupping each other in enthusiasm. His sideburns are two adolescent beards running down his cheeks to the bottom of his jaw. He smiles, look-ing every bit like a sturgeon eyeing a school of smelt.

Mr. Evans! Wonderful to see you again!

Carter, I'd like you to meet Miss Alliluyeva—did I pronounce that right, I hope?—a very important guest of ours.

Then an important guest of ours as well. Very pleased to meet you, ma'am. I hope you'll make yourself comfortable and let me know how I can be of assistance. Mr. Evans is one of our very best customers. Are you in the market for anything particular today?

Nothing particular, I answer, and then stand almost unnoticed, beside the point, as one after another dresses are brought out on hanging racks, and skirts, and a pantsuit in the color *desert rose*. I already know what I like and do not, what I intend to buy or not. But mostly what I am doing is watching Sid. His childlike pleasure in the clothes illuminates his eyes, dispelling all depression. It is he and not Mr. Carter who does the choosing. He moves purposefully among the racks and shelves. Before handing me one of his selec-tions, he holds it up. He rubs the material between his fingers and nods if he approves, as though it were telling him a secret. *Beauti-fully made . . . Feel this linen . . . This pattern is exquisite . . .* When

he is certain, a more intense focus hones his gaze, a gleam of cov-
etousness that seeks to include me in its thrill. In this way, five,
seven, ten garments of different styles are gathered and the three
of us, plus a tailor called Jesús, who materializes out of what appears to be a back closet, retreat to a changing area, little more
than a hanging curtain rod in front of a standing mirror, rather
cheap for all this finery. I step inside and pull the curtain as much
closed as it will go, which is not entirely: a glance through the gap
shows me a sliver of Sid's shoulder and the hand over the elbow
where his arms are crossed.

I unzip and step out of my dress. The dress I step into is the
same as on the window mannequin; for all I know, it is the very
one, pulled from the poor plastic girl's back, leaving her naked and
shamed before all Scottsdale. Though God knows, she is not shy
and never was.

Through the thin curtain I hear Mr. Carter's *So how's the fit?*
And the sound of Jesús the tailor rolling his soft measuring ribbon
back into its leather case. Only Sid is silent, stock-still: I can feel
him there breathing, waiting, separated but so close, hand on
elbow, icon of some kind of want I do not yet understand.

Mr. Carter wraps my two purchases in fine tissue paper, hands me
a shocking bill, brightly inquiring if I will be paying with cash or
by check.

Retrieving my Bank of Princeton checkbook from my purse, I
notice him discreetly slide a separate paper, with rows of prices
totaled at the bottom, across the counter to Sid, who with cursory
glance and vague air replies, *I'll be back in a week or two and we'll
settle up then, Carter, if you don't mind.* Which by the merchant's
suddenly deflated optimism—it has been a good day of business
after all, has it not, for how often does one sell the dress right off
the back of the plastic sexpot in the window?—I take to mean that
now is perhaps not the first time this fruitless economic dialogue
has been attempted or played out. I think over my five days in
Arizona thus far and realize that I have yet to see Sid wear the
same piece of clothing twice. He must be what they call a *clothes-
horse*. Though these clothes are not free, not in America, just ask

my new friend Jesús the tailor, they must be paid for sooner or later, by someone.

And seeing this weakness in this big strong man, I wish to help him. To protect him from his own generous instincts, under which he is clearly rather helpless.

With hardly a sigh, Mr. Carter retracts the record of ongoing credit until next time. *Of course, Mr. Evans.* He slips this in a leather binder with other such credits—the Widow's among them, I am beginning to imagine, and a whopper it must be—and turns to me in time to receive, with a flash of capitalist gratitude, the large check I have just written him for my new clothes.

My father never had a bank account. The State paid for everything, and the head of that State of course incurred no expenses of his own. He *was* the State, and anything he wanted he would simply order, and it would arrive or be done. He liked to keep a bit of petty cash in his pockets for appearances' sake, but he had no conception of money's true worth. He received a salary, but he did not know its value as currency, did not know what to do with it on any significant scale. So he did nothing. Every month a large packet filled with money was delivered to his home office, and there on his desk the unopened packets would accumulate, month after month after month, until with time they grew into a hazardous mountain that could be neither climbed nor ignored, at which point he ordered his bodyguard, Vlasik (who kept him supplied with the little trifles of cash that he liked to carry on his person), to unpile the large packets and move them to a storeroom, where they would be piled again and begin the wait to be joined by more large packets in the years to follow. Some of these disappeared into the trunk of Vlasik's car or into the dachas of commandants and generals. My father sensed these thefts but for all his suspicions could never prove them because every single item of the bookkeeping was faked anyway, lies upon lies without a trace, but mostly because he did not understand money in personal terms. This was the man, after all, who in the late 1940s, after the Soviet Union had won the war, as he was fond of saying, still mentally ascribed to the ruble its prerevolutionary value, when a hundred rubles might be considered a fortune, and wore the same musty, tobacco-smelling tunics as when my mother had believed him, in the glory days of the Party, a savior and hero of the people.

Do you need money? he would demand when I saw him then, once or twice a year. *How much?* There was nothing tender in the way he asked the question, nor did he wait for an answer. He would press into my palm, in a gruff handshake, two or three thousand rubles that he'd tugged from his pockets and send me on my way, somehow convincing himself that he'd just made me a millionaire.

Sid takes me next to his favorite jewelry shop. I tell him I would like to buy a ring or bracelet as a token of my visit to Arizona, and he says he will pick out for me something made by the local Indians filled with the spirit and beauty of this place.

The shop is small and narrow, owned by a husband and wife in early later age, quite a sweet pair, who after just a minute or two of talk volunteer the biographical detail that they fled to Scottsdale a decade ago from Chicago and its traumatic winters. I point out that Moscow has known some traumatic winters of its own, to say nothing of the Gulag, a remark that is met with either excessive gravity or none at all, they are such placid, sunny creatures in their permanent southwestern retirement mood that I cannot be certain.

Like Mr. Carter from the clothing store, the Kogans appear on warmly familiar terms with Sid and refer to him as their best customer. He has, I am to understand, a *house account.*

MR. KOGAN: *Sidney here has a magnificent eye for quality stones.*
MRS. KOGAN: *He certainly gives an awful lot of gifts.*

Sid remains humble in the face of such gushing, eyes downcast and already beginning to peruse the trays of turquoise and coral rings under the glass countertop. What he does not see, or does not care to see, is the pointed sideways eye look that Mrs. Kogan gives to her husband following her remark, as if she feels it prudent to remind him to be a firm businessman and hold his ground.

Mr. Kogan (clearing his smoker's throat): *Sure does. And he's collected some nice pieces for himself too. Helluva shopper, actually.*

This is not going to be a gift, I tell them, just to be clear. *This ring is something for myself. A memento.*

Ah . . . Mrs. Kogan says and beams. *Well, then.*

How about this one? Sid lifts a ring from the felt-covered tray that Mrs. Kogan has placed on the counter before us. The stone is turquoise, small, ovoid, polished, the silver band less bulky than some of the others, with tiny, delicate indentations that catch the light.

Mr. Kogan: *Go ahead, dear. Try it on.*
Mrs. Kogan: *That's the only way you can really tell.*

I hold up my left hand. This is not something I plan on doing, it merely happens. I am wearing a Timex watch but no other jewelry and hovering there now the hand looks plain and barren, crudely fashioned, something you might consider using in the kitchen but never in the dining room with important company. It is the hand too, I recognize, of another climate and culture, a winter hand of shameful pallor, with the odd little red blotch and a faint coarseness no cream can cure. I am about to change my mind and lower the offending object out of sight when Sid gently takes it, tilts it level, and, with no warning or ceremony, slips the ring on my middle finger.

Mr. Kogan: *You can't go wrong with that piece. Am I right? Pure Native Indian artistry.*
Mrs. Kogan: *Give the woman a moment, Larry. Let her think for herself. She knows what she wants.*
Mr. Kogan: *I'm just saying.*
Mrs. Kogan: *Exactly what always gets you into trouble.*

What do you think? Sid speaks to me softly and personally, as if the chattering sales couple were on a screen and not real.

I stare at my hand. It is no longer pale or blotchy or coarse. The blue of the turquoise is contradictory like myself, at once flat and deep. The silver band too, warm against the skin and not like metal. And all at once I am struck by the thought that I will marry him. Because he needs me.

MR. KOGAN: *What? What did she say?*
MRS. KOGAN: *She hasn't said anything yet, Larry. She's thinking, an activity I recommend. For God's sake, did you forget your hearing aids again?*

Only buy it if you really love it, Sid murmurs to me. *You're the one who's going to wear it.*

True. But he is the one who put it on my finger. I look up into his face to see if he understands this. He is staring at the ring, however, the piece of turquoise on my finger. It is beautiful to him. Some Indian dug it out of the ground, polished it, set it, and hammered the silver band with a native tool. All this Sid is perhaps seeing as he stares at the ring on my finger, believing in its beauty above all, unable to help himself. I would like to take my other hand now and place it around his big western jaw and force his eyes to look into mine.

I was dug out of the ground too, didn't you know? Oh yes: polished, set, hammered. Semiprecious. Half-loved. When I was still a girl, they named a perfume after me. Yes, it was called Svetlana. *Derived from the Slavic* svet, *meaning* light *or* world. *It had record sales that first year at the GUM in Kitai-gorod in Moscow. Lyusia hated the smell. He found it disgusting, an insult. He said they'd got me all wrong from the start and he was the only one who understood. He was right. After that, I never wore* Svetlana *again. The perfume, I believe, is no longer in production. Now will you look at me, Mr. Evans?*

I will take the ring, I say in Scottsdale, Arizona, to Mr. and Mrs. Kogan, formerly of Chicago.

MR. KOGAN: *Great choice. You won't be sorry.*
MRS. KOGAN: *Listen to King Tut over here. Why should she be sorry?*

The ring is an object of beauty, Sid says, looking relieved. *I'm so glad you're going to wear it.*

It is a gift to myself.

MRS. KOGAN: *What could be better? I admire an independent woman. Now, will that be cash or check?*

On our way out of town, Sid pulls the Cadillac over to the side of the road.

Early evening now, or rather long southwestern dusk: sky somewhere between flame and rust, tall cacti standing like burning totems as far out into the desert landscape as one can see. While closer, on the shoulder of the churning highway, gathered around a hand-built food stall as around a campfire in the wilderness, intimate groups of Mexicans and Native Indians sit on benches, drinking bottles of beer and eating filled tortillas from their laps.

You like tacos, Svetlana?

Sid's smile with its strong white teeth is slow to light but quick to generate heat, I am finding, an electric switch that warms me from the inside out.

Before I can answer, he gets out on his side of the car and walks around the long hood to open my door for me, then leads me by the hand to an empty spot on a bench and sits me down beside a Mexican man whose joy in the dripping, overstuffed taco he is eating is childlike and contagious. Instantly, I am ravenous.

Don't go anywhere. Sid smiles at me. *I'll be right back with dinner.*

I hope you had a good time today. I know I did.

His voice is quiet and deep. It is hours later, and only a little while ago now. My new ring on my finger; I bought it just for him. We are standing together inside my guest quarters, after delicious tacos and coldest beer and the open-air ride in his car back through darkening desert.

I tell him the truth: I have had such a good time this whole day, I am not ready for it to end.

In that case, he says, taking my face in both his hands and kissing me, *I'd like to see you in that dress you bought. Would that be all right?*

Yes.

And then, if you wouldn't mind, he murmurs, leaning in and kissing me again, *I'd like to take that dress right off you.*

22 March

Sid.

25 March

The sun is breaking over desert hills. Here in the luxuriously appointed guest quarters the lights are dim and soon will be useless. In the main house the elaborate Saturday night revelry has ended, I presume. People are sleeping things off. Men with women, men with men. According to Vanna (who speaks of this with proud knowledge), her mother takes a proprietary interest in the sexual lives of her charges, even going so far as to run impromptu seminars on the spiritual and physical benefits of healthy sexual practice when needed. She is a great admirer of the Greeks in these matters.

I try to imagine my father overseeing such a thing, but somehow, as they say here, I cannot get the math to work.

As for myself, I sit alone, writing in my underwear with a soft cotton blanket around my shoulders. The temperature in the guesthouse cool but not unpleasant. My toes reacquaint themselves with freedom after long imprisonment in Vanna's heels. Vanna's blue chiffon dress that she insisted I wear (despite my recent fashion purchases)—cut like a tunic and held together by a pin at the shoulder—now sleeps like a seraglio cat on the back of one of the Architect's famous chairs.

Sid left an hour ago to return to his own rooms.

If at times since my arrival I have perhaps felt myself to be in a play not of my own making, then last night must truly be considered a carnival. There were guests from Scottsdale and beyond.

This the Widow explained to me: *collectors, patrons, aficionados, conscientious objectors* (I must remember to ask Sid about this), *artists*, and the like. Apparently, they embark on this festive madness once every week. Roasted game meats and six kinds of pie. Music recitals and modern dance. Whole gardens' worth of picked flowers in Asiatic vases as tall as one's head. Women dressed to outdo those flowers, in gowns like wild orchids. Tuxedoed men posing as actors from old Hollywood movies or players at a royal croquet party held for no reason in the high desert. It was grand, thrilling, preposterous. A kind of drug for a while, until the drug wore off.

This *Fellowship* is the sort of place where you cannot start questioning why you are here because to be here is to have already absolved yourself of the question. Maybe it depresses me this morning to think that the Soviet Union is not the only nationalist entity that produces cul-de-sacs of moral inertia, where even those things that are good are routinely done for the wrong reasons.

After dinner, I stood watching Sid in his element. I had believed him rather shy among people generally, but here in the center of his home crowd, shaking hands, touching women's arms, laughing often, joining the Widow in praising with ringing sincerity the rich of Scottsdale (for none but the rich, I take it, are routinely welcomed through these doors for celebratory activities), occasionally twisting the immense gold ring he wears on the fourth finger of his right hand, he appeared eager, or at least determined, to sell his shyness to the highest bidder. By the evidence, the Widow was the platform from which he would launch himself into the social stratosphere. And he perhaps hers. How many times did I hear her pronounce to some socialite holding a champagne glass, *As Sid will tell you . . . My husband trusted Sid to see the world through his eyes . . . You must ask Sid, he knows everything about this place . . .*

Yes, I would have liked to ask Sid. To be alone with him. Or even simply to sit down, my feet were killing me in Vanna's shoes. But all the chairs and built-in sofas in the great room were occupied by rich guests, each piece so stridently and uniquely designed, so decisive in motive and taste, so exclusionary in its perfection as object, that anyone not already sitting on it was by definition an interloper. There was nothing to do about this, and eventually I wandered off.

One end of the living room gave onto a dimly lighted low-ceilinged hallway, small rooms branching off it in motel-like fashion. This was where the architects lived during the few hours when they were not performing indentured labor or participating in organized revelry at the Widow's behest. A couple of the doors stood open—a lapse of protocol, I imagined—and I could not resist poking my head into the empty rooms while I had the chance. In each case, the immediate impression was monastic. These were sacrificial people who prayed to a higher calling. For what else would it have been possible to do under such ceilings and in such oppressive light? Had I heard the scratching of scribes' quills and smelled melted sealing wax I would not have been terribly surprised.

Turning to go, I almost ran into the Widow, her dark/light eyes fixed on mine.

Enjoying yourself? she demanded.

I had not heard her come up behind me, and found being so close to her all at once disorienting.

I saw you wander off from the party and it worried me.

I am fine, thank you. I was just walking past these rooms . . . This is where the architects live when they are not working?

As you can see.

They do not find the spaces too cramped?

Cramped? The Widow's face was quite still; only her lips moved. *Why do you ask? Are your guesthouse accommodations uncomfortable?*

Oh no. I am very comfortable. Lavish, even.

I see. You are lavish. But these rooms here you find cramped.

Maybe cramped *is not the right word. It is my first time seeing* them.

Has Sid showed you his studio apartment?

Yes.

And what did you think?

He has a lovely terrace.

The terrace was my gift to him.

The rest of Sid's bachelor apartment was only one room, with not even a *kitchenette*. Beyond the main wall (against which his *sleeper-sofa* was placed) was the architectural office, so the noise of clacking typewriters and ringing telephones was ever-present. The ceiling was so low he had to duck constantly to avoid banging his head on the beams. And this for the Chief Architect of the firm! The whole living arrangement not at all un-Soviet, in fact, though when I tried to suggest as much to Sid, he showed no interest in pursuing the connection. *It's more than enough for me,* he replied. *Not that I couldn't imagine improving the place a bit if I had sufficient reason.*

What kind of reason? We were out on the terrace, enjoying the Widow's view, staring out at the desert moonscape.

He smiled then, and kissed me.

"La cumparsita!"

From the direction of the party, a cry went up. A woman (it sounded like Vanna) called out again: *Give us "La cumparsita"!*

Sí! "La cumparsita" or death! Laughter. *Ai, ai, ai! "La cumparsita!"*

Standing close to me in the confining hallway, the Widow offered no indication that she was hearing anything unusual.

What are they shouting for? I asked.

A famous song. They want to dance tango.

Tango! They know how?

Of course. She sounded annoyed that I should doubt the house repertoire, and I realized that she herself must be the tango teacher—as well as *doyenne* of healthy sexual practices, spiritual leader, clairvoyant, and so forth.

Mrs.—

Mother, she corrected.

I want to thank you sincerely for the visit and the kindness you have shown me here in this remarkable place. I will be sad to leave you all the day after tomorrow.

Leave? Out of the question.

My travel plans are to go on to Colorado and then—

Tell me, she broke in, taking me by the shoulders and pulling me closer, her eyes boring into mine. *Do you like Sid?*

Like Sid?

Don't just repeat my words. Do you like him? Do you enjoy his company? How does he make you feel?

He is very nice. A true gentleman.

He is a man, not a sheep.

I like him very much.

Then why the rush to leave? Stay longer.

I am afraid to stay. I looked at her in a kind of shock, as if she had stolen this confession from me against my own intentions.

But she merely nodded, as if she already knew. *All the more reason why you must stay*, she persisted. *There is still too much for you to do here. And see. And feel. Doors to be opened and connections deepened. Love to be made. You have barely scratched the surface of your next life.*

My next life? She had me by the shoulders and her eyes—I have said this before but must say it again—her eyes were gripping mine, plunging deeper into the private core of my self. As if taking up residence inside me. And I did not know, could not say, how she had gained such access, except by the sheer force of her will.

26 March

Tonight at dinner in Scottsdale, over a white tablecloth and bottle of California wine, attended intermittently by a Mexican waiter, Sid lifts the veil of his personal life. I am a little shocked, I confess, so reticent has he been about his most intimate experiences until this moment.

I feel I owe you a story, he says.

You cannot owe a story, I reply with a smile, hoping to lighten this grave mood that has come upon him. *A story must be given freely.*

He does not seem to hear me. He empties his wineglass, and when the waiter moves to refill it, Sid waves him off and does the job himself.

I was in the drafting room that morning, he begins. *This was in*

Spring Green. I was chief engineer back then, in charge more of the technical aspects of building. I remember I was standing by Jack's desk—

Who is Jack?

It doesn't matter. He's been gone a long time. I don't know where he is anymore. The only thing that matters about Jack now is that he and I were looking at cantilever specs that morning when the phone rang. It was probably ringing quite a while before anyone picked up. That's how it usually was. I heard my name called from the other end of the studio and I'll admit it annoyed the hell out of me, we were right in the middle of trying to hash out a very complex engineering problem, and when I walked down the room to take the call I passed Mr. W's drafting table. I'll never forget this. He looked up at me, looked me right in the eye, and said, Is it going to work, Sid? *And I said,* Yes sir, it's going to work. *Which in that case was not exactly the truth. And then I took the call.*

The waiter walks by our table and Sid calls out to him that we will have another bottle of wine, though the first bottle is still a quarter-full.

Sí, señor.

Sid is silent. His hand with his glittering gambler's ring looks misplaced on the table now. I put my hand—with my new ring—on top of his.

You took the call, I say.

Yes.

Who was on the phone?

Service station owner. He'd been driving his tow truck over the little bridge that crosses the runoff from the river. He looked over and saw . . . the Jeep. Upside down in the water.

He falls silent.

Sid, if you'd rather not . . .

No. I need to. For God's sake, it's almost a quarter century ago!

A woman with *beehive* hair and a lizard handbag is staring at us from her table in the corner, where her fat cat date is boring her into early spinsterhood. With one look, I send her back to her own affairs.

Svet never liked that soft-top Jeep, Sid says. *Didn't trust it. Said it was fine for the Army but in peacetime everyone deserved a real roof over their heads. I wouldn't listen.*

He twists the ring on his finger. Now my hand feels as though it's trapping his, pinning his life, so I pull it back.

We had a kitten, Sid says. Tiny little thing. Lloyd begged her to let it ride to town with them. Svet said absolutely not, then she gave in. Lloyd was four, you know, hard to refuse. He was always telling anyone who'd listen that he was teaching that kitten to play fetch.

Sid reaches for his glass. *They were on their way back from buying groceries. Somehow the kitten must've got loose while Svet was driving and jumped onto the back of her neck—they found scratches on her. She must've lost control of the wheel. The Jeep slammed into the abutment and flipped over into four feet of water . . .*

Sid reaches for his glass. *When I got there . . .*

He shakes his head and falls silent.

Sid . . .

You build a roof, he says. A real roof, I mean, not some fucking piece of worn cloth. The point of the roof is to protect the people inside from the elements. The people you love and have sworn to protect. You put a roof over their heads and maybe that's all you can do. But you do it. You don't not do it.

He reaches for his glass.

Lloyd was trapped under the Jeep in the water. You understand? He was drowned. Four years old.

He drinks.

And my wife . . . Svet's neck was broken and she died. She was seven months pregnant.

He drinks again.

The night it happened, I didn't sleep. Afraid of dreaming. Just spent hours wandering around the property. There was a single dim light on in the drafting room. I looked in and Mr. W was bent over one of the far tables, working on a design. Still had his wide-brimmed hat on. He didn't look up, and I wasn't going to disturb him.

Sid puts down his glass.

That was all that was left, he says.

He takes my hand.

That's what family is to me.

He asks me to marry him on the path outside the guesthouse. The climbing bougainvillea makes a small amphitheater around us.

We have known each other less than two weeks.

29 March

Peter?

Svetlana? Everything okay? Are you still in Arizona?

Yes, still here. And very all right, thank you. But, Peter, remember what you said? How I should call if I need anything?

I remember.

Well, I need something now.

Okay . . . Tell me.

Exactly the problem. I can't tell you why I need you.

You can't tell me?

Peter, you will simply have to trust me.

I do trust you, Svetlana.

No, I mean trust in a new way. With extras. All I can tell you is that I need your presence here on Saturday.

You're asking me to fly to Arizona this weekend, but you can't tell me the reason?

Let us say I prefer not to.

Hm.

Thank you with my heart, Peter. I knew you wouldn't let me down. I will meet you here at the compound late Saturday morning. Okay? I will be the one shouting happily at you in Russian.

I work in New York, Svetlana. People are always shouting at me in Russian and many other languages, though not necessarily happily. I'm going to have to break the news to Martha. She's expecting to go to Block Island Friday and she's going to want an explanation.

I'm sure you will think of something.

EDITOR'S NOTE

She was waiting for me by the entrance to the compound, wearing a pretty dress of seashell pink. Slimmer, tanned by the desert sun, brimming with a happiness that made her radiant.

Beside her, long arm disappearing behind her back, stood a tall broad-shouldered man with the sort of square-jawed American handsomeness found in John Ford westerns. Though perhaps my memory is overstating the case. He was maybe a dozen years older than she but physically fit, his face deeply lined by years in the desert sun. His clothes, cowboy boots included, were surprisingly, almost conspicuously fine and well tailored.

She came forward and kissed me affectionately on both cheeks. Close like this, she smelled of dry sunshine and something wonderfully fresh—cactus?—that was unknown to me.

"I still don't know why I'm here," I said.

She stepped back. "Peter," she announced, "this is Sid."

He approached in long strides, gave my hand a firm shake, and said he'd heard a great deal about me. Then he excused himself, adding with a smile to Svetlana that he had a few things to take care of, but promising that we would all be seeing each other soon.

Once we were alone, she put her hand on my elbow. "Did you bring the pink tie?"

"I did." The pink tie had been the subject of its own telegram.

"Good. Now I will show you your guesthouse."

I had done my homework and seen pictures of the famous property in architecture books. In person, I found that the desert rootedness of the buildings, while unquestionably impressive, resonated above all with the ego of the artist who'd set them there; one felt everywhere the oppressive aura of genius. Perhaps a similar feeling gnawed at Svetlana, for the Russian-accented tourguidisms she chattered at me as we walked along flower-lined paths gave the impression that she was proud of the history of this historic compound but wary of its reality, as if it were an ancient temple built by a demanding god and she had discovered herself already something less than a true believer.

She led me into the guest quarters, where the first things I noticed were low ceilings, unwelcoming furniture, an elaborate bar cart, and a complete lack of telephones.

"Would you like a drink?" she asked.

"No, thanks. But if I wanted to make a call . . . ?" Thinking about Dick Thompson, who before I'd left New York had asked me "as a personal favor" if I would check in with him and let him know how "our Russian friend" was getting along in the "high desert." (Was this the *high* desert? I had no idea.)

"I'm marrying Sid in an hour," Svetlana said.

Completely blindsided, I dropped my briefcase. "Sorry." I picked up the case and set it on a table, which gave me a moment to compose myself. "Well, I guess congratulations are in order. What's Sid's last name? I don't think you told me."

"Evans. Sidney Evans." She was looking at me closely. "Peter, will you give away my hand in marriage?"

"Of course." The words out before I could stop myself. But then, I was her lawyer—what choice did I have? Nothing to do but paste an idiot smile on my face and keep blundering forward. "Just your hand? Or the rest of you too? You know, if you don't mind, I think I *will* have that drink."

Martini for one. There was no shaker so I knew it wouldn't taste right, and she wasn't going to share it with me anyway. She said it was important that she "stay like myself" during her wedding, which was so soon, so she would not drink, or at least not yet, later yes absolutely, maybe some vodka, though I should please go ahead, there was so much to celebrate.

And I did go ahead, there was so much to celebrate. And the drink tasted off.

"Peter," she said as I emptied my glass, "Sid has known great sadness. I will tell you sometime how much. It makes me want to take care of him."

"He's a lucky man."

"Peter, I have been in this country barely three years."

"I know."

"I will always be grateful how you came and fetched me in secret. More than grateful."

"We took that flight together, it's true, Mrs. Staehelin. I won't ever forget it."

I had to turn away from her for a moment; the word *forget* was what stuck in the throat.

When I turned back, she was looking at me. It's called a brave face, I believe, that thing you wear when you're all out of arrows. I just couldn't tell, at that moment, which one of us was wearing it.

"You should probably get dressed," I said finally. "Wouldn't want to miss your own wedding."

She nodded, kissed me on the cheeks, and left. I drank half of a second bad martini, showered, put on my blue suit, and knotted my pink tie. I was all ready by the time I heard the knock on my door. It was one of the young apprentice architects—a tuxedo-clad Bolivian—come to collect me for the ceremony.

The great living room was like no other room I'd ever been in. A low articulated ceiling and high-positioned windows, architectural furniture and luxurious fabrics, and a grand hearth like a personal high altar, beside which sat, in a pose of victorious contemplation, a striking, slender older woman with jet-black hair dressed in a long black tunic. Mrs. Wright and a massive black Great Dane lying at her feet stood up together when they saw me.

"You are here," she announced, her voice carrying the length of the room without being loud, her very dark, heavily made-up eyes ferociously distinct at twenty paces. It was like running into an aging Mayan warrior at a cocktail party. "Come closer, Mr. Horvath. Let me meet you properly."

Her hand when I took it felt all thin bones and heavy rings, but strong. Tendons stood out along her dancer's neck. The skin of her face was as intricately wrinkled as a piece of papyrus I'd once seen in an Istanbul museum. Her beauty hung about her in severe remnants, yet emanating a strange, irresistible pull.

We were twenty-four in all. I was the bride's sole representative and friend. The majority of the guests in the great room were virtual strangers to her, local royalty—which is to say, obviously wealthy—whose access to this celebrity event had been arranged by Mrs. Wright. It all made quite an impression.

The wedding service had been carefully orchestrated from the top down. The vows had everything you could hope for except a single note of Russian, or any evidence of Svetlana's spirit.

She had asked me to give away her hand in marriage—something I had never done for anyone before, and which frankly I had always viewed as more of a romantic metaphor than a literal act. I didn't know how ignorant I was.

She was next to me, in a sleeveless white dress, hand resting on my forearm. And then the time came and I took her hand, and guided her to her new husband's side, and placed her hand in his.

And for a fleeting moment we were no longer at her wedding, or any wedding at all, but back on the tarmac at Kennedy Airport that day of her arrival. A part of history. And I was by her side. And she was facing—bravely, beautifully, honestly—the huge ravenous crowd of a new country, an enemy people no longer, every one of whom wanted something from her without knowing her, something they believed she was because of her name, something she was and wasn't, something she would never be able to give.

Then it was over. And just beginning.

1971

24 May
San Francisco

It is late finally and the hospital, or at least my room in it, seems to have taken a pause in its hectic life-and-deathness. Three days old, Yasha sleeps on my chest. The milk from my forty-five-year-old breasts—may wonders never cease—has stupefied him and now he dreams only of more, his lips making sucking noises though the meal is over. Thin cap of reddish brown hair soft and milky sweet against the tip of my nose. When I lift my head, his helpless scent mixes with the dense perfume of the elaborate bouquets, which Sid was having sent to me daily while he was in Iran on architecture business (who, if anyone, has paid the florist, I am afraid to ask) and which earlier today, upon seeing his new son for the first time, he and the local television crew he brought with him saw fit to rearrange around the room for *better viewing*.

Not just flowers my love was sending, but accompanying notes written before his departure with instructions for distribution according to a strict calendar, as I made my heavy way toward childbirth in his absence. Different days, though the same message each time: *I am missing you.* Fifty separate cards, which I will save always. He had deposited me, thirty-four weeks pregnant and round as a Russian oven, in the elegant Mill Valley home of his sister and brother-in-law. *For safekeeping,* he said. A word which, like the cards themselves, I confess touched me to the core of my feelings for him.

He came to the hospital this morning straight from the airport, having flown all night and half a day. Bearing one final bouquet of flowers, larger than all the others and this time delivered in person, he entered my hospital room looking older and more worn—more his true age—and yet more exuberantly hopeful than I had ever seen him before.

He could not stop smiling. *And this is Jacob,* he said with quiet pride.

Yes, I said. *This is our Yasha.*

Sid placed a hand over his heart and for a long while said nothing more.

He is a large man, as I have said, almost a foot taller than I am. We made room for each other on the hospital bed, my leg draped over his, our shoulders touching, with our beautiful infant son sleeping across both our chests.

Thank you, he whispered to me with a grateful smile.

For what? I replied, smiling back at him through my happiness.

For being strong enough to do this without me.

It was a strange reply, perhaps, though I didn't have more than a few seconds to reflect on it, because at that moment there came a knock on the door and a man carrying a television camera entered the room.

Mrs. Evans—is that the name she prefers?

The television producer's query was directed at Sid rather than me, as if I was but a piece of baby-holding furniture in the center of the room.

You may call me Lana Evans, I answered the man sternly, for this was something I'd decided on my own while Sid was away, and long before I ever set eyes on this media character with the cartoon facial hair. I glanced at Sid and found him looking rather pleased by my pronouncement, if a bit concerned, at the moment, by the tone in which it was delivered.

Great, remarked the TV man. *Sounds good. Okay, lights, camera— rolling. And what about your son, Mrs. Evans? His name's Jacob, right?*

Yasha had begun squirming in my arms. Could these people not see that their television spotlight, held by the producer's gum-chewing assistant, was assaulting my baby's face and making him unhappy?

Yes. After my oldest brother.

Your brother—Stalin's son?

No! I mean yes—Yakov was my brother's name, but this has nothing to do with anything.

Did you give your son any Russian middle names? Something from his grandfather?

My son's name is Jacob Evans! He has no other names. He is American citizen.

I was losing control of my temper, and Yasha producing gasps of irritation. I would have too, if I'd had the guts. Instead, as I became agitated, my English was shrinking. Sensing chaos, Sid signaled a nurse through the doorway—she entered and, without so much as a beg-your-pardon, whisked my son from my arms. And I let her do this, as the television producer with his caterpillar side-burns kept hounding me.

Mrs. Evans, do you really think your son can grow up in America without people connecting him to his grandfather Joseph Stalin?

After a moment's hesitation, Sid stepped forward. *Look, I'm very sorry but I think we'd better wrap this up. Mother and baby need some rest.*

But the truth was that after the TV people had packed up and left, Sid appeared deflated, as if disappointed in me for miscalculating a fine opportunity and casting a shadow over the event.

However, I confess to being then in no mood for such considerations.

This was a terrible mistake, I complained. *Now they will never leave him alone.*

Please don't talk like that.

It's true—their only interest was the grandfather. No mention of you, the American father. No mention of citizenship. Is it only my blood? Was this immaculate birth? Does the boy speak Russian? No, and he never will. I would drown him first.

Calm down, Sid pleaded. *Now look, I promised Mrs. W I'd call and tell her how the interview went. She's been incredibly considerate and interested in our welfare.*

I was silent. My breasts ached; I missed my baby.

I'll come back again after lunch, Sid added more gently. *You get some rest. I love you.*

I love you too.

He kissed me on the forehead and left.

He did come back as promised—a good and loyal husband—and then a short while later departed again. There was an interview to give to a San Francisco society magazine, and another call to make to the Widow. Sid assured me that all the press he'd arranged around the birth of our son was an important part of his responsibility to the Fellowship, a way of attracting attention and funds to the cause. Yes, I'm afraid that my husband is a great and honest believer in the hopeful American dictum that *there is no such thing as bad publicity.*

And I must bite my tongue not to point out to him that in the world my father made there also was no such thing as bad publicity. There were only people who officially deserved what had befallen them. And others, like my aunts and uncles, who simply disappeared with no publicity at all.

12 July
Taliesin East

The Architect's Welsh ancestors settled this green Wisconsin valley more than a century ago: these fields of wildflowers, Queen Anne's lace, chicory framed by oaks and elms, these sandy walking paths, these cornfields, these distant meadows studded with unmoving cattle. All this, I tell myself, will be Yasha's Motherland;

the imprint on his inmost dreams, the idea of place he will never be able to turn away from.

He is asleep now in the bassinet that I rock with my right foot while writing these words. I hear him sucking the back of his tiny fist like a lucky chestnut. And the sound of a typewriter clacking from the studio adjacent to our two-room apartment (one room more than in Arizona, so I will not complain), and a male voice, vaguely familiar, calling out, *Come and look at this, will you?* The Widow informs me—or rather, she informs Sid, who informs me—that Yasha is the first child born inside the Fellowship in a dozen years. Thus: wildflowers, cattle, and rich people, yes; children, no. But fortunately my son, bless him, does not yet comprehend the corrosive milieu in which he spends his infancy. It is not his presence required every evening at dinner with the Widow, Vanna, and the others of the *inner circle* as they compete to charm some local financial baron out of his wallet, or to inspire Sid to mush his poor architect slaves toward one more dogsled victory in the name of Truth.

Poor Sid. Can't he see that he is by now little more than a slave himself? The Widow's favorite, no question, and her most devoted, but no more the general of his own army than my brother Vasily was of his drinking. And still Sid insists—it's the greatest source of argument between us—that I present myself for the Widow's mysterious judgment each evening. These people unified in believing that their exceptionalism rests at least in part on this being not a commercial endeavor, oh no, but an artistic one, a way of living beholden to the spirit, rather than to capitalism or, God forbid, something more base. And yet, at least in my presence, all they seem to think about or imagine morning till night is money! Not enough of it, how to get more of it, how to conjure it out of thin air. If they could, they would print it themselves. They would walk miles for it, dig their hands deep underground to mine it at its source. To keep Genius alive! However, such extremes of action aren't necessary. No. For hallelujah, a *meal ticket* has been discovered.

In this morning's post, a letter from Peter:

Dear Svetlana,

I hope this finds you and Yasha comfortably settled in Wisconsin. The fact that I haven't heard a word from you since your arrival could tilt either way, I suppose, but for the moment I'm choosing to interpret it as a sign of calm and contentment. I hope you received the baby present from Martha and me.

I wanted to check in with you about a couple of important matters. Dick Thompson called the other day and we spoke for a long time concerning your inquiries about Josef and Katya. Lucas Wardlow and George Kennan have informally weighed in as well. We are all in agreement, and the conclusion will upset you. Dick is convinced that the Russian "journalist" periodically sending you encouragements "from" your son in Moscow is almost certainly working for the KGB and should under no account be engaged by you. Silence is the only recommended course of action. None of us of course is suggesting that Josef is aware of playing any role in this subterfuge. I know you'll be worried about him and what your silence might mean for him under the circumstances. But I urge you to consider the position that you would be putting both yourself and your new baby in were you to initiate a return correspondence, to say nothing of making plans for a potential rendezvous. You must assume that whatever Josef's true feelings, the messages he's sending you represent state influence, and thus are inauthentic in a personal sense.

I'm sorry to sound so much like your lawyer, but I feel to do or to be anything less would be to let you down. So while I'm already wearing my lawyer's crash helmet here, let me speak to you about a second subject of real concern. I've tried to keep some of this from you until now to spare your feelings, but perhaps that was a mistake.

As you know, I flatly rejected the Fellowship's request to Wardlow Jenks that you sign a contract donating $30,000 per annum of your money in perpetuity to the Fellowship. I explained that this was impossible—your publishing earnings were held in a charitable trust, much of which was already tied up in building a hospital in India under the name of your late common-law husband, Brajesh Singh. What I never told you was that on the very afternoon of your wedding, the deed on the land adjoining Taliesin East that Sid some years ago bought for the Fellowship (using virtually his entire personal inheritance, I believe) was legally transferred to the Fellowship, so that it could never be inherited by you (or now, by Yasha), no matter what should happen. Which means that the only asset of any kind currently owned by your husband is the nearby farm you bought for him last year, improvements for which you have since paid to the tune of over half a million dollars, despite the fact that the property has yet to bring in a cent of income.

I'm worried for you and Yasha and your financial future. I can't say it any more plainly than that. With your book out of print, and no more in the pipeline (at least none that you've told me about), you have no foreseeable means of replenishing your funds. And from what I can tell, you are spending (largely on Sid and his hobbies) at a rate clearly unsustainable for more than at most a year or so. If you keep going like this you'll end up impoverished by a husband whose intentions may well be decent, but who earns no income yet is an inveterate spendthrift; and by a woman (you know the one) who still appears to believe the insane myth that the reason you went to Switzerland when you defected was to recover legions of gold stashed there by your father.

It's late here, time for me to bring this monologue to a close. I feel quite helpless, you understand, that's what's driving me mad. The whole point of my becoming a lawyer was to somehow try to gain enough knowledge to be able to protect my clients from the systems and processes that threaten them. But in your case that seems the opposite of what I've managed to do, at least as things stand now. Of course, you must know, you are much more than a client to me. If you weren't my client, I would still do everything in my power to protect you. And there, you might say, is another of the stories between us that I will probably never write.
Ever yours,
Peter

16 July

Out on our daily constitutional, he perambulating in his pram, Yasha and I make our way up from the pond that once, historically, was a brook. I have picked a bouquet of wildflowers in the near meadow and these I dangle playfully in his eye line.

What he needs, declares an unmistakable voice, *is some real food.*

I glance ahead on the path . . . and there is the Widow. All in black, black Great Dane trotting ahead of her. Leaning on the arm of her *personal physician*, who I'm quite sure is a charlatan. Behind her, one of the more recent architectural servants—a strapping fellow I have seen around the property framing windows—has parked the golf cart that follows her everywhere she goes on the grounds, in case the old lady might need a rest.

The Widow and I regard each other coldly. We live in a Kremlin of gossip of her own design. And she has made it clear what she thinks of the practice of breast-feeding.

She nudges her doctor and he trudges her forward until her rice-paper mask of a face is peering down into my baby's eyes.

Has he lost weight?

I don't answer, nor does she expect me to. My son's weight is more than adequate, we both know.

He has his father's features, she observes pointedly.

I hope so.

Her eyes lock on mine suspiciously, as if I've just tried to slip an insult past her. *You're never at meals anymore.*

Yasha needs me. And I don't wish to disturb you or the others.

For some reason—perhaps what she perceives as my maternal arrogance mixed with a false, antagonistic humility—it is this banal remark that tips her over the edge.

I don't know why you're so ungrateful, she snaps. *We've given you everything. But I suppose I shouldn't be surprised, given your history.*

She's attacking me, not my baby. But every word strikes me as if it were directed at him. And this I will never accept. I look her straight in her eyes.

All cults are the same. All dictators too.

Her face goes rigid, grotesque. *What did you just call me?*

I called you nothing. Come, Yasha.

I wait until she removes her claws from the edge of the pram, and then I wheel my baby around her and on toward our quarters.

21 July

Today something happened—perhaps only inside me—and now I am afraid to sleep.

Earlier I wanted an errand, as so often I am looking for little trips or jobs to occupy Yasha and myself while Sid spends his days in consultations with the other architects or away in client meetings. I will do almost anything to remain absent from the great house at mealtimes, or from the kitchen in between times, since the Widow likes to go there for her *kitchen talks* with the other women—who is sleeping with whom and having what sort of sex.

I am missing the one friend I had in this strange, suffocating place. Jane Arnold, the wife of Nathaniel Arnold, one of the architect fellows, hailed from Nebraska, with a poet's gaze but a farm-wife's hands. She wore her hair as short as her husband's, smoked hand-rolled cigarettes, and liked to square-dance rather than tango. Willa Cather was her favorite author, she confided to me one evening when I found her sitting outside on the stone steps, reading *My Ántonia*.

Jane was not a fan of the kitchen talks, I came to understand, but an outlier like myself. The Widow's so-called marital advice to her female minions was meaningless to Jane, who had no worldly power except her certainty that she was no one's minion. The Widow, of course, perceived this silent rebellion and was threatened by it; her radar for independent thinking was as sensitive in its way as my father's ever was. And gradually, through the assigning of demeaning tasks and the spread of unflattering gossip, she began from her black heights to wage war against my friend's humble position in the group.

By the time I returned from California with my baby, Jane and her husband were gone.

Yasha and I are on our own now. And so today, with him beside me in his basket, I drive our Dodge to Dodgeville for a car wash. Not that I'm complaining: *My Dodge to Dodgeville for a car wash*—if this is not the very best errand in America, I don't know what is. Yasha enjoys sitting inside the car while the young men circulate their drying towels over the windows, their little squeaks and then the sudden windswept clearness. Later, at the chemist's in Spring Green, I buy a tin of lavender pastilles for Pam, my favorite of Yasha's teenage babysitters, and a tube of therapeutic hand cream for myself. The old man in the yellowing lab coat behind the counter, with his haunted eyes and time-spotted hands, reminds me of how Uncle Stanislav might have looked had he survived the Gulag.

The café in town has a nice tapioca pudding, I have discovered. I sit at a window table with a bowl of it, while Yasha studies a fat fly bouncing against the window glass, the few other patrons in their plaid clothing openly staring at us. I am a minor celebrity in this town less because of Josef Stalin or the Cold War, I suspect, than because of the trail of unpaid debts left by my husband and the Widow at merchants up and down Main Street. And perhaps they have heard the Widow's rumors about Swiss gold and Communist vaults. In any case, I am careful to always leave a generous tip for the waitress.

There is only one route back from town, a two-lane highway that runs over the same narrow river in which Sid's first wife and their son died in the car accident. This is not the first time I have driven over the truncated bridge. But never until today, for some reason, have I slowed my car and really looked at the killing water below, burned low by the summer heat.

Which perhaps is why, some minutes further on, observing from the highway the modest iron gate leading to Unity Chapel, where I happen to know the Architect himself lies buried, I find myself gripped by a powerful need to visit his place of eternal rest for the first time. As if tribute must be paid, or else.

And so I pull the Dodge to the side of the road, lift Yasha from his basket, and together we enter the grounds.

Midweek on a summer afternoon, we are the only visitors. The little graveyard lies to the side of the chapel that the Architect designed, with atypical humility, in a pastoral corner devoid of fanfare. The Architect's people, I have heard it told, were a proud and accomplished lot: farmers, educators, a minister or two, firebrands and Truth seekers in the American vein. You must walk through their generations to reach the Master himself, whose personal gravestone—asymmetrical and upside-down, rough-hewn, unexpectedly stirring—announces its own distinction. I stand before it a little while, but Yasha begins to fuss until, jiggling him in my arms, I move us on to the next stone. Obviously older and placed flat in the ground, this grave marker seems to speak a private language from all the others:

MAMAH BORTHWICK, 1869–1914

And suddenly I realize who this must be. The forbidden subject that some of the Fellows—never Sid—have made it a point of recounting to me out of the Widow's hearing and usually after a few drinks. Mamah Borthwick, the married woman from Oak Park, Illinois, scandalous love of the Architect's life, for whom he built the first Taliesin. A mad cook murdered her and her two children and burned down the house. An unbelievable story but true, unlike so many stories all too believable but false. In his grief, the Architect eventually rebuilt Taliesin as a vessel for her spirit, so the Fellows say. The Widow hates the Borthwick woman and would kill her again with her own hands if she could, some believe. At the very least, she will make sure one day that the Architect's bones are dug up and moved to lie beside her own sacred corpse in a better, truer place. Wherever that may be.

All this death is having an irritating effect on Yasha. Poor boy, he has to go everywhere I take him. He is hungry and tired. *Okay, I tell him, we're going.* I turn and start walking us back toward the chapel and the road. But as we go, we happen to pass two unequally sized gravestones tucked off along the edge of the Jones family plot. I look down at the larger of the two and shock seizes me by the throat. A terrible shudder runs through my body.

It is my own name, SVETLANA EVANS, etched on the gravestone.

There are birth and death dates too. But all I am able to take in is my name, along with the smaller, neighboring stone for my child.

Yasha does not understand his mother's sudden terror. Why in this empty peaceful place she would cry out and run as if from death itself. But run she does, carrying him in a jolting rush past God's house and out through the iron gate and across the two-lane highway to the parked car, where in a single motion she flings open the door and tosses her baby inside like a leaking sack of garbage. What kind of mother is this? Her baby is already crying. Who wouldn't be? But these early tears are nothing compared to the pain that assaults him the moment his bare legs come in contact with the sunbaked car seat—oh, then he shrieks bloody murder! Gives her a dose of her own medicine. And what does she do then? I'll tell you what she does. She grabs her baby in her monster's hands and screams into his face, in Russian, to shut up or by the love of God she will kill him.

8 August

I am afraid to drive Yasha anywhere. I do it when I must, and he has no choice but to come along for the ride, but the mental struggle disturbs us both. I've told no one about what happened at the Architect's family graveyard. Weakness is not something to trumpet in this poisoned atmosphere. And Sid, between his work, the Widow, the regular group dinners, and the Saturday evening beauty contests for prospective patrons, is too busy to notice.

It was his first wife—the other Svetlana—and their son whose graves I saw. I know this now. But it makes no difference. With my own eyes, I saw us buried in the ground.

This is my fixation. Perhaps I am not healthy in my thinking. But to be a mother is to be both cause and instrument of another's fate. To play God. Like my father, who did not believe in God but despised Him all the same.

What did I expect? I, who abandoned my first two children without even saying goodbye.

Did I honestly believe I would not be punished?

17 August

The light inside the Dodge is a trembling egg yolk, hardly strong enough to see by. Outside, midwestern night presses in. It was important to the Architect that the drab reality of a car park not impinge on the spatial perceptions of those living within his house. So I am well away from them now, the car's front seat pushed back as far as it will go. Doors and windows closed, the only sound this pen on paper. My dear nurse, I think, who was never properly educated but cared so much what I might become, would have been proud to know that I keep notebook and pen in the glove box of my vehicle at all times, for just such contingencies as this.

Why did I slap Sid tonight? I was enraged, yes—not from mere anger but from something more uncaged—but honestly I can't recall what he says to me that leads, a second later, to my hand striking his well-shaven cheek. So quick he doesn't have time even to look shocked. Not so the rest of the room—the rich patrons eating stuffed-pepper canapés prepared by overeducated kitchen slaves; the editor of the Spring Green *Home News;* Vanna and the three architects who fight over her attentions and her bed. All stare, mouths agape. The Widow, however, remains cool. Slowly she turns her gaze to me from across the long room, predatory satisfaction intensifying the yellowish gleam in her eyes. And I see that I have played right into her hands. Somehow through dark magic she has orchestrated this moment. She stands milking her visitors' stunned silence as long as she dares, before offering them an arched painted-on eyebrow and remarking, *As you can see, friends, concentrated passion lies at the heart of all we do here.*

In the wake of stilted laughter, Sid doesn't follow me out of the room. Pam is babysitting Yasha in our apartment, so I can't go there. It isn't until I've escaped the building and tucked myself inside the Dodge that I clearly see the kopek-size stain on the front of my dress. The dress Sid handpicked for me during our hurried courtship. Some bit of oil that will never come out.

And suddenly I remember what my husband said to me that made me an animal that had to strike him.

Look at you. You have gone and ruined another beautiful thing.

Look at me. I have gone and ruined another beautiful thing.

I must put down this pen and notebook. Hide them in the glove box, where they can do no further damage until next time. Get out of this car and breathe the night air. And the stars, yes, the stars, will be clear for once in their constellations, each a story that is also an uncorrupted memory, the same here as in Russia. And perhaps I will know then why I came to this godforsaken place to start a new life in the ashes of the old.

Late one afternoon in the fall of '71, a black Town Car pulled up in front of my office building, where I stood hunting in vain for a taxi to take me to Penn Station. The car's rear door swung open and Dick Thompson leaned out, mouth twisted in that half smile of ironic apology that he'd once referred to, modestly, as his "spook's calling card."

"Hello, Peter," he greeted me. "How about I buy you a martini, and you can take the seven-forty-nine instead?"

It was a rhetorical question, we both knew. Half an hour later, we were sipping drinks—always Jameson for him, neat—at a corner table in a crowded Irish bar near Penn Station. (Dick preferred the reliable din of such places.) After a minute or two of small talk, his internal timer went off, and he got down to business.

"When was the last you heard from her?" he began.

"A postcard when they arrived in Scottsdale last month," I told him.

"How'd she sound?"

"Hard to say. It was just a few lines."

"What was the picture?"

"Which picture?"

"On the postcard."

"I don't know . . . some kind of flowering cactus? Does it matter?"

Dick merely nodded as if the flowering cactus, if that's what it was, might well prove significant. "I gather the marriage is in trouble," he said. "And she and Wright's widow are fighting like Siamese fish. I think we both know who's going to win that war, and it isn't our Russian friend."

"You seem pretty well informed for someone who's never personally been to the *high* desert."

I thought he might crack a smile then, but he didn't. "Listen, Peter, Washington's concerned she might get kicked out by these cultists and end up drifting around the country with no money and a wagonload of grievances to air. Not what we need right now, under the circumstances."

"You know, Dick, you're starting to sound a little like your boss Nixon."

He shrugged, his expression suddenly tired. "Hazard of the trade these days, I guess."

"Well, you can tell 'Washington' that I share their concerns, though for different reasons."

He studied me a moment over the rim of his glass. "Care to elaborate?"

"Look," I said. "No question she can be impossible to deal with sometimes. But think what she's come from. It's amazing she's even sane."

"I agree with you, Peter, amazing she's sane. But it's early days. Down the road, that's the concern."

"What am I supposed to do?"

"Just continue to keep an eye on her. Let me know your thoughts now and then."

The 7:49 to Princeton was a more culturally mixed affair than the 6:01, which I took most evenings. We older types in dark suits with our briefcases stuffed with legal files and 10-Ks were joined by long-haired students heading back to campus after a day spent AWOL in the city. Paperbacks of Heller and Vonnegut, Roth and Barthelme were suddenly among us, and bright color flashes of scarves and, mingled with the usual cloud of cigarette smoke, the sheepy lanolin smell of heavy wool sweaters.

A couple of the women in my car that evening were frankly beautiful. I watched them in stolen glances through a scrim of men half my age, and tried to busy myself with the work I'd brought.

At New Brunswick, after the heavyset banker beside me disembarked, I allowed myself to spread out on my seat and close my eyes. Not to sleep, but to be alone. The train rocked a couple of times and began, as though embarrassed by itself, to drift forward, the first few crossrails thumping under the cars. One of the coeds laughed at something her boyfriend said. I opened my eyes and there was my own face, hollowed and paled, almost translucent, in the window dividing interior light from outer dark. I leaned closer, to see through myself. Pole lamps were shining every ten yards or so along the tracks, casting circles of polluted, diminishing light, making the industrial buildings that lined the route out of town appear ruined. And then, as we began to pick up speed, I noticed a small heart-shaped silhouette hanging in the night sky, affixed to the bristling train wires by an invisible thread. A balloon that had escaped some girl's birthday party, I imagined. Just a glimpse, then gone.

A Sunday morning. My father dead a month. His passing a relief, to be honest, he'd been ill for so long, unable during the last year to even lift his hands. And yet, since the funeral, my mother has hardly left her bedroom. After Kaddish and seven days of shivah, the house empty again but for the two of us. And we both know that this is how it is, and how it's going to be, so there is no need to talk about that, and we never will.

Unsupervised, cut loose, I pedal my bike in the cool early morning as far as it will take me—out beyond the town limits and the last dying factory, until the road narrows and becomes dirt and the planted fields are dense with green soy except where the brown furrows cut through. I pedal because the farther I go, the easier it is to forget what I've left behind. I pedal because ever since my father's death I've had a fantasy that if I can just keep pedaling, my bike will eventually carry me to a great city beyond the state I live in, New York perhaps, and there, recognizing my true destination, I will climb off my bike and stand on my own two feet as something other than what I am now. I don't know what this means; it's only a feeling that sits, aching and immutable, on my handlebars as I pump my legs in the cool morning air, seen by no one who will remember, the bike carrying me farther from my life with each minute, the road turning back to the dirt it came from, back to land, the green soy fields, empty at this hour, spreading out around me.

Martha had left the light in the foyer on for me; it was past ten o'clock and my wife and daughter were asleep upstairs. I hung my overcoat and scarf in the closet and walked into the kitchen.

Waiting in front of my place at the four-seat butcher block table, as I knew it would be, was a meatloaf sandwich on white bread on a white plate. Beside the sandwich was a quarter slice of pickle, and beside the plate was a paper napkin folded in a precise triangle, and a tall glass of tap water. Always the same dinner when I came home late. The sandwich appearing, beneath the unforgiving glare of the hanging light above the table, starkly naked, like something recently interrogated.

After eating, I washed my plate and glass and set them on the dish rack to dry. I switched off the kitchen and foyer lights and trudged up the stairs. Across from the second-floor landing Jean's door stood partially open. I hadn't seen her all day, and in the morning I'd be gone before she woke. I stood hesitating. And then I entered her room and sat on the edge of her bed to watch her sleep for a little while.

She was ten and a half, with my high forehead and dark brown hair and thin upper lip, fuller now in rest, and Martha's delicate ears and that expression of my wife's that made it seem as if she were perpetually studying, though never quite enough, for some imminent test. A recent growth spurt had taken Jean, in the space of a couple of months that I'd somehow missed, from cute to gangly, her surprisingly large feet now almost touching the end of the twin mattress on which she'd first slept when she was four. On the wall above her head was a poster of the singer Carly Simon, all lush hair, long limbs, and wide mouth. It had been reported to me by Martha that for Christmas (celebrated by us in nonreligious fashion, whatever that meant) Jean was hoping for tickets to a Carly Simon concert, as well as a new turntable and a gift certificate to Tower Records. That much I knew. And so I made a mental note to myself—receiver of secondhand lists and silent nighttime watcher in my own house—as my daughter slept.

1972

12 March
Arizona

Morning, ma'am. Is Mr. Evans here?

From my front porch, I stare at this young shrub of a reporter. Quite possibly, under normal circumstances, with his blue eyes and cherubic cheeks, cleanly shaved, he is a perfectly decent south-westerner, a *baseball dad* and *low-handicap bowler,* as well as an expert carver of Thanksgiving turkeys. But these are not normal times. Which he well knows. Else why brandish notebook and pen on my porch at seven-thirty in the morning?

I tell him that Mr. Evans has gone into town. I start to close the door of my new little house—everything in it, including this door with its heavy brass knob, still feeling foreign to the touch—but he's quicker than he looks and manages to get his foot in the way.

Is Mr. Evans residing here, ma'am? Are you two separated? Are you going to file for divorce?

Like all good hunters, he has been careful to catch his prey unawares. I stand before him in house clothes and callused bare feet, an owl's nest of hair. Such an awkward human picture that internally he's berating himself for not bringing a camera, I can see it in his eyes.

Absolutely not.

Then why are you living out here? Why aren't you at Taliesin?

The Fellowship believes in communal living, I attempt to educate him, *not in children or families. So my husband and myself, we agree it's better for our son to have separation from the Fellowship. We bought this house together.*

That's not what the Fellowship's saying. They've sent out a statement.

Statement? What statement? Who says this? I know nothing of any statement. Show it to me.

I don't have it on me, but it's definitely authentic. Official Fellowship stationery.

I know that stationery, I think, with the Architect's famous crest and lettering. The Widow loves nothing more than to disseminate her philosophies and revisionist histories to the public on its bleached surface.

I see. So what does it say, this statement?

It says you've abandoned your husband, Sid Evans, and he's seeking a divorce.

The woman's a liar.

Mrs. Wright? He seems genuinely shocked, as if I have just damned his queen to hell. Then he gathers himself, cheeks flushed by the prospect of imminent promotion at *The Arizona Republic*, and neatly flips open his notebook to jot down my remarkable words.

Two days later, I am holding an envelope of that very stationery, addressed to me in the Widow's black-inked hand. The stamp—she must have an awfully large supply of them—bears a likeness of her late husband, with his flamenco dancer's black hat and flowing mane of white hair. I ask Pam, who has come to live with us, if she would take over feeding Yasha his lunch, and I slit open the envelope with the tip of a paring knife and carry the Widow's letter out to the porch to read in private.

> *Your message has reached me as you intended. Rather than reply in kind, I invite you to return to the Fellowship for your husband's sake. Assuming, of course, that you will agree to live by our rules.*
>
> *From the beginning I offered you a mother's love, which you chose to spurn. Rest assured that the invitation I make to you today is of a purely practical nature and will never be repeated.*

I have no intention of returning to that place where one's freedom is forever chained to the iron peg of that woman's egotistical will. I want Sid to come to *me* of his own free thinking. Though with each week of separation that continues between us I am faced with the greater reality that our reunion will not happen. Never would I have imagined that this big strong educated man from the American West would prefer to live enslaved rather than free. But I must face the fact that he has lost his desire for independence, if indeed he ever had it. The chain has become his friend or, perhaps better, his lover. Or it has become himself, his very being, a thought that I tell you makes me sick to my soul because it means it is already too late for us, we are an ending without a story.

21 March

It's Yasha's pediatric nurse who suggests I see Dr. N. The nurse's name is Roberta, and she notices that I am not myself these days, a bit beleaguered, stumped by circumstance. Or it could be my hair, which admittedly is not looking superior. Or my cigarette smoking, a rejuvenated vice. But more than anything, I suspect, it is the pound and a half that Yasha has recently lost (to say nothing of the seven I have gained). Concerned, Roberta questions me about his feeding habits and digestion, and when I am not as clear in my answers as she expects, when I seem a step or two behind in my maternal comprehension, she opens a drawer in the examination room and takes out a card and hands it to me.

This is the name of someone to talk to, she tells me in confidential tones. *A psychiatrist. I think he might be able to help you.*

Dr. N is a phlegmatic middle-aged Jewish man, balding, round-faced, and deeply tanned. He has exchanged his dress shoes (I can see them neatly lined up by his desk) for gentleman's slippers. A bag of golf clubs leans against a corner of his soporific office.

Tell me a little about your family life, he begins, following ten minutes of informational this and that.

You mean Yasha?

Sorry, I meant your original family. Parents, and so forth. You're from the Soviet Union, I believe you said?

Is he suggesting that he has no idea who I am? *Why are you asking me this question?* I demand.

Despite my aggrieved tone, Dr. N's smile is patient, encouraging. He holds his tanned head perfectly still and waits for me to expose myself further.

I am here to save my marriage, I plead in a softer voice.

And if your marriage cannot be saved?

The question shocks me. *What do you mean? But this is why I have come to you.*

I understand, he says. *And if I can help you succeed in this, nothing would make me happier. But life is rarely so simple, I'm sure you know, or I'd be out of work. And if it turns out that your marriage can't be saved, for whatever reasons, you will still be you. Wherever you go. So that's the person I'm asking you about.*

I will never go back to Dr. N. Let us say that the person he insists on interrogating me about is not any person I wish to dine with again. And so I leave a figment of that hectored woman in his office, with the golf clubs and the slippers and the ingenious tan, and turn back on *my own resources,* as Americans are fond of saying—a turn of phrase that could have been invented only in a country with resources to burn.

2 April

I am folding baby socks. Yasha finally down for his afternoon nap, his wardrobe of miniaturized garments, still warm from the automatic drying machine, piled on the kitchen table before me. I think that breathing in the innocence of these clothes, their lack of mileage and cynicism, such repositories of love, is one of the few truly peaceful acts I have known. My American son asleep in the next room. For him, love is not yet knowing what is to come; for me, it is trying to forget what has passed. These two sides of our love, how we reach across time to be here together . . .

Never mind. I am thinking too much. Breathe; let go; fold; breathe . . .

In my driveway, where no visitor is expected, a car door slams.

I am on my front porch before the Widow can take two steps; I don't want her inside my house, near my child. Her turquoise chapeau, black woolen shawl, and wide-legged pants so elegant and preposterous as to seem part of some costume drama unfolding for no clear reason in my average desert yard. Her makeup too heavy for this afternoon matinee. Waving off her personal physician and architect *stud muffin*, who have driven her in her dead husband's *Cherokee red* Mercedes (he collected them, he collected them all), she walks slowly, fiercely upright and unaccompanied, trailing an aura of cold triumph, from the car to my porch. In her hands a small box wrapped in exquisite handmade paper.

So. You have made me come to you.

There is no point, I warn her.

There is always a point, if people are open to reason. Won't you invite me inside? As you can see, I've brought a gift for Jacob.

I square my body in front of the door to keep her out, amazed that she still believes I can be bought for what she's selling. *Yasha is taking a nap.*

Sid will be disappointed. I wait, but she makes no move to leave. *I promised him I would say hello to his son,* she persists.

Why doesn't he come himself?

He feels unwelcome. And he's extremely busy. Did you know he was in Iran again? The Fellowship is thriving. Projects are abundant, creative spirits more deeply engaged than ever. Of course, raising funds for our great work remains a constant challenge. And yet, out of all this, there is only one thing that disappoints. Do you know what it is? I'm quite serious. You must stop slandering me to the public. Immediately.

You are the ones telling lies to the press, not me.

Oh, I think you know the truth. She takes another step forward, her face now so close to mine I can see the crevices in her forehead, which no paint can fill. *Listen to me carefully, Svetlana. We come from the same part of the world, you and I. Of all the people you will meet in this country, I am the one who knows what you really are. In the end, you're just a murderer's daughter, aren't you?*

I raise my hand to strike her. I would crush that face, those brown eyes streaked with yellow. She does not flinch because she knows I lack the conviction to go through with it; she has poisoned me with my own doubt. Behind her the handsome fellow who does or does not know he's a lackey has leapt from the car, prepared to take the threatened blow instead of his dominatrix, while the personal physician, secure in his seat, doesn't move a muscle.

The gift is for the boy, the Widow hisses like a Gypsy curse. She turns stiffly and signals the young man. *Help me down these stairs!*

Once they're gone, I tear off the exquisite wrapping and open the box. Inside, on a bed of cotton, is a framed photograph of the Widow and the Architect—an image captured, one could fairly say, during their glory years. Across the bottom of the photograph, written in oil pencil, an inscription: *For Jacob—Truth Against the World.*

I return to my kitchen. Seeing it now for what it truly is. I have lived here no time at all. To call this home is to not know what home is. Only my son's clothes on the table, light as they are, have any reality, any heft. I put my hand on the jumbled pile and feel how the warmth has left them. If you do not catch innocence as it happens, can it be said to ever have existed? My father loved me once, I know he did. I think of him forever having Kuntsevo torn down and rebuilt again around the single room he lived and worked in, the one room he never allowed to be changed. He must have guessed that it was the only room where what little that was human in him still resided, and known that if he ever destroyed that too, there would be nothing left.

14 April

My marriage to Sid is over.

I should not have gone to see him tonight. It was weak of me, but I needed to know. I could not continue existing in this limbo between our polar realities, ignored into inconsequence as if I'd never happened to him at all. As if our child had never happened. As if I had made it all up in my own head.

I asked Pam if she would watch Yasha for an hour or two. When she hesitated—it was her night off and she was dressed to go out to dinner with friends—I said I'd pay her double her usual salary. It was crude and thoughtless of me, and it offended her; after months of working for us, she has come to feel like part of our little family. Still, she agreed, hugging me as if I were the wounded one. *Of course,* she said. *Do whatever you need to. I'll stay with Yasha.* And I grabbed the car keys and went out.

Twenty minutes later, I was turning the Dodge off the highway, hearing the fenders scraping and grating over the unwelcoming rocks of Taliesin road. The moon high and full, its cold light throwing the cacti into long shadows. I parked on the side of the road and stepped out. The stars were quilted overhead. From my daily peregrinations with Yasha I was familiar with every hillock and shrub of this landscape, none of it as strange as the life I'd led here. I began to walk. There was no one about at this hour, and my footsteps were muted.

Our apartment overlooked the road through a sliding glass door. At certain times I'd hated that door—groups of tourists constantly peering in from the outside as if we were apes in a zoo. Other times, though, I came to feel that the desert view the door afforded was the anchoring point of my sanity: as long as I could apprehend it, it must be real; and if it was real, then I must be real as well.

While I was having these thoughts, my foot painfully struck

something on the ground: a rock about the size of my hand. For no reason I was aware of, I picked it up and continued walking. Soon our apartment came into view, its one illuminated room and that glass door staring back at me like the lens of some giant camera. In the dark, outside, I could get close enough to observe intimate details of the life going on within.

Sid had changed nothing about the place since I'd left. (In truth, he'd changed little after I'd first arrived.) Hanging on the wall among an assortment of antique weapons was the sword he'd been given by the Iranian government in gratitude for his work there, a string of dried flowers dangling from its curved blade. His collection of rock crystals and geologic *nodules* (a word he taught me) were still arranged on shelves, along with his library of art and architecture books.

He was sitting with his back to me. Wearing a dressing gown, his feet bare, watching some show on television.

He must have heard the glass door slide open, must have known it was me, but he did not turn his head. He did not move. For some time we remained like that—I standing just inside the door, he facing the television as if I weren't there; the show's mindless, fake laughter. And then, slowly, I moved closer, until I was close enough to touch him. And still he did not turn his head.

Sid, I said. I had begun to weep, but quietly. I put my hand on his shoulder from behind. And still he did not respond.

Sid, I'm leaving. I'm taking Yasha to Princeton. I will divorce you, if that's what you want.

His head sank—perhaps a nod, perhaps a surrender. And still without looking at me, he reached back for my hand on his shoulder.

I left my desert rock on a table on my way out. For his collection.

PART THREE

EDITOR'S NOTE

She decides she wants her old house in Princeton back, the little white house on Wilson Road. The familiar, some sense of a place she's already been in a country she no longer knows, if she ever did. Lucky for her the married academics she sold her Cape Cod to eighteen months earlier, soon to retire to Key West, are only too happy to sell it back to her at a modest markup. The down payment further depletes what's left of her savings after the paying off of Sid's exorbitant debts in their divorce settlement, but Svetlana doesn't think twice about the money. She wants to be American. Isn't owning one's home and castle the essence of the American dream? And why should such a life, the very antithesis of the Soviet plan, be any less manifest for her than for anyone else? Within a single month, in 1972, she signs contracts for the sale of her Arizona property (occupied but a few months) and the repurchase of 50 Wilson Road. Though I am not a real estate attorney, I counsel her on the transactions as best I can. Meaning that I offer some advice and say a few factual things in discreet tones, and then she goes ahead and does what she's going to do anyway.

Perhaps unavoidably, her relocation to town is noted by the local newspaper, *The Princeton Packet*, the last week of May, if only as a rather cheeky addendum to its lead article on Nixon and Brezhnev's historic signing of the ABM Treaty. You have to navigate the "continued on p. A-5" before finding, in the piece's final paragraph, the following digestif:

> *In other, more local affairs relating to the Soviet Union, Lana Evans, formerly known as Svetlana Alliluyeva, and, previously and more notoriously, as Svetlana Stalin, only daughter of Joseph Stalin the deceased Soviet tyrant, is reported to have moved back to Princeton following her separation from architect Sidney L. Evans, with whom she has a one-year-old son. Mrs. Evans, who defected to the United States in 1967, spent the previous two years living with her husband at the Taliesin Fellowship, the alternative-minded architectural school established by Frank Lloyd Wright in Wisconsin and Arizona, where Mr. Evans is currently Chief Architect. According to Mrs. Evans's attorney, local resident Peter Horvath, the timing of her return to the East Coast "obviously has no connection whatever" to the signing of the Anti-Ballistic Missile Treaty between the United States and her native country.*

Yes, thank heavens for good old Peter Horvath: always around to set the record straight.

Svetlana moves back into her former home. But somehow the place, the longed-for domestic comfort, is not quite as she remembers it. The interim residents made certain alterations, added on a screened porch and a two-car garage, ruining symmetry, spatially impinging on her beloved backyard. The neighbors have built an "aggressive" fence. Other additions and subtractions as well, too obscure for me to register. At least her beloved dogwood tree is still standing: she can see it from her bedroom window. Taller, fuller than before. Symbol of memory and hope.

Unopened boxes are still in evidence in her new/old house as Yasha approaches his second birthday. "Don't worry, Peter," she assures me, "we celebrate. Nothing grandiose. We are simple people,

Yasha and I, and he's only two. As his godfather, of course you are with us." Godfather? This is news to me. But yes, I am with them. And over the phone the handsome architect-cowboy Sid Evans tells her that he plans to fly in, of course he will, just needs to straighten out a knot in his work schedule. Right up until the morning of the event, in fact, she believes that Sid will magically appear so they might celebrate their son's birthday together. When instead of her ex-husband, however, a delivery boy from Princeton's most expensive children's-wear shop, bearing a wrapped and beribboned box, rings her doorbell on the big day, Svetlana finally understands that Sid is not going to come.

Inside the gift box is a beautiful, toddler-size sweater, robin's egg blue. And a card from the shop describing the tiny Scottish isle on which, in some craggy, windswept cottage, a very old Scotswoman knit this garment from wool sheared off her very own sheep. And so forth. *Happy Birthday, Jacob, from your proud father . . .*

"Sid always has beautiful taste," Svetlana says, voice as bleak as the Siberian steppe.

She gets vodka from the freezer and pours small glasses for us both. Sticks a birthday candle in a blue-frosted cupcake from the Acme market and places it on the plastic tray of the high chair where Yasha sits eating apple slices, lights the candle with a match from a book that says PEKING PALACE, and begins to sing "Happy Birthday" to her son, her Russian accent stronger than ever. I join her, our voices not quite synchronizing. She gently orders Yasha to make a wish, but he is not speaking yet, and the notion of a wish is too abstract for him anyway, so his mother closes her eyes and silently invokes one on his behalf. (I have often wondered what it was.) With a blunt Russian breath, she blows out his candle. We down our vodka shots, which she immediately refills. And she looks at me, unbowed, as if to say: *You see, Peter? American birthday. I am learning.*

That summer I see her rarely. On each occasion I observe her acting out the role of American woman, mother, homeowner happy with her situation. And while this unlikely self-representation ought to alert me to its own lie, for various reasons I am feeling somewhat caged and awkward in my own life and so perhaps not looking closely enough. Martha too, as it happens, is a loyal reader of *The Princeton Packet*. And my wife has suddenly decided that this is the summer we are going to renovate—at our own expense, though we are renters—the guest room in our Block Island cottage. Meaning that, unlike Svetlana's first American summer, we will be unable to have guests stay with us during our monthlong vacation.

Back in town, second weekend of September, Svetlana throws an "open welcome party," as she advertises it, for her friends and neighbors. I have never enjoyed such forced community endeavors, but uncertain how many friends she still has left in Princeton—the fact is, with her well-earned reputation for being a fascinating but at times "challenging" woman, many of her former crowd no longer invite her to their dinners or barbecues—or who her neighbors are, I feel compelled, on protective grounds, to attend. As it turns out, unsurprisingly, Martha is struck down with a last-minute migraine, and Jean has a sleepover at a friend's. So I venture over to Wilson Road by myself.

Six o'clock on a balmy, end-of-summer evening. She's mowed her yard with her brand-new lawnmower, bought full price from friendly Mrs. Urken at Urken Hardware; wisps of cut grass clinging to the edges of the bluestone walkway and the tips of my loafers, the cooling air pearled green with it. She always leaves the door to her house unlocked "on principle," she has told me, "so why not anybody—the washing woman, you understand, Peter, the man who cleans the chimney, college professors, a Negro from Chicago, all of them, they can walk into my house as they like and find me where I am."

This is part of what I love about her, I realize, this relentless democratic dreaming expressed in her own particular American idiom. The daughter of a monster, okay, but she refuses to be held back, this forty-seven-year-old single mother of a baby boy, in a foreign country, by the bridge that can't be built, the door that can't be opened.

"Peter!" she greets me with warm cheek kisses as I enter her living room, where a small group of guests—two old Christian Science biddies; a Polish astrophysicist; a Native American garage mechanic; a couple of academic types; and, yes, a black man from Chicago—stand uneasily mingling under what feels like a general cloud of diminished social expectation. "Here you are. What again, no Martha? Another headache? Well, never mind. Come and have some punch. I got recipe out of stupid ladies' magazine, but actually it's not so bad."

I go in. And she is right about the punch. And soon I find myself smiling like a teenager, because I have missed her.

1974

12 June
Princeton

I have a new friend. Dottie, wife of the new assistant minister at
All Saints' Church, where, when the mood strikes, Yasha and I
may be found in attendance, fifth pew on the right, nearest the
aisle. I always bring a box of raisins for Yasha to snack on when he
starts getting restless. (He enjoys the music too.) Dottie's bony,
balding, ministerial husband has a soothing voice and prominent
front teeth. During his maiden sermon to the congregation, he
spoke about the decade that he and his wife and two children
spent as missionaries in Uganda before coming to Princeton (no
wonder he looks so underfed, poor man), and how the experience
of being an outsider in life, that is, a person without community
who must seek community in all its flavors, is in its way a gift from
God. At that moment, I glanced at the side pew by the pulpit and
discovered a slight woman with bright eyes and a flange of dark
springy hair corralled into a bun staring back through the seated
faces directly at me—a welcoming nod of the head from her, which

I was unsure what to do with, before she turned her attention back to the speaker. Yasha required another raisin then, and I did not think about the woman again until I found her approaching me on the lawn outside the church after the service was over.

My husband was a bit nervous today were her disarming first words.

The minister is your husband?

Assistant minister, I should say. She extended her hand. *Dottie Carpenter. Like you, Mrs. Evans, we are not from here.*

You know my name? My voice perhaps suspicious, though I shook her hand.

Oh, I know more than your name. I've read your book. What an extraordinary life you've led. May I ask how long you've been worshipping at All Saints'?

I told her—honest about my irregular church attendance, but declining to give the reason: that I consider the physical place of worship irrelevant, be it All Saints' or no saints; for God, at least as I understand Him at this moment, is the same everywhere, He is no demagogue. Just as all religions are equal, none above the other.

Yasha, pulling at my skirt, wanted more raisins. I gave him some.

And this must be your son, Dottie Carpenter said, bending down to get eye level with him.

Yes, this is my Yasha.

Hello, Yasha. Did you enjoy the music?

A shy paroxysm, then Yasha handed the odd church lady one of his precious raisins.

Why, thank you. Aren't you a polite boy. And handsome too, with those big black eyes.

Yasha emitted a reply that, while full of meaning, was nothing like speech. He wandered a few feet away to pick a tiny butter flower that somehow had escaped the lawnmower's guillotine.

My son doesn't speak yet, I said. Never intending to make such a confession, let alone to a stranger; but once it was out, I tasted bittersweet relief in my mouth.

The assistant minister's wife placed her hand on my arm. *You mustn't worry. Think of Einstein—not a word till he was three, then all at once whole paragraphs bubbling out of his mouth. I'm sure your son will start speaking soon, Mrs. Evans. He looks like he has a lot to say.*

And I did: I thought of Einstein. We were in Princeton, after all. Then I came back to earth.

His school recommended a speech therapist. You know the Morris School? After what I have seen, Mrs. Carpenter, I refuse to send my child to state education. State anything.

I can imagine.

You agree about the speech therapist? It's a good idea?

I believe the best idea of all is God's love, Mrs. Evans, Dottie Carpenter observed with a calm smile. *But I'm sure the rest can't hurt.*

24 June

In the speech therapist's waiting room, Yasha amuses himself on the floor with a toy fire engine and a lollipop with its wrapper still on. We are the only patients. A receptionist of the *Woodstock generation*—complete absence of brassiere support and hoops for earrings that might fit around my wrists—coolly buffs her nails, ignoring us as I sit struggling with the *parental questionnaire,* five pages long and full of intimate invasions:

> Subject's parents' ages?
> Any family history of mental illness?
> Any family history of alcoholism or drug addiction?
> Any particular stresses in the child's home life?

Answers to which have taken me a lifetime. And yet here I am supposed to regurgitate them on command, like some mother seagull being pecked at by her chick? For a doctor's exorbitant fee, no less. Well, I do my best. The thought of there being something wrong with Yasha, some tainted packet of his grandfather that I have brought with me across the ocean, nauseates me to the core. I look over, find him watching me, my little human questionnaire, and muster a smile from nowhere.

The doctor will see you now, says the receptionist in the Janis Joplin Halloween costume. I hand her the paperwork and gather Yasha by the hand, and we follow her into a room that is like Dr. N's psychiatric office in Scottsdale, minus golf clubs and life-threatening cactus, but with the addition of a paper-covered examination table.

The speech doctor himself is hardly much older than Janis, bearded and wearing an ill-fitting half-length lab coat over brown corduroy trousers. No wonder he has no other patients. After a carefully enunciated greeting, he disappears into my questionnaire as if it were some paperback *bodice ripper.* I pull the wrapper off Yasha's lollipop and pop it into his eager, speechless mouth. He starts sucking this way and that, registering the pleasant rush of sweetness, then pulling the candy out again to inspect its properties.

Grape, I whisper to my son, hopefully. *Guh-rape.* He smiles as if Mommy has made a funny joke.

The speech doctor lowers the questionnaire and wheels his medical stool over to where we sit on the examination table. His manner now uneasy, jettisoning his default certitude that he can solve our problems.

So, Mrs. Evans, what exactly is it that has brought you and your son to see me?

Yasha is doing fine at the Morris School, I explain. *You know it, yes? Top school, very expensive. His teachers praise his intelligence and quickness for his age, his remarkable vitality.*

This is all true, even if the doctor's mouth currently inhabits a knife's edge between encouragement and skepticism.

But I am worried, Doctor. Yasha doesn't speak. Not at school or home. All the other children are speaking, yelling with words, but not him.

I see. The doctor scans the questionnaire again. And I glimpse the dirty evidence of my family history in his hands:

Subject's parents: biologically OLD.
Subject's grandfather on mother's side: _____.

Subject's grandmother on mother's side: nervous breakdown, followed by eventual gunshot suicide.

Subject's half uncle on mother's side: died German concentration camp, technical suicide, though wartime conditions, etc., must be taken into consideration.

Subject's uncle on mother's side: died alcoholism age 41 following time in prison for manic insubordination after father's death.

Subject's mother: separated from subject's father, not unfamiliar herself with alcohol, but rather not specify at present time.

Home life stresses: normal for situations described above, plus other complications.

The speech doctor's expression by now a death mask of Hippocratic concern. If indeed he knows who my father was, he is a most malicious stage actor. He turns to my little boy and says, *So, young fellow, I hear you're very bright* . . . And thus begins his investigation. While my thoughts catalyze and ricochet between electric points of dread, backward, forward, but always backward, to a stone hovel in Gori where a drunken cobbler beats his son to within an inch of his life, to a Tbilisi alleyway where the son shoots his first victim in the name of revolution, to my mother's life bleeding into the mattress through the hole she shot in her heart, to Zubalovo, to Kuntsevo, to Sochi, Beria with his gleaming pince-nez, the Kremlin, Lubyanka Lubyanka Lubyanka, to Vorkuta, to Inta, and Aunt Anna and Uncle Stanislav, *We don't have exile. We just disappear*, and my father's blunt palm slapping my face, I am sixteen, *Look at you! You look like a whore! Who would want you, anyway—*

Mrs. Evans?

The speech doctor speaking to me.

I asked if you've had your son's hearing checked. It's something we'll want to rule out first.

I tell him my son's hearing is one hundred percent fine, I do not need a doctor to know this.

The speech doctor stares at me in confusion, perhaps alarm. And I realize that I have just spoken to him in Russian.

17 July

Peter telephones from Block Island, where they have been on their annual holiday since the beginning of the month. I tell him I can't talk long, I have a friend over for a visit—Dottie right now in my living room perusing the American volume of Akhmatova that I pressed on her after she ignorantly attempted to praise Tsvetayeva as the greater poet—and he rather defensively says, *I was just checking in*, as if the call is nothing but an extension of his job, billed by the hour. Even as I hear a door closing on his end and know he must be calling from the phone in his and Martha's upstairs bedroom, where he is attempting to seclude himself for a few minutes of private talk, forgetting that the walls of their island cottage are as thin as those of any Soviet building designed for eavesdropping by the hidden powers of the State.

What did the doctor say about Yasha?

He said there is nothing "definitive" and the situation is worth "monitoring."

Well, at least that's better than you feared, right?

Perhaps my son will speak and perhaps he will not—either way, one hundred and twenty-five bucks cash, thank you very much.

You sound pretty angry.

No, Peter, this is simply my new American voice.

Come on now, Svetlana.

It's a long hot summer, Peter. At least here, where we do not have the luxury of the Atlantic Ocean and the odd Russian émigré living in the blue bloods' house.

Okay, I'll let you go.

I'm sorry. You know I don't mean anything. How is Jean?

Jean's fine. Tell me what's going on with you. That's why I called. You sound upset about something.

I have a friend here.

Okay, I'll get off then.

No, Peter, wait . . .

What?

Nothing.

I'll call again soon.

Peter? Thank you.

No need to thank me. I like talking to you, it's not a job. In case you don't know that by now.

He hangs up.

Back in the living room, I find Dottie on the couch, Akhmatova on her lap and a mug of Lipton on the coffee table. Perhaps she observes complications in my face, but she does not inquire. The woman spent ten years in war-torn Uganda and knows how to be discreet with other people's sentiments.

Do you know Akhmatova's Requiem? I ask her.

As if fearing I'm about to give her an exam on the subject, Dottie Carpenter replies meekly, *Not really.*

During the Great Terror—yes, my father's—Akhmatova's only son, Lev, was arrested for counterrevolutionary activities. They sent him first to Leningrad prison. Every day for seventeen months his mother lines up outside the prison walls along with the other sufferers— mothers, wives, daughters—hoping to deliver packages of food and clothes to their men. This poem, this requiem, begins on the day when an old woman standing in line next to Akhmatova tugs on her coat sleeve and whispers: "Can you describe this?" And Akhmatova, just another mother among thousands, looks back at the old woman and says, "Yes, I can." And so it begins:

> *Seventeen months I've pleaded*
> *for you to come home.*
> *Flung myself at the hangman's feet.*
> *My terror, oh my son.*
> *And I can't understand.*
> *Now all's eternal confusion.*
> *Who's beast, and who's man?*
> *How long till execution?*

I am crying now, I can't help it. And clearly moved herself, Dottie asks, *Does she get her son back?*

I stare at my new Princeton friend, wife of the assistant minister of the All Saints' Church. A compassionate lady, doubtless.

Uganda, et cetera. And still, how does one . . . If you are not a poet. If you never stood in line.

Her son, Lev, spent nineteen years in the Gulag. He was not released until 1956.

Relief softens Dottie's thin face, brightens her eyes to a fever of hope again. *But he* was *released. Eventually she got her son back. The poem worked.*

No, I correct her, perhaps too severely. *Poems don't work or not work. They either survive or they don't—like Russians. When Lev finally returned from the camps, he felt only great bitterness toward his mother. He felt she should have been doing more to save him instead of writing poetry all those years. He never forgave her.*

How terribly unfair.

Maybe.

I can see that my new friend is ready to leave. I lead her outside with promises for another visit soon, then walk upstairs to Yasha's room, where he has been down for a nap. Thinking now not about my little boy but about my half brother Yakov—the earlier Yasha—and his wife, Yulia. Yakov was captured by the Nazis in July 1941. In August of that year, our father issued Order 270, declaring that all Soviet soldiers who surrendered to the enemy or were captured were *traitors to the Motherland.* Wives of these traitor soldiers were not exempt—they too would be treated as traitors and arrested. No exceptions would be made, not even for the *vozhd's* son and daughter-in-law.

For eighteen months Yulia was kept in solitary confinement in Lubyanka, and later, with the Germans pressing deeper into Russia, she was transferred to a prison in Engels, on the Volga. Then, in the spring of '43, for no reason that was ever explained to her, she was allowed to walk free. She made her way back home, where her and Yakov's daughter, Gulia, now five years old, did not recognize her.

It was that same spring, the ghosts tell us, after the unmitigated carnage of Stalingrad, that my father refused the prisoner exchange that would have brought his firstborn son, Yakov Dzhugashvili, home. A month later, my dearest brother was dead.

Now Yasha murmurs something, opens sleep-glazed eyes. *Hello, my darling. Mama's here. Did you have a nice nap? Apple juice.*

I stare at him, doubting my own ears. *Say that again? Apple. Juice. Mama.*

9 August

President Nixon has resigned. On TV in my living room, drinking Miller High Life, *the Champagne of Beers,* to help me through the proceedings, I watch the President of the United States of America declare that he is quitting, though he *isn't a quitter.* Good to know. Seated in the Oval Office, the disgraced leader informs us that he is confident he is leaving the world *a safer place for the people of all nations.* Of course, no mention of what mischief he got up to with FBI, CIA, Internal Revenue Service during his time as Leader of the Free World.

A bit later, Vice President Ford speaks from in front of what must be his charming private home purchased with his own significant wealth. He seems an alarmingly mild fellow. He will become president now. And I say good luck to him.

27 August

After eleven o'clock at night and still a good eighty degrees hot outside, humidity so thick you could drink the air if you were desperate enough. Which I might be, if not for the vodka and beer that I keep always too well stocked in case I start brooding about Josef and Katya again. Once more tonight, after Yasha was down to sleep, I carried my drink over to the chair by the television and planted myself for the duration. A habit I must stop. I feel it in my physical heart sometimes—drink, sitting, stupidity, thickening me like goulash. Watching this Archie Bunker, who is all mouth. Mary Tyler Moore, who would not survive a single day in Minsk. Some child-man called *the Fonz.* I am just about to beg for mercy when my cultural savior Dick Cavett appears with his ironic delivery and intellectual programming, helping me to remember that I am not a transplanted idiot.

A wonderful lineup of guests on tonight's show: that magnificent boxer Muhammad Ali, most beautiful Negro the world has ever seen; some impressive woman who performs what she calls *political vaudeville theater* (now a redundant art form); and finally, Jerzy Kosinski, dashing and slim in European sport jacket and silk foulard tie, yet still looking, with his cunning pained smile and seagull's nose, like a count in permanent search of his lost castle. There is talk out there—I have heard it myself recently from Dick Thompson, who always knows more than he says—that Jerzy did not actually write his famous book *The Painted Bird* himself, or that at the very least the horrors he said he endured as a Jewish boy passing as Christian during the war in Poland did not happen to him, or that perhaps he is not even Jerzy Kosinski at all. Cavett, of course, does not bring up these accusations—this is a friendly interview, not like the kind I get nowadays, when they happen at all—though skepticism can be heard humming in the televised atmosphere, giving the moment its satisfying undertow of tension.

I find I can't take my eyes off this charming literary refugee with the coal-black eyes, the intoxicating impression he gives of a doomed man standing in front of a closed curtain, daring us to look behind it. Naturally I regret the humiliating letter I wrote him after we met that time at Edmund Wilson's three or four years ago. But the conversation had flowed so freely between us, felt so light-footed and intelligent, we felt so close in spirit, that I suppose I can forgive myself for believing more lay underneath. Not the first time I have been disappointed by someone who turned out to be less than he seemed and whose story was not his own.

But what is the point of thinking about all this now? I must not drink so much. It's because Peter is not here.

Where is he? He promised he would come see me after his return from Block Island, but he has not come, damn him, he has not come but instead has left me with this helpless feeling that I have always hated of waiting for a man who does not and will not relieve me of my vulnerability of needing him. A man who wields his absence as a power, whether he knows it or not, a man self-satisfied in his own family castle, father and husband, while I sit here with television and sweating glass and little boy upstairs and this restless fucking desire that has nowhere to go.

Something is wrong with the electric fan—blade tick-ticking against its metal cage as if trying to escape. I yank the plug from the wall . . . And through half-open window blinds see my neighbor, distinguished astrophysicist Roman Smoluchowski, walking his dog down my street. One of those little black tailless creatures bred to live on barges in Dutch canals. Smoluchowski gazing straight up at the heavens as he goes—all the way to the stars, I presume, in their infinite mystery.

14 September

I am buying my *New York Times* at the kiosk in town when Smoluchowski waves to me from across the street. He is alone today, in houndstooth sport jacket and olive green fedora, with no little dog on a leash.

Svetlana, he says rather conspiratorially, closing the distance between us in a few strides, *I have been looking for you.*

Looking for *me?* I regard him. On the whole, I think Smoluchowski a gentleman and an intellectual, with his fine Slavic forehead, trimmed silver beard, and quite good posture for someone his age.

I am right here, Roman. Buying my newspaper as usual. How is your dog?

Bruno is healthy for his years, thank you. Listen, I want to talk to you about something important. Can we go somewhere for coffee?

With Yasha in school until noon, I am unoccupied. Roman and I go to the café on the next block, settle into a booth, and order two coffees, black. He leans forward, his manner scientific yet human.

I am just back from an astrophysics conference in Moscow, he says. *At this conference, one day I was approached over lunch by a colleague I had never met. A Russian named Karpovsky. You know him?*

I do not.

The man was aware that I teach at Princeton. And he'd heard that the daughter of Stalin is again living here as well. He asked— quietly—if I happen to know you personally. In which case, will I agree to pass on to you some news about your children?

My children? I grab my good neighbor's wrist where it lies on the table between us—with more strength than is feminine, perhaps, because I see him flinch. *Roman, you must tell me now. Are my children safe?*

They are safe. Feeling suddenly light-headed, I release his wrist. Now the waitress interrupts with our coffees, and Roman waits until she leaves before adding, *According to this man Karpovsky, your daughter—*

My daughter, Katya?

Your daughter received her degree in geophysics from Moscow University. Now she is teaching, also geophysics.

Katya was always smart. Is she married?

No. Apparently, she lives with her grandmother.

I am appalled by this revelation but say nothing aloud. My former mother-in-law, a bully and a loudmouth, was the main reason I divorced Katya's father. *And Josef?* I ask with trepidation. *What about my son?*

According to Karpovsky, your son Josef is a doctor at one of the better clinics in Moscow.

This takes a moment to sink in.

What sort of doctor?

Some aspect of cardiology, is what I understood.

Is he married?

He was. But now divorced.

I shake my head in dismay. *From the time he was small, I warned him not to marry young as I did.*

Men who spend their lives peering at the stars are by nature optimists, I have found. And I see now that it pleases Roman to be able to deliver his news to a lady in emotional turmoil such as myself, so that he might comfort me. I do not blame him for this. It is how men are.

There's more, my neighbor continues. *Svetlana, according to this Karpovsky, your son Josef is a father. He has a four-year-old son.*

Now I can only stare at him.

That's what I wanted to tell you, my dear. You're a grandmother.

29 September

A hole is growing in my backyard. More than a hole—a pit. And unlike those mass graves my father is now said by historians to have been so partial to, none of this minor suburban excavation, I can tell you, is to be found at Communist prices. The labor here, even Guatemalan or what-have-you, is certainly not cheap; the *backhoe* is not cheap. I am paying for my American swimming pool the *good old-fashioned way*—on the installment plan. This is how people do it here, the pool company salesman assures me. Of course he is corrupt, and Peter is apoplectic (for Peter, I mean) at my lack of financial sense, but why should Yasha not have a pool to swim in during these long hot New Jersey summers, when so many of his little classmates at the Morris School have theirs? Or their *country clubs,* which are not open to all people.

Nelson, head laborer of the three amiable fellows who now seem to live in my yard while destroying it, was born in Guatemala City, which he informs me rather shyly is a place best known for its high rate of murders. Well, he is here now, all five feet, four inches of him (information he volunteered with perhaps a dose of male hyperbole), a survivor and illegal immigrant to whom I am happy enough to give work. He brings his lunch in a metal pail and shares it with his equally small-statured compatriots at 11:00 sharp each morning, three fellows sitting on the curb out front with their feet on Wilson Road. A generous and satisfying lunch, from what I've seen; and so it pleases me to imagine that Nelson has a wife who loves him.

Meanwhile, I have stopped checking my bank account except when absolutely necessary. I must be honest with myself: I have allowed this installment situation to grow into a many-headed snake. I say nothing of the mortgage on the property as a whole, an eye-watering debt, which, I am constantly being told, is actually a sign of good financial health. No, the true Hydra begins with the lawnmower, the Maytag washer and dryer machines, the General

Electric dishwasher. The Electrolux Swedish vacuum cleaner, known to be the best in the world for *real shag* carpeting. And now, pièce de résistance, the swimming pool with *California blue* bottom, which if it ever gets finished (and paid for) will require a *pool boy* to go with it all, some resident genius to manipulate the filters and heaters and such.

But what else did I expect? Is capitalism not what I aspired to? So much time spent going after <u>things.</u>

And I am no different: I desire these things too—perhaps more than they do. Each sparkling, never-before-needed thing with its price. Each price attached to its system of payment. Each system of payment waiting on wallet, checkbook, bankbook, membership, prayer, victory.

So if I'm winning the lottery and the whole damn show, as supposedly I am, why doesn't it feel better?

That is no pool in my yard. That is a pit.

23 October

I met Max Kirschner, the journalist and professor, three weeks ago at George and Annalise Kennan's. *Oh, you'll love Max,* Annalise promised me before the other guests arrived, *he's a force of nature. And he knows all about Russia.* And it was true, this I could see the moment he walked into the room that evening: a man of formidable years (seventy, according to Annalise) whose lifetime of experience in the world was a raging fire inside him still: tall and imposing, with a brow like a gorgeous ship, he strode right up to me and declared, *You and I have a lot to talk about.*

Yes? I replied, unable to take my eyes off him.

He was from Philadelphia, he told me, the son of Russian Jews. *Crazy about the Revolution,* as he described himself in his youth, he'd left to report from Moscow in the 1920s, married a Russian woman, and had two children there. But my father's Great Terror had driven him out—first without his family, though eventually they were able to follow him to the States.

And where are they now? I asked. *Your wife and children?*

Here and there.

He went on to tell me about his work with Hemingway, Dos Passos, Malraux; biographies of Gandhi and Churchill.

You've read my Stalin book?

No.

I had a six-hour interview with him in 1927.

The year after I was born.

I know. Your father was "unsentimental, steel-willed, unscrupulous, and irresistible." I'm quoting from my book. But when he talked about you, he couldn't stop smiling.

It is possible that the immediate impression made on me by Max was not entirely unlike his description of my father. He was seated next to me at dinner; we talked all evening. Dessert was still on the table when he leaned close and said, *Shall I drop you home?*

His fondness for women, his visceral physicality, was as much his calling card as the cataloging of his own brilliant adventures in my bed that night: this he wanted known, and I knew it; and I suppose I have fallen for him at least in part because of it.

26 October

Max stands at his kitchen-counter *island,* shoveling chicken chow mein directly from the container into his mouth with deftly wielded chopsticks, managing at the same time to refill our glasses from a bulbous jug of Chianti dressed in a straw basket.

So you see this as a new book?

He is referring to the pages of writing that, at his urging, I recently sent him for his opinion—pages now laid out on the counter between us, amid packets of *duck sauce* and hot Chinese mustard.

Trying not to sound too defensive, I reply that I don't yet know what these pages will be—precisely why I asked him to read them in the first place.

Because to speak frankly, Svetlana, based on what I've read so far, I'd think twice before trying to publish this material in its present state.

I assure you, Max, I say crisply, *I have thought more than twice.*

It's a figure of speech.

I am not allowed to criticize this country?

I didn't say that.

Maybe you misunderstand my English.

In that case, maybe you should go back to writing in Russian.

Max, I am sick of Russian.

You might be sick of Russian, but it's the Russian in you that people still want to hear about.

Give me back my pages.

Now don't overreact. And suddenly Max is smiling, as if he's just thought of the perfect gift to give me that will make everything better. *Tell you what,* he says. *We'll write a book together.*

I eye him suspiciously. *A book about what?*

He puts down the carton of Chinese-American food and drains his glass of Italian red wine. He circles the counter in three confident steps and slides his arms around my waist, his warm breath pulsing against my ear.

Oh, I can think of a few things. Can't you?

1 November

Last night, Max knocked on my door wearing—it took me a moment to understand—a Halloween costume.

A long flowing beard, a wig of thick unkempt hair, and a peasant's tunic.

I laughed, impressed. *Tolstoy?*

He looked hurt. *Rasputin.*

Ah . . .

And who are you?

Akhmatova, I answered, as though it were obvious.

Later, at the Halloween party he brought me to, we were able to laugh together at the fact that no one present was able to successfully identify either of the characters we were playing. There was a Pocahontas, a Lincoln, a Theodore Roosevelt, an Elvis in attendance, but no Russians.

As the evening wore on, though, and this was unexpected, I found the idea of impersonating one of my own people, especially one I revered, even in such surface fashion, to be a disturbingly alienating experience; I began, in the midst of all those adults playing make-believe like children, to feel homesick.

After only an hour or so, I found Max across the room talking to two women dressed like *flappers* from the 1920s, or some such. I told him that I wanted to leave.

Have a drink, he said, frowning.

I've had a drink.

Anna Akhmatova, he introduced me to his two companions, *meet Louise Brooks and Mae West.*

Max, I want to go. Please take me home.

His jaw clenched and he sighed loudly through his nose. *Be back soon, ladies,* he said to them.

The ten-minute ride to Wilson Road was tense between us.

I felt myself sinking. I said quietly, *Leaving my children in Russia was an unforgivable mistake.*

For God's sake, Svetlana. It was just a fucking party.

We reached my street. He pulled over in front of my house, but kept the engine running.

I'm heading back to the festivities.

His voice held no warmth. Perfunctory as an afterthought, he leaned across the seat to give me a quick kiss goodbye.

His lips would have brushed my cheek, but I was no longer in the car.

EDITOR'S NOTE

November. The month of her mother's suicide. The month which all her life will arrive like a cuckoo clock of despair, calling, *You are alone, you are alone, you are alone.* This year no better, maybe even a bit worse: she has told me (under the rubric of lawyer-client privilege, I assume) of her recent all-too-brief affair with the journalist Max Kirschner and how it ended. Kirschner is already rumored to be sleeping with his new research assistant, a grad student a third his age.

And Peter Horvath, Esquire? Kind of you to ask. No such romantic entanglements for him. Behold him in early middle age, tucked away in his Park Avenue office, sticking diligently to the professional script as it once was written for young men like himself in the vaunted halls of the nation's finest law schools. His mentor, Lucas Wardlow, is semiretired and rarely in the building anymore. And without the famous attorney's worldly encouragement and sophisticated bonhomie to guide his fortunes, it is fair to say that almost the entirety of Horvath's more civic-minded (i.e., pro bono) practice at Wardlow Jenks has gradually been squeezed aside by routine corporate work, financial contracts, negotiations, and the like, which pay the firm's and his own hefty bills well enough, but leave him somewhat less than proud.

Among his many clients, however, there remains one notable exception to this rule of widgets and monotony. (Hint: she is Russian.)

She is the client—the only one—whom he regularly telephones during nonoffice hours (and always on a private line, with the door closed), simply to "check in." The client whose roller-coaster moods he has come to be able to read with the nuance of an expert seismologist. The client whose always undiluted opinions about people, places, nations, politics he has begun—much to his surprise, alarm, and, yes, occasional amusement—to absorb as his own. The client whose level of emotional energy has become the barometer that tells him the atmospheric pressure of his day. The client whose memories of her traumatic past—whether in fact she herself perceives how traumatic—have increasingly come to weigh on him too, as if (though he knows this is fantasy) he were not a relatively recent addition to her life but rather an old and intimate conspirator, someone who had been at her side from the beginning, in a country far from his own, inseparable from the joys and hurts of her foreign, inconceivable life.

And yet for all this, a neutral observer, if such a person existed, might have remarked how during these crucial weeks of our story Peter Horvath himself, ever the professional, continued to conduct his public life without the appearance of any major disturbance of the heart.

But hold on a minute: yes, out there, a wind is beginning to blow.

Thus we arrive at the Thursday before Thanksgiving, 1974. The phone buzzes and my secretary, Beverly, informs me that Mrs. Evans is on the line.

"Put her through."

"Peter, is that you?"

"I have it, Beverly, thanks. I'm here, Svetlana. Everything all right?"

"Peter, do you have special recipe for cooking turkey?"

A surprising urgency to her question, as if I'm being asked for the nuclear launch codes. "You mean for Thanksgiving?"

"Of course Thanksgiving, what else? I am talking real American turkey."

"Hmm. Sort of outside my field of expertise. I could ask Martha, if you'd like."

"Never mind. I can see you have no idea."

"You're right," I quickly agree, relieved to drop the matter.

"Fine, then." She actually sounds put out that I don't have a turkey recipe up my sleeve. "Peter?"

"What?"

"You know Bonhoeffer?"

"Bon-*who*?"

"*Bonhoeffer*. Theologian. German, but against Nazis. My new friend Dottie lends him to me. His book calls what is happening to me a *crisis of faith*. *Temptation of the spirit*, he says. The kind of alone you only feel when God has left."

"God hasn't left you, Svetlana. If He was with you before, He's with you now. God knows I'm no expert on God or Bon-what's-his-name, but I know that's how it works. Most of all, I know *you*."

A sudden *crack* on the other end of the line, followed by a buzzing wisp of static. And oddly, as if I were at her side, I can picture in my mind exactly what's happened: the telephone receiver has fallen out of her hand and landed on the linoleum. I can picture where she's standing in her kitchen, the twisted length of phone cord. And now I hear what can only be the unscrewing of a certain kind of bottle cap—Smirnoff's—followed by the unmistakable sound of liquor being poured over cubes of ice.

According to the silver clock on my desk (from Martha, Tiffany's, engraved for our tenth wedding anniversary), it's a quarter past three. "Svetlana, are you drinking? It's the afternoon. Look, maybe it's none of my business—"

"Why not, if it makes me feel better?" she snaps. (There's my girl: daughter of the *vozhd*.)

"For Yasha's sake," I remind her. "And because you know as well as I do that drinking's not going to make you feel better. It's going to make you feel worse."

"What the hell do you know? I'm a bad mother. I never learn."

"You're *not* a bad mother. You're just having a rough time."

She blows her nose.

"You're crying."

"No."

"Listen, I'll stop over and see you this evening. Okay? From the station. I don't know how I'll work it out, but I will."

"You'll *check* on me," she accuses me bitterly. "My Park Avenue lawyer."

"Did it ever occur to you that if I *check* on you, as you call it, maybe it's because I actually—"

"Sure. Jenks Wardlow. One hundred seventy-five bucks an hour and all-you-can-eat buffet."

"It's Wardlow Jenks, not Jenks Wardlow. And fuck you." Enraged, without thinking, I hang up on her. (Sixteen years practicing law, and she's the first client I have ever hung up on.) Pulse still racing, I stare dumbly at the black phone on my desk.

Scared out of my wits, because I'd been about to say that I loved her.

A minute later, the phone buzzes. "Mr. Horvath, Mrs. Evans is on the line again."

"Tell her I've left for the day."

The holidays pass with no word from her. Has she fired me? Relieved me of my obligations to her, professional and otherwise? The prospect, the silence, the darkness have a paralyzing effect, making me outwardly quiet and dull, a dead man walking in my own home. Carving a fifteen-pound bird at the sideboard in our dining room, Martha's parents and unmarried sister at the table discussing Watergate and how to get tickets to the Broadway revival of *Gypsy*, I let my mind drift to wondering what sort of turkey Svetlana ended up cooking after all, and for whom.

"*Peter.*"

I come to: Martha beside me, holding a stack of plates.

"What's wrong with you? I've been standing here for about a minute."

"Sorry."

She hands me the top plate and stares at me a few moments longer—as if reading my mind—before saying, "Remember, Mother prefers dark meat."

And now it's Christmas. Jean no longer likes Carly Simon, she likes Led Zeppelin. It is New Year's. Nineteen seventy-five, the year the Vietnam war will finally end and my daughter will turn fourteen and I, her father, will turn forty-two.

Svetlana will be forty-nine.

February 6, 1975

Dear Mr. Horvath,

My husband and I are giving a small birthday dinner for our friend Lana Evans on the 28th of the month. When I asked Lana which guests she would like me to invite, the only people she specifically mentioned were you and your wife. Would you come? I'm sure it would make her happy. The evening will be a simple affair, as my husband, Thomas, and I—he is Assistant Minister at All Saints' Church here in town, you may have heard—are not fancy people. But it would be our pleasure to meet you and your wife, and to welcome you to our home.
Sincerely,
Dottie Carpenter

Some evenings now, when I sit in my living room listening to Glenn Gould playing the Goldberg Variations late in his career, the pianist's ghostly, animalistic moans emanating from the exquisite formal arithmetic of Bach's musical line, I find myself getting lost not in the ever-extending correspondences of notes but rather in the raw, inchoate exhalations of a man quite obviously on the cusp of some kind of madness. Ecstatic madness, perhaps, but madness all the same. And this reminds me of something, a time and place. Of certain desperate, uncontainable feelings I have known—on whose behalf I see that I too was capable of being a bully and a fool.

Back then, of course, I didn't explain it to myself this way. A social invitation had been received. There were reasons—good, solid, *professional* reasons, I insisted—for accepting it, and what was clear to me, possibly the only thing that was clear, was that, because she was my wife, it was Martha's duty to assist me in this endeavor, *for the good of my career* and thus, ergo, *for the benefit of our family*. Oh, I doubt she believed a word of this crap. But then, as I presented it to her over three nights running, gradually, quietly (were we not quiet, polite people?) bullying her into submission, she didn't have to believe it. She didn't have to believe anything at all. She didn't even have to believe in *me*. All she had to do was agree to go.

As it turns out, Dottie Carpenter's description of the birthday dinner for Svetlana as "small" is no mere figure of speech. Martha and I are still in the Carpenters' front hall, handing coats and scarves to Thomas ("Reverend Tom"?) Carpenter, when I notice the grim resentment in my wife's expression—up to now visible only to me, I believe—suddenly threatening to become explicit. I follow her gaze to the living room and there, standing by herself with martini glass already well in hand (this is not a dry house, I'm relieved to see), is the woman of the hour, wearing a red cardigan sweater over a brown woolen dress.

"Are we early?" Martha's polite smile evaporating.

"You're right on time," Mrs. Carpenter assures her. Then in a lower voice adding: "The other couple had to cancel at the last minute. Their son has tonsillitis."

"Oh. I'm sorry to hear that."

The Carpenters' two preteen children, boy and girl, pale and earnest, appear and make respectful hellos to the guests, then start drifting back up the staircase.

"Billy," the mother calls lightly to the flannel-shirted boy, "don't forget your guitar." The boy nods once, and is gone.

Turning back, I find Svetlana kissing my wife's cheeks—once, twice, three times.

"Martha, you are good to help celebrate my old age! That beautiful blouse you are wearing."

"Happy birthday, Svetlana."

"Yes, happy." The guest of honor's martini glass is nearly empty. "And you, Peter, what a strange face you have tonight. But you are here, that's the main thing after such long absence. While we are both not too old to still enjoy life a little, hm?"

"Happy birthday, Svetlana."

"So people keep telling me. Now, Mr. Staehelin, you must have a drink with me on my special anniversary."

"Certainly, Mrs. Staehelin."

It's not the little smile that's just popped onto my lips that catches Martha's attention, I imagine, so much as this exchange of private names that she's never heard before, uttered in public. Our hosts don't seem to have noticed, but my wife's face has morphed into an ominous mask, fitted so as to allow light neither in nor out.

"Why don't we go into the sitting room for the hors d'oeuvres?" Dottie Carpenter suggests.

On the coffee table sits a spinach and Velveeta cheese dip and a plate of Triscuits. "Dip?" Dottie Carpenter offers. It looks like a bowl of goose guano but is actually not half-bad. Between slathering crackers with green-and-orange goo, Reverend Tom asks Martha if we have ever attended service at All Saints' Church, and she responds that, to tell the truth, her relationship with organized religion has never been especially pleasant.

"Then perhaps on one of my better Sundays, Mrs. Horvath," the minister remarks with sly humility, "I hope I might have the opportunity of attempting to change your mind on the matter."

My wife makes no further comment.

"It was at our church that I first met Svetlana," Dottie Carpenter tells Martha. "I looked over and thought, *Who is that remarkable-looking woman?* You know what I mean, Mrs. Horvath. That combination of strength and vulnerability she radiates. A person with the courage to look her own monstrous history right in the eye without blinking. It reminded me a little of some faces we used to see among the Ugandans. Wouldn't you agree, Thomas?"

I don't catch the rest because I've joined Svetlana at the bar cart in the corner of the room, where she's taken it upon herself to mix her second martini and my first. If nothing else in America, I note with a certain pride, she has learned how to make our national drink with the necessary degree of hubris. Her idea of vermouth is a vanquished dream that never was.

"You're not still angry about our phone call, Peter?"

"I'm not angry. I'm embarrassed. I've never lost my temper like that with anyone."

"Because I am not a normal client. And you were being human and emotional—not always usual with you. But listen, I've told you this before. Don't get stuck on little words I throw out between big feelings. Sometimes my brain can be like a fist. A thing which, how do you say . . . ?"

"Clenches?"

"Clenches. So my feelings come out too strong. But you must realize I'm no fist. That was my father. I am more my mother. A turtle, with the soft belly underneath."

"Okay, turtle."

She laughs—the sound an unvarnished story flung from deep within her chest; also a gauntlet thrown down. A bit of martini sloshes over the rim of her glass onto my shoe, though somehow this too is charming. We are on the plane from Zurich again, two bank robbers on the lam, making our break for freedom.

She takes a swallow of drink and turns back into the room. "Has Peter not told you, Dottie and Thomas, how he fetched me from Switzerland during my defection?"

"Let's not bore them with that," I interject with a quick glance at my wife, whose gaze is chilling my toes from ten feet away.

"Yes," Martha agrees, "let's not."

But Dottie Carpenter is studying me with newfound interest. "That was *you*?"

"I will tell you how it was done." A note of rare triumph in Svetlana's voice as she plops herself on the couch next to Martha and launches once more into our tale of magical, heroic escape from her past.

And so . . . forward. Time for cake. Somehow we have got through split-pea soup; ham and sweet potatoes; iceberg lettuce with "Russian" dressing. The dishes have been cleared, a cloudy pause fallen over the table, the sky just before lightning. I become aware without exactly being aware that Martha—seated at the round dining table between Dottie and Reverend Tom—has uttered hardly more than a brief sentence or two these last twenty minutes. While Svetlana, placed between Dottie Carpenter and myself and still floating on the ebbing tide of her two early martinis, seems content to let the conversation go where it will (or won't). The ship of international hospitality is sinking, in other words. But our faithful skipper will not let her go down without a fight.

Captain Dottie emerges from the kitchen bearing a home-made vanilla-frosted cake with a single candle burning on top. Behind her, holding a three-quarters-size guitar and looking full of regret for someone who can't be much more than twelve, comes her son. "Billy." Dottie Carpenter nods at him as she sets the cake on the table in front of Svetlana. And Billy commences, somewhat haltingly, to play "Happy Birthday" on his instrument.

We sing, of course. Even Martha does more than lip-synch. And when it's over and the wish has been silently invoked and the candle extinguished, Reverend Tom says to the boy, "Now, Billy, how about 'Hey Jude' for the guests?" And then to us: "Billy's crazy about the Beatles."

But crazy or not, Billy shakes his head. He doesn't want to play "Hey Jude" or anything else for the guests, whoever the hell we might be.

"Come on, William," his father insists, a note of Episcopal sternness entering his voice. "One song for the table."

"For God's sake, leave the boy alone!"

The voice loud. And Russian.

"I beg your pardon?" sputters the Reverend.

"He doesn't want to sing. So leave him alone now."

"I'm sure I don't know who you think you're speaking to, Mrs. Evans. I'm the boy's father."

"That is your problem." Svetlana scrapes back her chair and stands. The rest of us, even young Billy, remain nailed to our stations. "Reverend, in your own house I will tell you something, since you don't ask. When I was your son's age, my father would have his dinners and parties. The whole Politburo would be there, sometimes others too. I would be off by myself, quiet, reading or just thinking, sometimes already asleep and—and suddenly there he was, deciding it was time for me to sing and dance for his crowd, simply because that's what he wanted. My hair was in braids then. *Pig*tails. And he would grab my pigtails like this"—with a vicious double-handed yank, she mimes the pulling-back of her head— "and drag me onto floor in front of everyone. He would make me sing and dance for him while they all watched. Can you imagine such a thing for a child, Reverend? No? Then I will show you."

She stalks from the room. No one else stirs. Through the doorway I watch her open the front hall closet and rummage around inside.

I have an inkling then. But I do nothing to stop what's happening. I just sit there.

She reenters the dining room wearing a man's gray fedora and holding a black furled umbrella. The hat too large for her and partially covering her eyes, which are wide but taking no notice of any of us, as though she is seeing into the heart of some awful waking dream.

"Watch how I danced for my father."

She begins to kick out her legs, first one, then the other. Hard to describe, even now, how cruelly pathetic. Twirling the umbrella like a parade baton, she performs a half turn and then more kicks, following some routine drilled into her long ago and never forgotten. A small skip to one side, a hop; then back, another turn—and now she stumbles, almost toppling over—before somehow righting herself with the umbrella and managing a last, broken pirouette.

Tears are streaming down her flushed cheeks.

Beside me, Dottie Carpenter's gasp suggests the purest pity. Across the table, the minister fervently regards his lap, praying to his own corporeal reality. And young Billy has fled the premises; the future has defected. Only my wife—leaning back in her chair, chin slightly raised, lips parted, eyes bright with spectacle—seems ready to embrace the horrible strangeness of the moment, this utter humiliation of a once-feared rival.

I can't stand another second of it. "That's enough." I get up and go to Svetlana, now bent over and weeping. Gently I pull the hat off her head and the umbrella out of her fist and drop them on the floor. "I'm taking you home."

"*Peter*," Martha snaps—on her feet, mouth a hard thin line.

"Sit down, Martha."

"Peter, this is totally inappropriate."

"I said *sit down*."

And my wife, pink-faced as if she's just been slapped by a stranger, sits back down.

"I'm driving Svetlana home in her car," I announce to the room. "I'll call a cab from there."

I glare around the table. The Carpenters are gawking like rude children, but for once I don't give a fuck.

"Mr. and Mrs. Carpenter, Svetlana thanks you for dinner. We all do. You're good people and this is no one's fault. Come on, Svetlana, let's go."

We do not speak on the way to her house. I am driving her beloved green Dodge. How she has managed to hold on to it through all the moves and mistakes, the makings and breakings of the last few years is anybody's guess. But somehow she has, and now we are under its cover, moving, the heater struggling to warm us. The starless sky eggshell white, promising snow. Signs of a student party, loud beautiful bodies spilling off the front porch of a townhouse, slide by: not for us. Farther on, we pass a Jersey Central Power & Light truck, men in hardhats preparing for a cold night of work. We are invisible. I fish a white handkerchief out of my pocket and hand it to her. She does not ask, as an American might, whether it is clean. She does not care. She wipes her eyes and blows her nose. Her tears are gone. And soon we are at her house.

"You will come in."

It is not a question.

The babysitter a neighbor's daughter, a year or two older than Jean. While Svetlana searches for her wallet, I wait awkwardly with the girl in the living room, finding it impossible not to notice, even obliquely, her firm new breasts under her tight cable sweater. Then catching myself and thinking: *I wouldn't want my daughter showing herself off like that.*

No? the girl's expression says back, when our eyes briefly intersect. *And who the fuck are you, mister, and what the fuck are you doing here?*

"You are okay walking?" Svetlana asks, pressing some bills into the girl's hand.

"I'm okay, Mrs. Evans, thanks. It's just two blocks and my mom's waiting."

The girl leaves, a gust of cold air entering the house on her way out. And what will she tell her mother, if anything, about the evening?

"I will check on Yasha," Svetlana says.

I nod vaguely, listening to her steps, a bit heavier from drink, climbing the stairs. Lost in my own fugue state. As if I've never been in this house before, yet know it intimately. Like a dream in which every detail of a landscape is at once completely new and completely familiar, and the hand one sees reaching into the unfolding narrative is one's own, yet different.

I discover an LP cover left out beside the turntable on the shelf. *Classic Russian Songs:* one of those generic compilations of kitsch that music companies are always putting together and selling on late-night television. The jacket art shows a photograph of a man dressed exactly like one of the waiters from the Russian Tea Room on Fifty-seventh Street.

There's a knot in my throat I don't know what to make of.

In her kitchen, I find vodka in the freezer and pour myself a drink. Raising the glass to my lips, I notice my hand trembling.

"One for me?"

While upstairs, she's removed her cardigan; her arms are bare to the shoulders and pricked with goosebumps. Strong arms still, but softer now in places. Like the brown wool of her sleeveless dress, which looks both coarse and fine. Eight years older than when I first laid eyes on her that morning in the Zurich airport. Both of us. Though what strikes me in the heart is not pity or shame—the wisps of gray in our hair, the few added pounds around our middles—but how she grasped that little dinner gathering of cowardly stiffs (myself included) by the scruffs of our necks and shook us until the masks of our hypocritical composure cracked and fell away, showing us, for just an instant, our true faces. Unlike her own face, which—love it or leave it—has in my experience only ever been true.

That face that I have come to love, and cannot leave.

"Take mine," I say, handing her the drink. "I've had enough."

But instead of drinking, she sets the glass on the counter and looks right into me.

"So, Peter. What do you think?"

"What do I think about what?"

"Don't be stupid. You don't do it very well."

We are standing very close. Whether I will ever feel more alive than I do at this moment is a question for another day. But now, slowly, her eyes leading mine, she takes my hands and places them on her full, womanly breasts.

"This," she says. "What do you think about *this*?"

1975

11 March

Let us call Peter's body a contradictory series of reluctantly divulged messages. His waist narrow and still boyish, but his chest—with little help from its owner, one assumes, other than the odd game of legal tennis—rather naturally broad and muscular. His biceps on the lax side, as if they could not be bothered to do more; his subtly impressive thighs, however, appearing ready to press above their weight. And where his chest and legs wear a thin but masculine carpeting of hair the color of chestnuts, the areas around his hip bones are as endearingly pale and smooth, I suspect, as when he was a boy.

More contradictions. His shyness at being seen fully naked versus his completely unexpected lack of inhibition in the way of noise at the *moment of crisis* (my nurse's phrase, when she finally understood, without a word passing between us, that I was no longer a *virgin of the Motherland*). Peter's prized Enlightenment virtues—thoughtfulness, rationality, science—of which he really is quite vain, versus his simmering anger against the timid of the world, himself perhaps included, which he has borne as long as he can remember. His passion versus his fear of passion. His secret desire for dominance. His private wish to break and hurt, however quietly, versus his public inclination to fix and heal. His rigid view of himself as a *good husband and father* and what this means in the life he has constructed versus the imaginative courage he must have needed to escape his oppressive childhood and which, he must already sense, he will need once again if he is to ever truly break free of what binds him.

17 March

The train to Penn Station; a taxi to West Forty-seventh Street and the Edison Hotel; pick up the lobby phone and ask for Mr. Horvath.

These were my directions.

Peter, it's me.

Have you eaten lunch?

Not yet.

Good. The tension in his voice jumping through the line into my ear. He clears his throat as if there's something stuck in it. *I've ordered room service. Come up to 1412.*

I pass through the lobby to the elevators. The lighting everywhere on the brown side of dim, as if the Great Depression never ended. The loiterers mostly out-of-town people, I would guess, Broadway ticket holders and old Jewish men in hats. This establishment not in danger of being mistaken for the Plaza, certainly, or the Pierre, or the famous Carlyle with that delightful black singer Bobby Short singing Cole Porter with martini in hand—not that I expected such luxuries. But then neither, I confess, did I quite envision *A Diamond District Depot* as my cabdriver referred to this establishment, with a cheery grimace, when I gave him the address. What diamonds I don't know, I'm sure. The music in the elevator is jazz, at least, lifting my heart, while my nose does battle with the lingering odors of potato latkes and other fried traditions wafting up from the kitchens below.

———

Is this your regular hotel?

I don't have a regular hotel, Peter says in a defensive tone. *This isn't something I'm in the habit of doing.*

You have never stayed here before?

No.

I believe him. *However,* I can't help pointing out, *we are not really staying here, are we?*

His only reply is to pull up the corner of the bedsheet so it covers more of his bare chest.

A moment later, to lighten the mood, I pull the same corner of sheet back down to his navel.

He tugs it up again . . .

I yank it down . . .

Both of us laughing now as I roll on top of him. And to my surprise—neither of us any sort of *spring chicken*—I feel him saluting me down there, battle-station ready. *You again?* I say with a cheeky smile, for we have been through this happy dance just a bit earlier, before the lunch of blinis and Bulgarian caviar sent up by room service; the bottle of French champagne with the flowers on the label; his attempt at calming his nerves by making small talk— *Did you know Johnny Burnette of the Rock and Roll Trio used to be the elevator operator here?*—his flinching when I tried to loosen his necktie because it looked as though it was strangling him; his fumbling his way through the relative delicacy of my new French brassiere to reach, hungrily, my middle-aged breasts, which had been waiting for him. And even as my body moves over him this second time, slower and more knowing than before, I find myself thrown back to our beginning together, that first summer on the porch of the cottage on Block Island, the crickets clamoring all around and Martha and little Jean—little Jean with her nightmares—asleep upstairs, and Peter grabbing my hair, twisting my head around, kissing me hard on the mouth, and running away.

Peter . . .

Oh, Jesus, he groans, as if he is dying.

Then it's separate trains home to separate houses: late afternoon for me, early evening for him. I ride pressed in among the commuter types. Unshowered, fragrant with him, but otherwise well enough disguised. The fellow next to me—camel hair coat, English bulldogs on his necktie—politely offers me a section of his *New York Times*, which I politely decline.

Ravished and unclean, hardly caring where I am going, I sit with this happiness, my airy new friend, hanging on to its balloon string with both hands.

21 March

Ten minutes past noon my doorbell rings. At first wary—Yasha is at school and perhaps something has happened?—I am then quite astonished.

Peter.

Sorry, but I had to see you.

His overcoat already off, here in my foyer, followed by his suit jacket. Now his necktie, flapping shirttails, shoes hitting the floor.

We never make it upstairs. Afterward, I ask if he would like lunch or coffee while he's here. He says he would like nothing more than to stay and stay, but he must go, he'll just make the 1:15 train back to work.

Be careful who sees you, I warn him.

From his expression I can tell that he misunderstands and thinks I mean Martha or Jean, or perhaps local gossips. But that is not who I mean. There are things going on lately that I have told no one about, not even him, certain unknown individuals in the area who have no business paying attention to my doings yet pay attention all the same in ways they assume I do not recognize—they do not know that I am onto them, and I intend to keep it that way.

Dressed and ready to return to the office, Peter opens my front door. A taxi is already waiting at the curb; he must have called it while I was in the bathroom.

You know you make me very happy? he says, giving me a last kiss before departing.

And though I am not his wife, I straighten his tie for him and place my hand flat against his chest, just over his heart, wanting so much to feel the vivid life that thrums inside him at this very moment, silently beating my name.

24 March

In a recent issue of *Partisan Review*—sent to me *out of respect*, supposedly, by one of the editors—my former lover Alexsei Kapler gives the following brief interview concerning my defection:

> *When I heard of her departure I couldn't believe it. I have my own ideas about Russian women; I have known many. And I believe something terrible, something abnormal must have happened to Svetlana. What she did is unforgivable.*

29 March

Someone is watching me. All morning a black sedan of some American make—Chevy *Monte Carlo*? Oldsmobile *Cutlass Supreme*?—has been parked on the other side of Wilson Road, about thirty degrees to the left of my front door. Inside a man wearing a tan raincoat and black heavy-framed eyeglasses appearing to read the newspaper, but more accurately using it to shield his face from my position at the window in Yasha's room. Yasha, thank goodness, is at school. If he were here, God help me, I do not know what I would do.

Careful not to make myself visible through the windows, I go to the phone in my room and dial Peter's office.

Good morning, Wardlow Jenks and Hayes, Peter Horvath's office.

Beverly, I must speak to Peter right away.

I'm afraid he's in a meeting, Mrs. Evans.

Please understand, it must be right this second. My life may be at stake.

Now a little pause. For Beverly the secretary already has ideas about me, this I know, theories honed from many such humorless exchanges in the past and her watchdog role in Peter's affairs. I once imagined that she was in love with Peter to some pathological degree; but when finally I met her with her helmet of dull brown hair and her proper string of family pearls, I understood that her fighting over his turf was more likely a repressed form of class vanity. For all I know, her mother's maiden name is Jenks.

Fortunately, she's too well mannered to sigh out loud. *I'll see what I can do. Please hold.*

This verb *hold*, once archaically tender, even romantic in its implications, now a chiseling tool designed to pry my client fingers off the phone. (To say nothing of the contradictory attack of the word *please*.) Followed by a most insistent piece of recorded Mozart, until Peter's voice comes breaking through:

Beverly says your life is in danger? What the hell's going on?

I tell him about the man with the black glasses and the fake newspaper in the Chevy *Impala, Bel Air, Caprice . . .*

Maybe he's just waiting for the street cleaner, Peter suggests, no longer sounding much concerned.

I point out that today is not an official street-cleaning day on Wilson Road.

Or he had a fight with his wife and just feels like reading the newspaper in peace, Peter says. *I'd put money on it.*

I am the only house he's watching like this.

Peter allows himself a very faint grunt of frustration. *Okay . . . So what would you like me to do?*

Ask Dick Thompson.

I'd rather not bother Dick with something like this unless absolutely necessary.

Or Kennan. I have George's number and will call myself.

Please don't do that. I'll call Dick. Wait by the phone. He hangs up.

Not feeling better yet, heart racing, I use the time to return to Yasha's room and peek out the window again.

The black sedan is gone.

The phone rings. *Dick says he's sending someone over to check on the situation. He should be there in about twenty minutes.*

It left.

What?

The car has driven away.

Peter's silence now like a stone dropped from the heights of Olympus. *I'll tell Dick it was a false alarm,* he says tersely.

What if the man goes to Yasha's school and kidnaps him?

I promise you that's not going to happen in a million years. I have to go now, Svetlana. I've already missed half my meeting. We'll talk later.

3 April

I went down to Urken Hardware to buy a *peephole* for my front door. This was Dick Thompson's idea of comfort for me after he finally heard from Peter about my alarming visitor the other day. Though Dick did not offer to pay for my peephole. What's more, it strikes me that if peepholes are the best the CIA can come up with to protect its charges, the Cold War must not be going very well on this side of the ocean.

Mr. Urken himself came over to install the apparatus, complimented me on my new backyard swimming pool (covered with a tarpaulin ever since completion last fall), and as he was getting into his pickup truck to leave asked if I'd heard the news that my pool laborer, Nelson, was deported back to Guatemala last month. I said no, I had not heard, what a terrible disgusting thing for the American government—any government—to do to a nice hardworking man like that. And Mr. Urken, for his part, did not reply, did not in fact seem clear in his own mind that this deporting of my Nelson back to a country with the highest murder rate in the world was a terrible disgusting thing. And then he drove away.

I think I will take my hardware business somewhere else from now on. Although it may be difficult to fully separate from Urken; it is a complicated arrangement that we now have one way and another, all these installment payments I owe for my various pieces of home equipment. Very capitalist, indeed.

7 April

Mama, why are we here?

It's a friend's house, I explain to Yasha, curled up beside me in the front seat of the Dodge, which is parked, in the fading twilight, in a street unfamiliar to him, across from a house he does not know.

Is someone sick?

No, darling. Don't worry. We'll go home soon, I promise. Try and go back to sleep.

I watch my son until his eyes close again.

Across the road, in Peter's house, lights have come on. That must be the kitchen, I realize.

And Martha, setting the table for dinner.

10 April

Seen through my new peephole, Dottie Carpenter looms larger and more influential than I recall from real life.

I consider not opening my door to her, but in truth my options are limited. She will have seen my shadow blocking the peephole; yes, my shadow, like a calling card with no person behind it.

Hello, Dottie. I do not smile.

How are you, Lana? I just thought I'd take the plunge and drop by. I haven't seen you in weeks. Oh, and I brought this. She holds out something not previously captured by the peephole.

A *home-baked* apple pie.

I invite her in to tea. Will she take a spoonful of jam? She will. And a slice of her pie? Well, if I insist . . . She and Thomas have missed me at All Saints'. Am I truly all right? And Yasha? Truly? Yes, yes, and yes, I answer her. She hopes—doesn't want to assume, of course, but hopes—that no feelings of lingering embarrassment or . . . or anything like that from my birthday dinner might be keeping me from expressing my faith at church? Because the last thing she or Thomas would ever want is to think that they might have somehow inadvertently . . . *impeded* . . . rather than *encouraged*—do I understand?—my faith in the Holy Spirit.

My faith is not impeded, I assure her. *It is very much the same as it was before. More pie?*

As soon as I can, I walk her out to the street. Practically hand her into her car.

Your son . . . I say.

Billy? What about him?

Please tell Billy from me that he is a brave boy. Please tell him that from Mrs. Evans.

Dottie Carpenter's face hardens. And I am suddenly quite satisfied that this is the last truly personal exchange we will ever have together.

13 April

I'm being watched, Dick.

I don't think so, Svetlana—we've checked it out carefully.

You think I'm inventing this black car?

Inventing? No. But you're under a good deal of stress. And it's natural that this stress might make you sensitive to certain . . . let's just say, certain threats that understandably feel real but aren't.

You agree with this, Peter?

A brief pause from Peter, weighing his words on a scale. *I think Dick's right, Svetlana.*

You think he's right. Then why would the same car always be parked so near my house?

Many possible reasons. And many possible cars, Dick answered. *But believe me, Svetlana, the least likely of all the reasons—by far—is that the KGB is pursuing you in broad daylight. They're not that stupid.*

No, I agree. They're not stupid.

Dick pats my hand and tries on a smile. *Feel better?*

A little, I reply, which is almost true.

Well, says Peter grimly. *Why don't we order?*

Good idea, Dick agrees, scribbling his name and member number on a lined card with a truncated pencil. *What'll everyone have? Chicken pot pie's always reliable. And the crab cakes. Lobster bisque is good too.*

Just the bisque for me, thanks, Peter says.

Come on there, Pete. You're too skinny to be on a diet. Dick is teasing his compatriot, I see, though Peter doesn't smile. *Suit yourself.* Dick writes down the order. *How about you, Svetlana?*

Crab cakes, thank you, Dick. And one vodka martini, please.

Two sets of eyes, which they think I don't notice, land on me at once. "*1 Vodka martini,*" Dick writes in his spy's cryptic hand, along with iced teas for himself and Peter, and passes the card to a waiter in a beige jacket.

Our table sits in the corner of a high-ceilinged side room lit by brass chandeliers and one extremely tall window. Like most Party officials and *mafia dons,* Dick tends to position himself with walls protecting his back. His university club is said to have a number of authors and diplomats in its members book, rather than assassins or spies, though looking around the place I see no *boldface names* that immediately spring to mind. I confess I find it surprising that my CIA minder would ask me to lunch in a place of such public visibility—his usual preferred atmosphere being a bit more surreptitious, not to say cheaper—but then perhaps today's setting reflects some accounting on his part of my own diminished celebrity in this country.

I think Jasper Penshaw is a member here, Peter remarks. *Isn't he, Dick?* He turns to me. *You remember Jasper and his wife, Raisa Malinov, from Block Island? They gave that dinner for you.*

At the memory of that night on Block Island, Peter's and my eyes connect across the table, two torn halves of a postcard suddenly fitted together. A method of mutual secret recognition, I suddenly recall, not unknown to KGB men and those poor Rosenbergs.

Dick, ever vigilant at reading others' thoughts, segues as if on cue: *Since we're discussing transplanted Russians, I'll get to the reason for our lunch today. Peter?*

Peter, head still intertwined with mine on his island porch, appears taken aback by Dick's sudden reversal; then he recovers and, with a tender warning glance at me, pulls an envelope out of his briefcase and slides it across the table.

This was delivered to my office a few days ago.

Something in his voice; the sight of the envelope. And suddenly I am frightened.

It was addressed to me. Peter hesitates. *But it concerns you and Josef.*

The waiter, an emergency room Dionysus, has appeared beside our table with three glasses on a small round tray. *Vodka martini?*

For me. My hand shakes only a little as I swallow a third of the drink. Only then do I feel able to slip the letter from its cover and begin reading to myself:

"Dear Mr. Horvath: I am writing on behalf of Joseph G. Alliluyev, who has asked that I get in touch with his mother regarding his desire to visit the U.S."

I stare at Peter.

Read the rest.

I put down the letter, nauseated from hope.

Svetlana, Dick steps in, *whoever wrote this claims to be an American journalist, but he won't identify himself. He's passing on what he reports to be a confidential request from Josef that you obtain a three-month tourist visa for him. He says Josef teaches medicine at the First Moscow Institute and is divorced with a five-year-old son. Our sources have confirmed the latter facts.*

Yes, Roman Smoluchowski told me.

Who? I notice Dick already scribbling down my good neighbor's name—and suddenly we are back in the USSR, in any café or living room you care to name, and there is my father's picture staring down at us from the wall.

It doesn't matter, I tell him. *Josef denounced me, you remember, the year I arrived here.*

According to the letter, Peter explains, *Josef now admits to being coerced into denouncing you by pressure from the Soviet government. But he says he's fully changed his mind and wants to see you.*

According to the letter, Dick repeats pointedly.

Peter reaches over then, because I have not moved a finger, and turns the envelope upside down so that a small photograph falls onto the table.

And there is my Josef. A handsome grown man with beautiful

sad eyes—his father Grigori's eyes—holding his Soviet passport up to the camera.

The question, I'm afraid, Dick says, *is whether the letter's real author isn't this supposed American journalist, whoever he is, or your son, but rather Yuri Andropov and the KGB.*

I stare at my CIA minder as if he has just spit on my shoes. *Or if it's true and my son is desperate to join me as he says?*

This one's a hard nut to crack, Svetlana. But think how the Soviets could be playing this: Stalin's daughter, already a pawn of American intelligence and now trying to recruit her son as well. Which, think about it, it allows them to turn the tables on us by having your own son—Stalin's grandson, no less—expose you for the traitor they say you really are.

Dick, Peter says in a low voice, *I think you've made your point.*

You're right. I apologize. I simply wanted to make sure that our friend here sees the bigger picture.

She more than sees it—she's living it.

But they are both mistaken. The only picture I am seeing and living at this moment is the small black-and-white photograph in my hand.

My son has grown a mustache, I observe to no one in particular. And then I start to cry.

1 May

The last Americans have left Saigon. And so the Vietnam disaster ends like most disasters: a foolish nightmare whose terrors continue to haunt the survivors long after waking.

13 May

I am growing almost cruel with Peter. Sometimes I think he knows that some deep part of me perhaps wants to punish him for reasons that are no real fault of his own, may in fact have nothing to do with him. Yet it is this very part that now and again he seems to need to batter himself against like a wave crashing against a rocky shore. The other day, after taking the early train home from work so we can steal eighteen minutes in my bed while across the hall Yasha watches yet another rerun of *The Beverly Hillbillies*, Peter, like some misplaced Romantic poet, declares he doesn't *give a fuck* what happens now, he simply wants to feel *alive* because all around us the world is *dying*. He rolls off me—the clock ticking, always ticking, Martha and little Jean any minute starting dinner without him and *The Beverly Hillbillies* about to end—and sits at the edge of my bed, sits there naked with his head in his hands, either more or less like himself than at any time in his known history, it's hard to say, and tells me that he is thinking about leaving his marriage. And when I just lie there, naked like him and unresponsive, he turns and looks at me with desperate, unhappy eyes. And in a tired voice I say, *So you are asking me to tell you what you must do?* Which I believe is what he knew he would get from me, and I believe in this case even wanted.

We have been twice more in the afternoon to the Edison Hotel, with its lovers and latkes and old Jews in hats. Peter Horvath, Esquire, has played *hooky* from his demanding, highly remunerative legal job to take me hiking and make love to me in the Pine Barrens of New Jersey. And he has given me a copy of E. L. Doctorow's *Ragtime* inscribed *with love, Peter.* In the novel, which I read with admiration, the rich husband of a former chorus girl and American cultural sensation murders his wife's rich lover. I don't know what to make of this, I must say. But then perhaps a patience with historical metaphors is not in my blood.

Or patience, period.

So I could be more loving to him, yes. Which in turn makes me feel cruel. Which in turn reminds me of familial/historical connections that naturally I harbor but he does not, cannot, connections he thinks he has begun to fathom and would like somehow to share with me, as if to take some of their weight from my heart. Because he is a good man. And I love him for this, yes I do.

No, it is not Peter's fault that the letter about my Josef was sent to him rather than to me. It is not Peter's fault that in order to protect my son in case the letter is real, I have been forced to act as though it is false. It is not Peter's fault, therefore, that I have done nothing to respond to my son's entreaties for love and attention from the mother who abandoned him and his sister. It is not Peter's fault that with each succeeding year since my defection, I have had to face the nauseating probability that the dreamed epiphany about my children's futures that came to me while I was in India—the rationale I offered myself for abandoning them—was far more dream than epiphany. Nor is it Peter's fault that so much of what energy I possess anymore—no longer what it was even when I was forty—has been redirected away from my abandoned first two children, spent elsewhere in my attempt (failed) to be a wife again and now the mother, the only mother, that Yasha needs. No, none of these things could possibly be Peter's fault.

And yet aside from loving him for who he is, which I do because he is a good man and closer to me than anyone else, I confess to blaming him more than a little for these same things that are not his fault and that he has not done. And yes, sometimes perhaps I wish to punish him, because I have not the fucking courage to punish myself as I should be punished.

22 May

Today, Josef's thirtieth birthday, I no longer felt able to control myself. I picked up the telephone and called him.

When he was very young, tiny I mean, just a scrap of human belief, I called my firstborn *Bunny*. It was a name he loved, I am certain, for every single time I used it his face would light into a smile.

I can no longer remember when or for what reason I stopped calling him *Bunny*. Only that I did.

Seventy-five hundred kilometers away, I heard the familiar double click of the line connecting:

Who is it?

Bunny, is that really you?

I heard my son pause and think. Then I heard him make his choice, biting down hard on each word with his teeth:

It has been eight years. Do you think you sound the same?

And the line went dead.

EDITOR'S NOTE

"Your mother?"

My father's language, like his limbs at this late stage of illness, hardly functions anymore. Even when healthy, he was a reticent man. Now he exists on the cusp of a permanent silence that, frankly, is sometimes a guilty relief to us both.

"She said she had a meeting in town," I tell him. "She'll be home late."

He looks at me as if he would say something more if he had the energy. He is forty-four years old. The eyes staring out at me appear twice that.

"Can you take a little more broth?" I say, to move him off the subject. My mother has had a lot of "meetings" lately, that is just a fact.

With my hand supporting the back of his head, I tip him forward until his mouth reaches the straw I've offered. He makes a halfhearted suck, my mother's homemade chicken stock darkening the waxed paper tube like urine. Then his eyes close, our signal for "no more." I ease him back on the pillow. His helpless exhaustion a familiar specter, afterimage of himself that none of us will ever be able to edit out of the negative that was once his life.

I am at the door of his sickroom off the parlor, where he has lived these last six months, about to switch off the light, when I hear him murmur something.

"What, Dad?"

"Your mother," he gasps.

"What about her?"

"I understand."

I am thirteen years old. I do not ask what it is he understands about her. I say good night and turn out the lamp and leave him there in the darkness.

It is not long afterward—in my memory the same night, but that must be wrong—that I wake in my room on the second floor of the house to find my mother quietly weeping at the foot of my bed.

"Mom, what is it? Is Dad dead?"

She shakes her head, which she's holding in her hands. "No. But I wish I was."

"Don't say that."

"Why the hell not, if it's true?"

"Are you drunk?"

"Listen to me, Peter. Are you listening? This might be the most important thing I'm ever going to tell you about myself."

In the light from the hallway, I see that her mascara has started to run under her left eye. She has painted her nails, which she almost never does; they are gleaming faintly at the tips of her fingers like the carapaces of ten beetles. She has done her hair too, and the smell of her perfume, which she rarely wears, is in the room with us, and all of it is strange.

"You should go to sleep," I say, as though I were the parent.

"*No.* Listen to me. I felt . . ."

"Mom, I don't want to know."

"Peter, listen to me now. I ended it tonight. But I need you to understand. If I didn't get some love, just a little bit of love in my life, I felt I would die."

I recall a Senate hearing that was aired live on television not so long ago. They seem to occur almost weekly now, these staged gladiatorial inquests, there are so many channels to fill with "content" so many hours of the day, and God knows I have time to watch. The issue being investigated on this particular morning was some gross malfeasance on the part of powerful government officials toward those weaker and more vulnerable citizens they were duty bound to protect. (There's a surprise.) I do not recall the details of the case or the names of the two men called to testify that day. What I recall are their voices, their faces, and their manners.

The first official had his lawyer sitting beside him; every so often they would incline their heads toward each other and confer in tones too low to be caught by the microphones. It was like witnessing lovers, almost, or a rabbinical confession exposed to the public. After which, and so counseled, in every case the man testifying went on to reply to the question without actually answering it.

The afternoon session found a different official in the chair facing the senators. This second man had a lawyer beside him too. Yet at no point during his two and a half hours before the committee did he consult his legal counsel, or even glance in his direction. He met each question with his shoulders squared and his gaze direct on the speaker. He never once looked away. He took responsibility for his actions while at the same time calling on other responsible parties to do the same. It was his opinion, he stated, that in this particular tragedy there were no innocent parties. And from listening to his voice, watching his face, this is what I remember, wherever you happened to be or whatever you happened to be doing, through electrical wires, silicon chips, the warping mysteries of radio waves, it was impossible not to understand that here before you was a person speaking the truth. And if this person were speaking the truth, which he was, then that first man, that government official with the lawyer in his pocket, could not have been speaking the truth.

My mother ended her affair. Whoever he was. Whatever it was, love or something like it, someone's touch, that kept her alive while my father was slowly dying in the room off the parlor. After that night, we never spoke about it again. She had ended it, and yet she went on. How else to describe it? We all went on, except my father, who died that spring. And the following spring, in our same house where love had died but we had gone on, inexplicably, my mother and I were having breakfast early one morning before I went to school. I was studying at the table, an American history textbook open next to my plate of toast. My mother was reading the local paper with a mug of black coffee and a cigarette. Actually, I remember, it was yesterday's newspaper, we always got it a day late because it was cheaper that way.

"I'm going to lie down," she announced quite suddenly. And I saw that there were tears in her eyes. Before I could ask what had happened, she got up and left the kitchen. Left behind her cigarette, still burning in the ashtray, and the newspaper, still open to the page she'd been looking at.

My mother had been reading a wedding announcement—the type of news item I could not recall her ever paying the slightest attention to before.

Local dentist Carl Drummond, a thirty-eight-year-old widower, had married twenty-six-year-old Frieda Shepherd, who managed a flower shop. The bride had met her husband just three months earlier, when she'd gone in to have a cracked molar repaired. It was, she declared, "literally love at first sight."

The photograph of Carl Drummond with his arm around his new wife made him seem a handsome man who could not believe his good fortune.

"Anything you want to tell me?" Dick Thompson opened our conversation once the waitress (Mexican, wearing what looked like some sort of Irish Renaissance costume, with fitted bodice and puffed sleeves) had left us our drinks and gone away.

"You called me," I pointed out.

"Come on, Peter. This is what I do for a living, remember."

"Irish bars with Mexican waitresses?"

Dick smiled enigmatically. "Secrets."

"Ah."

"I'm going to level with you. Our Russian friend's looking increasingly unstable. I'm telling you, Pete, if you're not careful you're going to end up inside her head, seeing the world the way she does."

I was silent.

"Think of Martha and Jean, at least," Dick said.

"You think I don't?"

"Don't get testy. I'm trying to help."

"I never asked her to leave her country, Dick. Or to come to this one. It wasn't my idea. I never wanted to get involved in any of it."

"History doesn't happen because we ask for it, Peter. It just fucking happens. We all deal with it as best we can."

Before I left for Penn Station, Dick handed me an unmarked envelope. "For the train," he said, patting me sympathetically on the shoulder. "Do me a favor and burn it all when you get home."

Every seat on the 7:49 to Princeton was full; to find any privacy I had to go stand in the clattering vestibule between cars. The envelope I'd been given contained copies of four classified documents relating to Josef Alliluyev, thirty-year-old son of Svetlana Alliluyeva and her first husband, Grigori Morozov, and his repeated but thus far failed attempts over the previous two years to open channels of communication with his mother in the United States through the intermediation of someone named Krimsky— the same "American journalist" who'd written the note I'd received at my office concerning Josef's desire to visit his mother in America, and whom Dick Thompson deemed likely to be in the employ of the KGB. According to the very brief note I was now reading on the New Jersey Transit train as it rattled away from Manhattan, also from Krimsky, "Josef Alliluyev has lately been expressing deep concern, even panic, about possible punishments befalling him if he does not cease all attempts to visit his mother immediately."

The second document was a copied translation of an undated memo to the Central Committee of the Communist Party by KGB head Yuri Andropov:

> In a letter that we intercepted, Josef Alliluev [sic] complains about his loneliness after the divorce from his wife, about how he misses his mother, wants to see her. It is established that he has intentions to go abroad. In the past years, Josef Alliluev developed irritation, lost interest in social life, abuses alcoholic beverages. It seems rational for the Ministry of Health of the USSR to offer him more attention as a young doctor and for the Ministry of Health of the USSR to exchange his apartment for a better one.

The third document was a copy of an internal CIA memo confirming another, more recently intercepted note from Krimsky stating that Josef Alliluyev not only had broken off all contact with him (Krimsky) and was no longer seeking to reunite with his mother but had just moved into a new apartment, significantly nicer than his previous residence, made available to him by the Soviet government.

Affixed to this third document by a paper clip was a fourth—a plain white index card on which Dick Thompson had written:

"So Krimsky not on other team after all. JA staying put. Preferable for you to be one to tell S."

She greeted me at the front door of her house with a long vodka kiss, ice cubes rattling in the tall glass she was holding.

"Peter, what a nice surprise. Drink?"

"Maybe in a minute."

She put her hand under my suit jacket, flat against my chest, then tilted her head back and gave me a long look; for an unpleasant moment, I thought she'd somehow guessed why I'd come. But no, it was just the vodka shining through, and as I followed her into her living room I felt the gratifying reprieve of wanting her all over again.

"How long can you stay?"

"I'm not in a hurry."

"We can watch Dick Cavett together." A sly, booze-lit smile. "Maybe try some other things too."

Downing the last of her drink, she turned and kissed me again, the vodka metallic and cool in the heat of her mouth. Her movements looser from the alcohol, I could feel it, her temperature warmer. And the truth was that, as Dick Thompson's documents burned a hole in my briefcase, her buzz excited me while giving me an uneasy pause of foreboding. I wanted to hold her and make love to her. But I also knew that however happy she was to see me right now, however passionate and loving, the moment she recollected that Dick and I had told her to act as if Josef's intentions to see her weren't genuine, forcing her to turn her back on his pleas, the very intensity of her emotional high would turn on itself, and something darker and raging would appear in her heart.

"You like this Barry Manilow?"

"Who?"

As I spoke, I realized that the TV was on and tuned, as ever, to *The Dick Cavett Show*—where some skinny guy with a mop of blond hair, wearing a sequined tuxedo, was nasally belting out a pop ballad:

Well you came and you gave without taking
But I sent you away, ohhh Mandy
And you kissed me and stopped me from shaking
And I need you today, ohhh Mandy . . .

"Not especially."

"I like him," she announced. "Even if this Mandy is kind of a simpleton. But the man himself has a good heart, don't you think?"

"I'll take your word for it."

"So you'll have a drink with me?"

I had to smile. "Why not?"

"Why not, indeed. But first, my dear lawyer, you must relax and stay awhile in my company. Take off your tie and jacket. And let's put this down, hm?"

Before I understood what was happening, she had begun tugging gently at the briefcase in my hands, trying to take it from me.

"Come now, Mr. Horvath," she teased. "Work is over for the day. Everything here is for free."

"I'm sorry," I said tightly. "It's just . . . I have some papers I need to show you."

Instantly, her face became a tense question.

"What papers?" she demanded.

I looked at her.

"Svetlana, Dick wanted me to show you some documents."

"Which documents?"

"They concern Josef."

"My Josef?"

"Yes."

Now her eyes—those eyes with their untamable streaks of yellow—appeared lacquered with suspicion in the room's light.

"So after all, Peter, this was why you came to my house tonight," she concluded quietly. "To show me documents."

"Yes."

"Very well. So show them to me."

Having stepped into this blind alleyway, I didn't see what else I could do. I opened my briefcase, removed the papers, and handed them to her.

"They're copies," I explained, as if that made a difference.

She read them as I had—one at a time, in order.

And I watched as an understanding of the situation hit her in stages, like a series of small, invisibly landed blows. Until, at last, her body was bent at the waist in a mother's anguish.

"I will never see my son again."

"You don't know that."

"Yes, I do. I know." She moaned softly. "Oh, my Josef. My son."

Her grief, which I had delivered to her, was awful to witness. I had no idea how to comfort her.

"Let me hold you."

But as I held her, I could feel her begin to change. Like water freezing to ice, she turned rigid and cold, bristling with suspicion and rage—until, without a word having passed between us, it was clear to me that, just as I'd always dreaded, I was now her enemy.

I let her go. "Svetlana . . ."

"No," she snapped. "*You* did this, Peter—you and that spy Dick Thompson."

"Svetlana, that's not true."

"It *is* true."

"You're upset. I understand, but you have to believe me, it isn't what you think."

"What I *think*?" She practically spit at me. "I'll tell you what I think. I think my son wanted to come to me here in America. After everything I did to him, leaving him and his sister in Russia, he wanted to come. But you and your spy friend, you sons of bitches, decided this story cannot be true—no, it must be the fucking KGB that told my son to ask for me. So you slam the door on him for good. And now he'll never come. Never! I will never see him again in my life."

"Things can change."

"Not this. These things will never change. You have always known it. You and the spy."

"Stop saying that."

"I read the fucking documents, Peter! I'm not an idiot. I know proof when I see it."

"Calm down and please just listen to me."

"I *have* listened. My mistake. You and your fucking CIA."

"Goddamnit, you know who I am. I'm not the CIA."

"No?"

"Svetlana—"

"No more."

"No more what?"

"Get out of my house."

"Svetlana, listen to me—"

"I said get out of my house, damn you—you and your fucking lies!"

She hurled the CIA documents in my face: I felt a nick on my cheek, and watched the papers flutter helplessly to the floor.

And I tell you, whoever you are, that as in a nightmare, I could not believe what was happening. That still to this day, forty years later, I am left with the indelible image of myself getting down on my knees to retrieve those spilled pages from her floor, my tears frozen solid behind my eyes and my voice shamefully murmuring, "I'm sorry, Svetlana, I'm so sorry, but I can't leave these here."

"What the hell did you say to her?" Dick Thompson barked in my ear three days later, the moment I picked up the phone in my office.

"Beverly, I've got it." I heard the click as my secretary switched off the line. "Nothing," I told Dick bitterly. "I did what you asked me to do. I showed her the documents."

"Well, she's gone."

"What do you mean she's gone?"

"I mean, Peter, her house is empty. Not a stick of furniture left. And there's a For Sale sign on the lawn. And we don't have a fucking clue where in the world she's taken her son, or what she plans to do."

Thinking I was about to be sick then, I hung up before he could say any more.

LETTER

14 October 1975
Oceanside, CA

Dear Peter,
I understand if you may not wish to hear from me. I am very sorry that I took Yasha and disappeared so abruptly from Princeton after I threw you out, and that you have not heard from me until now. I have been in a state of almost perpetual confusion, with no real sense of clarity to offer you, which has made me too ashamed to write.

I have not been healthy in my mind, exactly. But I am trying.
Here is what I wish to say, my dearest, if you will listen:
Though I'm gone, I do not forget you. I can never forget you. What I cannot seem to do is love you well enough to stop running. Your loving
Svetlana

LETTER

17 December 1975
Carlsbad, CA

Dear Peter,

Merry happy Christmas—or what you and Martha and not-so-little Jean make of non-Jewish holidays these days, I myself am not so clear on this point anymore, or anything else. Here in Paradise, on the other hand, where Mr. Santa Claus wears sunglasses and surfing shorts, we are in states of perpetual ennui. So I am told. And that is the polite word.

California is cheaper than New Jersey, but not so cheap that money grows rather than disappears. I would give you our latest address and hope you visit but we are moving again soon. Because it's on the ground floor this apartment is gloomy and too open to invasive neighbors who are not always what they say. However, one of my nice women at Christian Science church here told me about this apartment on the other side of town that could be better for us. I will go tomorrow and look. You will sniff at this *idea of Christian Science, Peter—I can hear you, sniff-sniff—and I will not claim I believe all they preach or do, but there is <u>struc-ture</u> to their rules and regulations that I find helpful with my drinking too much and even, let me say, some days I find it al-most consoling. Some form and structure I mean in this freewheel-ing universe of California sun. On this boundless earth we must find help where each of us can, do you not agree? I have removed the vodka from the glove box of my Dodge. I am no longer waking myself at night with helpless questionings, spoken aloud, to my dear nurse, Alexandra Andreevna, about when my mother is going to come home to me and whether she was still bleeding after she was dead. I am trying not to torture myself too much with thoughts about how one day on the banks of the Ganges I man-aged to convince my brain that to leave Josef and Katya in Mos-cow was to free them—what a martyr I thought I was—when in fact I might as well have locked them away in Lubyanka with my own hands.*

No, for my mental health, I must try to give time now only to those thoughts of daily motherhood that prove me trustworthy in my own home. Otherwise how can I be alone with Yasha, this innocent child who needs me most urgently? And he with me? How can he rely on me to do what is right and good? What will we do?

I tell you, my dearest Peter, and only you, that every day I fear they will come and take him away from me. Every single day. And every single day, sometime or else, a part of me believes it would be better for him if they did.
Your loving
Svetlana

EDITOR'S NOTE

Two days before Christmas, 1975: I caught the last train from the city bearing late-found gifts for Martha and Jean. Home past ten, I tucked the Bergdorf's bag in the foyer closet with my coat and scarf, and entered the kitchen, expecting to find, as ever, a single place setting and a meatloaf sandwich.

"Sit down, Peter," Martha said in a quiet, firm voice.

On the table before her was a letter and a half-torn envelope. From two yards away, instantly, I recognized Svetlana's handwriting.

I cleared my throat. "Martha . . ."

"Do you honestly think, Peter," she interrupted me, "that I don't know?"

She was dressed as though we'd planned an evening at home together—black slacks and brown cashmere sweater, proper heels—but her hair, always carefully arranged, had not been brushed, and her eyes were red.

"You always wanted to be a hero," she said. "I know that, even if you don't. You probably never thought you'd get the chance.

Always so good and quiet. The clever stoic. Afraid to get sent out of the classroom for saying the wrong thing. You've always hated that about yourself. And here she comes as if on cue, the tyrant's daughter, the little Slavic princess making her dash for freedom, in need of a trusted counselor. I mean it's almost like you invented her. Sexy. Outspoken. Demanding. Just crazy enough to make you feel needed and important. The kind of gross egotism that for a little while, if you're blind, might get mistaken for courage."

"Martha . . ."

Martha raised a hand. "I'm not finished. You think she can love you back the way you want to be loved? Think there's room in that mountainous ego of hers for you to even get a toehold? You're not used to asking much for yourself. You're not very good at it. And you're going to start now, in middle age? Is she even listening? Does she even give a damn?"

"I don't know."

"What a hero you are, Peter. What a man."

Martha got to her feet.

"I don't ever intend to talk about this again. Just don't ever think—not for one minute—that I don't know who you are and why you want her. Now I'm going to bed."

LETTER

2 March 1976
La Jolla, CA

Dear Peter,
You are the only one I can tell. This morning in our small apart-
ment I lost control of myself and—how can I write this?—I
slapped my Yasha across his face.

    The sound of the blow, his awful cry—not just the pain but
such shock at my betrayal—the hideous red welt in the shape of
my own hand that instantly appeared on his blameless skin . . .
I was so horrified at what I'd done that I ran from the building.
Yes, I left my five-year-old son alone. I got in my car and drove
away. I tell you, Peter, I should be locked up. I drove to the beach,
the very edge of this country, where the road ends in a parking lot
by the Pacific Ocean. And there for nearly an hour, while my
son faced oblivion, I did nothing but sit on the hood of my car
and hug myself, the tide coming in, the waves growing bigger and
louder, shuddering the coastline in this land of earthquakes and

fault lines, this place where, when Yasha and I first arrived, the scent of the trees—the pine, the eucalyptus, the lemon, the orange—made me remember, oh, God how I remembered, the Black Sea of my childhood.

Yasha was watching cartoons on TV when I returned. It almost seemed he hadn't noticed. But when I got on my knees and embraced him, sobbing, he began to cry so hard I thought he would never stop.

I miss you, my Peter. But please understand, I could not bear to have you see me like this.
Your loving
Svetlana

PART FOUR

1983: ENGLAND

16 October
Cambridge

They advise me that if I am going to write anything serious now, it ought to be in Russian, not English. That Russian is the door to my "authentic" voice and therefore most likely to produce the "authentic" me in any "authentic" literary work that I, Lana Evans (not the name they're interested in), might write. The great Latvian-born "Sir" Isaiah Berlin tells me this, when he thinks to tell me anything anymore, he has been so sly with his esteemed intellectual presence ever since I came to this country, certainly more fox than hedgehog. The ostensible publisher of my next book—not a single word of which has yet been written in either Russian or English—Hugo Brunner, also tells me this, as a way, he believes, of encouraging me to new depths of expression with perhaps, though not necessarily, the promise of a book advance at the end of it.

But neither of these men nor any of the others—<u>none</u>— understands my pain when I write Russian, my father's language;

or for that matter the guilt which burns within me when I choose
<u>not</u> to write Russian, the language of the last words my mother
ever spoke to me, whatever they were, God help me I wish I could
remember; or even, as with these most recent years, which have
seen me turn fifty and older, when I have chosen to write no language of any kind, to myself or others.

It was my Russian voice I could not stand anymore and chron-
ically attempted to abandon, like some trunk in an Edgar Allan Poe
story filled with poisoned memories, which I tried to lose at every
station of my long wayward journey, only to find upon opening the
door of my new house in a new town (whichever new house in
whichever new town, there have been so many in Arizona, California, New Jersey) that, lo, the trunk was there. Indeed, sometimes it was the only thing there, waiting for me, having mysteriously
arrived in advance, and at the expense, of every other memory and
language I ever possessed.

And so, here in my little attic flat with the perpetual hot water
problem on the edge of Cambridge University, founded in the year
1209, which my dear Akhmatova never saw, I open this notebook
and begin again. Continue again. In my own language, this Russian
I brought with me from my native sadness.

My American son, on the other hand, not even twelve and currently being educated thanks to a most generous scholarship by
the Quakers at the Friends' School in the medieval market town
of Saffron Walden, England, Great Britain, speaks and writes only
in English.

Long live my unsilent son.

30 October

My beloved Dodge gone forever (last-ditch sale price of $350 *hard
cash* handed to me on the eve of our departure to England by an
unsavory fellow wearing a track suit and half-gold dentures, but no
matter), I take the train to Essex, and from there a local bus to Saffron Walden to pick up Yasha for his half-term holiday. The Friends'
School, founded 1702, one of those formidable brick piles the
English once did so well, with clean flat quadrants of lawn green-

ing the spaces in between the piles. In this case, however, I am pleased to find the architectural certainties of Western empire leavened by a warm Quaker humility that, as we Americans like to say, *takes all comers*. To think of my son sitting in Silent Meeting each morning, surrounded I hope by new *mates* while enveloped simultaneously by the weight of this academic history on the one hand and these welcoming, peace-loving Quaker arms on the other, makes me feel again that probably I have made the proper choice in bringing him to this country, where he might receive the sort of education that a free citizen of the thinking world must and should have if he is to make something of himself in these catastrophic times.

Before meeting Yasha in his dormitory, I stop by the administration building for a prearranged chat with the Head of School. Mrs. Gwendolyn Channing greets me dressed all in comforting Quaker woolens. The point of this meeting to rededicate the personal promise she made me upon my application to the school (and again upon their granting Yasha the generous scholarship) that under no circumstances will my son be exposed to the knowledge (which up to now I have rigorously kept from him) of his grandfather's infamous name. He will, in short, be protected from unwanted—which is to say, any—publicity from the world outside these peaceable walls.

Mrs. Channing assures me that *all is well*. There was a *rather challenging* first month, during which, out of a natural state of anxiety at finding himself *thrust into a foreign situation, Jacob was perhaps overemphasizing certain, shall we say, American aspects of his personality*, but he now seems to be *settling in quite happily* and making a number of new friends.

One such friend, presumably, is the quiet Indian boy sitting with Yasha on the front steps of the dormitory building as I approach. My son—my height now, with evidence of Sid's long arms and stretched legs and a healthy mop of dark hair curling over forehead and ears—offers me a lanky hug and mumbled *Hi, Mom* (or is it *Mum* I hear in some sort of borrowed Cockney mush?), followed by an introduction to his new chum Rog, whose real name, I learn once I have installed the three of us at a table in the

Old English Gentleman pub in town for steak-and-kidney pies and boiled peas on toast, is really Rajesh. Rog's parents are back in Bombay, it seems, and will not be over until Christmas. I would invite him to spend the break with us in Cambridge if we had room, but we don't, and if we did not live in an attic, as we do, and if we did not have cold winds already blowing through the "ventilation" holes behind our gas stove, and so forth. After my pint of brown ale I tell young Rajesh, who is as short as my son is tall, that I had an Indian friend once, more than a friend actually, a husband in fact, even if bloody Kosygin and his people refused to acknowledge our relationship in its true form and only reluctantly and for their own political calculations allowed me permission to travel, after dear Brajesh's death, to his homeland so that, along with his enormous grieving family, I might pour my dear companion's ashes back into the river of his birth. Yes, Rajesh can't imagine it, but I had gone to India once, and a heart-wrenching and momentous journey it turned out to be.

My children knew Brajesh, I hear myself telling Rajesh/Rog, before correcting my mistake. *My first two children, I mean. In the Soviet Union.*

As it happens, I have an old picture of Josef in my purse (the one of him holding his Soviet passport), and this I pull out now to show the Indian boy in the English pub that I am no mere lunatic woman or liar, saying, *This is my eldest. My Josef. A doctor in Moscow, you see? Yasha—I mean Jacob—has never met his brother, but one day I hope he will. And his dear sister, Katya, too.*

And poor little Rajesh/Rog with his brown skin and serious brown eyes, probably already dreaming of the long Christmas break when his parents or someone, anyone, might come and fetch him from this Orwellian Quaker nightmare, Rajesh nods—what else can he do?—and continues to stare at my son's photograph until finally I slip it back into my purse, releasing him.

India, I announce to Rajesh, and perhaps I sound a bit angry now, I can no longer tell, *is where I changed my life forever.*

Can we go? demands Yasha with furious embarrassment, looking not at me but out the window to the gray English street.

Of course, I agree. *Forgive me for remembering.*

I pay the bill, counting out the pounds and shillings. In my head I still do math in Russian.

3 November

I miss Peter. He is the one, the only one, who knows all the characters of my story and takes them to heart. Who might fight for and against them as I would, as real people instead of tilted windmills. Times, I confess, often late in the evening with Yasha away at school, when some nagging, pitiful one-sided conversation insinuates itself into my thoughts and remains there like a thread crying out to be pulled—and before I know it I find myself with phone in hand, ready to call out to the only man in the world who might tell me once again, selflessly and with absolute conviction, not to yank like a frightened child on the very thing that will be my undoing.

But I don't call. Because each time there comes at the last second a flash of lightning in my storming brain that is a picture of him sitting in his lawyer's office calmly offering his paid counsel over the phone to someone else, another client who is not me, and Beverly just outside the door eavesdropping on every word. And each time the recognition of this other, formal existence of his hurls me first into panic—if he is hiding in there behind his cold professional walls, every client equal and the same, then where and who am I?—and finally into anger—how <u>dare</u> he treat me like this?—until I slam down the phone without calling.

Which leaves me alone and without him. And so it has been for a long time now.

Too often like this: two dangerous seas colliding in my head.

I don't know why.

22 November

Yesterday there was a screening of *Oblomov* (with subtitles) organized by the Cambridge University Russian Society. I was not specially invited—almost no one in this city knows my real identity—but rather attended as the guest of my downstairs neighbor, Mrs. Fiona Driscoll, retired librarian originally from the county of Cork, Ireland. Fiona occasionally invites me down for tea while Yasha is away at school. She makes a strong *cuppa*, as they say, which she serves with thick tea biscuits, good for not being too sweet. Her gas fire gives off precious little heat, but at least she has one.

Fiona knows who my father was. I told her myself after confirming that (a) she is quite a solitary person and not prone to gossip; and (b) she isn't inclined to relish the information for any lurid historical aspect, but rather as a curious fact of the kind she regularly had access to during her decades of service in the Cambridge University Library and that, now as a pensioner, she often employs in solving the crossword puzzles that are her primary source of entertainment.

She had no particular interest in *Oblomov* but assumed, because it was Russian, that I might. Still, she was surprised on our walk to the screening venue when I told her that I was acquainted from my college days with both the director, Mikhalkov, and the star, Tabakov.

You know them?

Mikhalkov had a run-in with the Soviet censors, I explained to her. He managed to continue making films only by telling stories about the seasons with no people in them and virtually no dialogue.

Stories about the seasons? cried Fiona, horrified. *Not a whiff of dialogue or people, you say? Dear me, what have I gotten us into?*

We persevered. The cinema rather makeshift, more academic than social. It was only about half-full, something I would be grateful for later.

Some English don with an eggplant nose stood up and delivered a few words about Oblomov and the nineteenth-century Russian literary idea of the *Superfluous Man;* about Mikhalkov and the *current state of Soviet cinema.* I wasn't really listening. And then, before I was quite expecting it, the man sat down, the room darkened, and the screen filled with light.

A flashback in time.

A beautiful little boy with reddish curls in a linen nightshirt wakes alone in his big cozy bed. It is Oblomov as a child, one knows instantly.

And now he is running down a long hallway.

And now being bathed in a round wooden tub by his dear old nurse.

And now she touches him with such ancient tenderness.

And now, and now . . .

He is running out, out, alive and smiling, into an endless green meadow.

Lana? Lana, are you all right?

Fiona much concerned, ancient librarian's hand light as a feather on my back, though tactile through the wool of my coat, which I never did take off, for I am always cold in this bloody country where it never has the guts to snow; yes, I am cold.

Lana, tell me what I should do.

But this I cannot tell her, because I do not know.

The film is over. It ended, I suddenly remember, with me so overwhelmed by emotion that I was hyperventilating, unable to rise from my seat. I am breathing a bit easier now, it seems, but we are the last two people in the theater.

That little boy, I gasp.

The wee child at the beginning? He's but a dream, Fiona assures me. *Oblo—how d'you pronounce his name again? Well, he's only dreaming about himself back when he was a boy. Quite tender, really. His old governess tells him his mother's just back from her long trip and whatever he does, he'd best not wake her.*

Yes, it's coming back now: he is a good boy and does not wake her. Neither in his dream at the beginning, nor in his dream at the end. Good little Oblomov, before he grows up and becomes the Superfluous Man. And so returned to him but unwoken, his mother never does appear in the film. She is the dream that refuses to take shape, the fiction that will not rectify itself into reality. She remains forever the pure product of his anticipation, his aching desire to be reunited with her, his agony and joy, which, equally, are the exact dimensions of the hole scythed in his heart by her absence.

Back in my ever-chilly flat, Fiona soon begs off. I remain alone in my kitchen, coat still buttoned, staring at the clock on the wall the way earlier I stared at young Oblomov.

Nine P.M. in Cambridge. Eleven P.M. in Moscow.

I pour myself a drink, just the one, and sit down by the heavy black telephone to wait for the dream to end.

EDITOR'S NOTE

December 10, 1983

Dear S—
Since I haven't heard from you in many months, I'm sending this to the last address I have for you in Cambridge.

Paper boat in an ocean.

At least I'm not your lawyer anymore. (The one letter of yours that reached me, thanks.) So we don't have to argue about that.

The meter's no longer running. There's no "conflict of interest." No bills to send or pay. Not Wardlow, not Jenks: just Horvath.

I'm in my office now, the door closed.

I don't think this feeling is ever going away. I'm tired of trying to understand it.

Write me sometime, will you? Or call. Tell me what to do.

Love,
Peter

It was Vera Dubov, the translator of Svetlana's journals, who, twenty-nine years after it was written, delivered this letter back to me. She was perhaps six months into her challenging translation task, so at the time we were rarely in contact; she was doing her work and I was doing mine (though in fact, being retired, I had nothing special to do). It must have been after 5:00 that day, because I was fixing myself a martini when my doorbell rang.

"Professor Dubov," I said, surprised. "Did we have an appointment?"

She shook her head, clearly uncomfortable. "I'm sorry, Mr. Horvath. I should have called first."

"What can I do for you?"

"I have found something I think may belong to you."

Reaching into her shoulder bag, she produced a letter, sans envelope. I immediately recognized the old Wardlow Jenks stationery: bone-white weave, Tiffany watermark, and—visible in reverse through the backside of the folded single sheet—the firm's name in the fourteen-point Garamond type that Lucas Wardlow always preferred.

"Where did you get that?"

My voice sharper than intended; I saw color rise in Slavic cheeks. The hair at Vera Dubov's temples lately starting to gray, I noticed. Six months living inside Svetlana's head could do that to you.

"It was stuck between the pages of one of her journals," she said. "Like this, no envelope."

I took the letter from her hand, but didn't bother unfolding it.

"You're not going to look at it?" Whatever melodrama she'd been expecting, she couldn't hide her disappointment.

"Not necessary, thanks. I know what it is."

"Mr. Horvath, I want you to know that I stopped reading the instant I realized you might be the author. That the letter was . . . intimate."

I let the depiction hang. From where I was standing I had a clear view past my visitor to the dogwood tree in my yard: late fall, branches shorn of decoration. Stab of grief so sharp behind my eyes I had to bite down on the inside of my lip to keep back the tears.

"Mr. Horvath, are you okay?"

"It was a long time ago," I managed to say.

The Russia scholar looked me straight in the eye then. How much more interesting I was to her now than I'd been before she'd found the letter. Before she'd read the letter; I was sure she'd read the entire thing. I know I certainly would have, had I been in her place.

"Have a good night, Miss Dubov," I said, before she could say anything more. "And thank you."

1984: ENGLAND

7 January

Most days are not to be remembered. Believed, yes, but not re-membered.

Then there are days like today. Days like unicorns, not to be believed with one's own eyes. Days of radical incredulity. Days that could not have happened. And so it is as though they never happened.

These are the days one never forgets.

A pot of my barley soup simmering on the stove. A cooking glove—no, *oven mitt*—on one hand as I bend to take a tray of *heat-and-serve* rolls out of the oven. Yasha still home for Christmas holiday, now upstairs *dilly-dallying* (his new most popular word other than *shit cock fuck*), and these are his favorite rolls, served with loads of English butter. The phone rings, but I'm not expect-ing anything—the day thus far I mean, while perfectly nice, has been of the credible and forgettable kind, and so I finish removing the rolls from the oven and even give the soup a couple of stirs with my long wooden spoon before walking over to the phone table and answering.

Hello, yes?

Mother?

In his grown man's Russian the word is still a sound before it is a word. The way my boy was once a spirit in my womb before ever he was a boy.

Mother, it's me.

Josef . . . ? In my breast, my own heart is eating me alive.

Mother, I'm writing a paper for a medical journal and there's a study I can't get hold of because it was done in England. Cambridge University. It would be very helpful for what I'm writing—for my position, you understand? Do you think you might be able to find a copy and send it to me?

His tone astonishingly routine, as if we'd been speaking just the other week, rather than the other decade. As if we'd been in the middle of some pleasant conversation only he remembered.

All right, I . . . Some kind of medical study, you say?

Yes. Thanks, Mother. Do you have a pen? I'll give you the details.

I wrote them down. Good thing, because only a few hours later I can't remember any distinct fact about his urgent paper. On the liver? The kidney? The heart? What I remember is the sound of my son's Russian voice speaking to me as a son would speak to his mother—just that. And then, once the call was over, breaking out in sobs there in the kitchen, with my oven mitt still on.

Because of a set of instructions.

No. Because he is still my son.

11 January

Somehow Yasha's idea of Christmas break does not include hours spent deep in the intestines of Cambridge University Library, haranguing one librarian's assistant after another until finally, just in time for tea, the obscure yet much-desired study of some kind of plaque-eating microbe comes wheeling toward us on a cart. A drab little thing, after all that. Then a long line for the copy machine before we can escape to open air. By now the post office is closed; Josef's mailing instructions, in any case, are too complicated for me to maneuver in a single day. As recompense for his frustration, I take Yasha to a tea shop for a cuppa and a splurge on *clotted* cream and *thrice-baked* scones. I don't tell him—not today, anyway—how low the money is running, even with his scholarship.

Of course, he has questions about these siblings he's never met and practically never heard about. And fortunately I have a bit more to tell him. For yesterday a letter from Josef arrived in my postbox—for it to follow so quick on the heels of his phone call, I assume but would never risk saying aloud, he must have received official sanction to reopen contact with me—in which he preemptively offered answers to certain basic wonderings I had not yet had occasion to share with him myself. My grandson, Ilya, for example, whose existence until now I've heard about only from my stargazing Princeton neighbor Roman Smoluchowski, is today thirteen and living, it concerns me to learn, not with Josef and his new wife, Lyuda (whoever she is), but rather with his ex-wife, Elena (whoever she was).

And speaking of depressing news, Josef wrote that he would tell me what he could about our beloved Katya, though this would not amount to very much, for he regretted to say that he and his sister were no longer in touch. Some time ago, her work as a geophysicist had taken her to some rancid Siberian outpost called Kamchatka. He did not know what she did there exactly, but he thought it had something to do with volcanic gases. How reassuring. Katya is married and has a daughter, my granddaughter, whose name Josef did not supply perhaps because he does not know, or does not care to know, the name of his only niece.

And reading my son's letter, I thought of my infant daughter in her hospital incubator only hours after her birth, the size of my hand and already struggling to insist herself on the world. That those days of miraculous survival should have led, after so much frightened love, to these decades of profound absence and familial dislocation feels now, I tell you, like nothing less than a crime against humanity, the true guilt for which can be laid at the feet of only one person. And that person is me.

The photo of himself that Josef chose to include with his letter presented its own documentary case for the effects of unhappy living (or perhaps the unhappy effects of living). My first nauseating impression was that I was looking at a photograph of my alcoholic brother Vasily in the months after his return from prison. But this middle-aged man, my Josef, rather, for all his mournful, balding dissolution, gave off none of Vasily's desperate insubordination. My boy looked ill and weary and sad.

I could not help myself. If I could not save my Russian daughter, I could still save my Russian son. I went straight to the phone. He'd given me his number and I dialed it with clumsy fingers. The Soviet tone: four, five times resounding and with each one the bloody KGB pounding on your door, then the double click—

Hello?

Josef, you stop your drinking!

Mother?

You stop it, Bunny! Do you hear me? Now pull yourself together. You'll die if you keep on like this. I can see it in your face.

Mother, it's the middle of the night.

So it was.

So the three of us, we've all got different dads, Yasha observes in faux Cockney, trying to scoop the last of the thrice-baked crumbs off his tea plate and into his mouth.

I look at him. Is he bitter? Perhaps not yet, but that is no guarantee of anything. Hungry, yes. Growing so fast he will have tree rings inside his legs.

You already know this, I say as gently as I can, in fact not sure whether I have been clear about the countless things that I have tried to hide from him for his own protection.

My youngest child shakes his head in frustration.

What do I tell him? What do I tell any of my children?

3 April

The thing that I feared has happened.

On Friday my phone rang early in the morning while I was still drinking my coffee and trying to get warm. A male voice with a pub accent on the other end of the line.

Am I speaking with Svetlana Stalin?

Who is this? For a moment, the bizarre half hope that I was enduring an April Fools' prank. But then the voice continued:

Svetlana Alliluyeva? The blistering idiot pronounced my mother's family name like *hallelujah*.

Whoever you are, you are mistaken, I insisted. *My name is Lana Evans. I am an American citizen living in Britain. Call the embassy if you have questions. But do not call this number again!*

I slammed down the phone receiver. But the call had shaken me. The next day I was planning to take the train to Saffron Walden to fetch Yasha for his Easter break. I decided I would not set foot outside my building until then.

Like the feeling one gets when one looks up in a barren landscape and finds a crow flying close overhead. The ominous creature has no business being there, is all one knows. One shudders, and for good reason.

I spotted the first reporter on the street in front of my building just past seven the next morning. I pulled the shade down over my kitchen window and went directly out of my flat and downstairs to ring Fiona's buzzer.

It took her a minute to open the door. Heavy Irish cardigan thrown over her shoulders, smelling of old sheep, her thin gray hair out of sorts.

Lana, she said, clearly surprised. *So early? Everything all right?*

Fiona, you must not speak to anyone.

Oh, I wouldn't. I don't usually see many people as it is. What's this about, dear?

No one outside. No one with the press.

The press? Lord, no. Why would I? No one with the press has any interest in me, that's for sure.

Satisfied, I went back upstairs and dialed Yasha's school. The line rang and rang. On my third frantic try a receptionist answered. I told her I must speak with Mrs. Channing, it was an emergency.

However, I was too late. Mrs. Channing came on the line already talking:

Mrs. Evans, I was just about to ring you. I'm afraid a most unfortunate situation has arisen.

Not expecting me to pick him up until later that day, Yasha was naturally alarmed when his Latin teacher, Mr. Logan, appeared in his room before breakfast and announced that there'd been a change of plans: I would not be coming and instead he, Mr. Logan, would be driving Yasha to Cambridge. My son was confused. (All this recounted to me once he was home.) Had he done something wrong? This was the start of Easter break, classes were out, and he'd handed in his last assignment as expected. Yet here in his room was old Mr. Logan, a Scottish Quaker, this morning especially taciturn, urgent, and pale-faced.

When are we going? asked Yasha.

Right this minute, replied the teacher.

The Latin man placed Yasha's small suitcase in his rusticated Volkswagen Golf. Once Yasha had climbed into the backseat, he was told, *Now lie down and spread that blanket over yourself.*

The seat fabric of Logan's car, Yasha noted from under the heavy woolen blanket, smelled faintly of dead fish.

Stay down, Logan ordered, as the car passed through the gates of the school and between the clamoring crowd of paparazzi gathered there—adding under his breath, *Bloody parasite reporters.*

The drive to Cambridge took an hour and a half. Once they were safe beyond Saffron Walden, Yasha was told he could take off the blanket and sit up. He found the English sky as usual depressive and damp, yet glaring. When twice during the journey he asked his teacher what was going on, each time the reply was a muttered quote in Greek from Marcus Aurelius:

1. Everything we hear is an opinion, not a fact. Everything we see is a perspective, not the truth.

2. You have power over your mind—not outside events. Realize this, and you will find strength.

Finally, they reached Cambridge. *Time to hit the deck again, Jacob,* Mr. Logan instructed. *Don't forget the blanket.*

Another phalanx of paparazzi, this one outside our home at number 12b Chaucer Road, where they'd been agitating since dawn. Wielding history textbooks as much as cameras and pens, stalking my son with their flashbulbs and their shouted questions—no, not questions, indictments:

—*Jacob, what do you think of your grandfather?*
—*Would you call him a mass murderer? Worse than Hitler?*
—*Why'd you and your mother change your names?*
—*Tell your mum to come out and speak to us!*
—*Have you ever been to the Soviet Union?*
—*Are you a Communist?*
—*Jacob, over here!*

By this time I'd emerged on the sidewalk myself and was struggling through hostile bodies to reach Yasha, still trapped inside the car parked at the curb. A man with a large Nikon jumped in my face and I shoved him back with both hands, harder than either of us expected, in the process knocking his expensive camera to the ground.

Cunt! he growled. *I'll get you fuckin' deported for that.*

I leave when I want! I screamed at him, cursing him in Russian, suddenly so enraged I could no longer claim to be right in my own head.

And here was Logan, master of dead languages, leaping from his fishy car. *Mrs. Evans, for God's sake get him in the house quickly!*

Yanking open the rear door, he hauled Yasha out. I could see immediately how frightened my son was.

Mom, what's going on?

There was no time to answer him, and how could I anyway? Taking him by the hand, I fought our way through the shouting mob that stood between him and that priceless freedom to be a child that will never again be his.

4 April

That, I say nervously, touching the black-and-white photograph, *was your grandfather.*

Who was he? Yasha wants to know, at once curious and perhaps already faintly, though still unconsciously, troubled. For the image I have just handed him, while famous the world over as a document of history, is to him wholly unfamiliar: Stalin, Churchill, and Truman at the Potsdam Conference, circa late July 1945.

Your grandfather was the leader of the Soviet Union all through my childhood, until his death in 1953.

Only when I do not speak the name and get away with it, at least for the moment, does it become fully confirmed in my mind that my son has never actually heard his grandfather's name, does not know it or connect himself with it, still considers it, as it were, an unknown fiction, that historical asterisk of a name that even children in Cameroon and farthest Indonesia and the highest mountain reaches of Nepal know to despise.

The leader? Like the president?

You could say that. But the differences are important.

That's Churchill next to him?

Yes, Winston Churchill. Prime Minister of Britain during the war. I met him when I was just a few years older than you.

You met Winston Churchill?

Only for a minute. He told me that before he went bald his hair was red like mine used to be. And that man there—

That's Harry Truman.

Yes.

So these are the leaders who beat Hitler and won World War II.

You're right, I say to my son.

And he was my grandfather? That's pretty cool. I can't believe you never told me any of this.

Yasha, listen to me. There is only one thing you need to know. You are American. *Your father is American, and so are you. I am now an American citizen. But you, you were American from the second you were born.*

I get it, Mom. I'm American.

Of course, he did not *get it*, not yet, because I had spent his entire life to that point making sure never to give it to him to get. Had kept him growing always in the dark, as a hypocrite farmer, congratulating himself for being humane, might keep his prize hog locked in the barn before the slaughter.

But now, thanks to the supposed journalist Mr. Malcolm Muggeridge (friendly enough to me when I first landed, but whom Fiona says she heard last evening gossiping disgracefully about me and my father on BBC Radio) and his tribe of Fleet Street arsonists, my son's last vestige of innocence will be consumed by their flames in a matter of days, if not hours. And there is nothing I can do to stop it. And there is nowhere for us to go.

13 June

Today a letter from Josef. The Soviet government will allow him to travel to Helsinki, where he and I can meet.

I write this miraculous news again, to show myself it is real: The Soviet government will allow my son to travel to Helsinki, where he and I can meet.

Helsinki, Finland.

I could copy the words a hundred times and still not truly believe. He promises another letter as soon as he has more details. Okay. I can wait, knowing I will see him soon.

My firstborn. My son.

The time has come.

I wrote that at one in the morning. Now it is three and I have begun to doubt. Familiar disease, blowing under my closed door. I have not slept. Because I know the people in charge there. Oh, some of them have died, some have changed; but I know them. And they think they know me. They think they understand a mother's love.

They have no idea what I'm willing to do for my children.

I have the most recent photo of Josef propped on my knees so I can look at his face and see the painful and unhealthy life I abandoned him to. See that if there was ever a boy who needed his mother, it is this boy. This man. My Josef.

Daylight. Fell asleep just before dawn and dreamed of a place called Helsinki. Winter, clean and cold and harshly bright, so blinding I can't look without shading my eyes with my hands and squinting.

And now through this hellish glare I see what looms ahead of me:

An entirely empty airport.

29 June

I give you the curse of believing. The curse of fucking Helsinki. The curse of a photograph of my son that is not my son. For even in that photograph he looked sick and old before his time, a son in need of his mother.

Being examined by experts, he writes. *Medically unable to work . . . Unable to travel.*

So disappointed . . . Wanted to see you so much.

I drop his letter on the kitchen floor—spotless for once because I have recently cleaned it, imagining as I pushed the mop here and there of being in Helsinki with my son, bringing him home with me. But there is no Helsinki. Helsinki was a curse. So there is no home. There is only this letter on my clean floor as I dial his Moscow phone number and let it ring and ring. No answer in the USSR. I hang up, dial again, it's the bloody same, and I go on like this dialing, listening, hanging up, dialing, until finally I hear the double click I have been praying for, followed by the voice of a dying patient.

Mother?

Bunny, I cry, *I'm coming to take care of you!*

_____

And the moment I speak them, I know these words are the very truth that I have carried and planned for since my unforgivable mistake all those years ago, abandoning my children for what I assured myself was their own good. For never in his life—never in his life—has Josef needed me more than he needs me now.

I am his mother. And I must find a way to go to him, whatever the consequences.

LETTER

17 October 1984
Chaucer Road, Cambridge

Dear Peter,
You will be home by now. Will you have told Martha, after all, that you came to see me during your business trip to England? I wonder. But then you are probably regretting in any case that the visit was not as you hoped. I am sorry that after the joys of seeing each other again after so long; after getting to hold you again as I often imagined but never expected; after physical and emotional honesties between us—that all this should have ended, stupidly, in an argument at the very last minute.

I did not mean what I said. You must know this. You are not a spy or enemy; you could never be that to me. I am under increasing amounts of stress, and anger sometimes is the result. You once told me, back at the beginning, that you have a terror of feeling trapped. Well, it is the same for me. I am good and trapped now, Peter. I have tried my hardest to make certain things possi-

ble in this part of the world for myself and Yasha, you know I have, and you have seen with your own eyes how it has not worked out. And when one is older, you also know, one's mistakes become magnified within one's history; they are easily made catastrophic. And so I realize my situation to be now. The sacrifices I have made for Yasha's schooling have had some beneficial effects—you witness how he has grown in body and mind—but they also I think created the illusion that there was a chance to outrun my father's ghost and establish some permanent life of peace for myself and my son. And this was a lie. It cannot happen in the West, I _finally_ see that; too many betrayals have occurred, with only more to come. (I don't mean _you_.) The illusion is over. Perhaps just as well. You asked me—you were angry—what the hell was I going to do now that I was determined to "burn every last bridge" in my life. I told you that I didn't know. But I do know, Peter. And when you learn what it is, you will want nothing to do with me ever again. And that, for me, you must believe, is a terrible cost to pay. But what else can I do? I have made mistakes no mother should make.

Whatever you may hear or read about me in the coming weeks, please please do not dwell on the argument we had in my kitchen, with the taxi waiting outside and your suitcase packed by the door. Think instead of the night we spent together in my creaky bed, holding each other with tenderness and passion. That was me too. When I was young, people were always leaving without explanation. Most never returned. I have forever hated the sound of closing doors and the view of people's backs. Perhaps I can't be counted on, but I can be trusted; I hope you can see the difference. So trust my heart, Peter, and forget what comes out of my mouth. Remember how we held and touched each other. Leave if you must, but I beg you, don't ever abandon me.
Your loving
Svetlana

PART FIVE

EDITOR'S NOTE

On November 16, 1984, flanked by officials from the Soviet Foreign Ministry, Svetlana Alliluyeva appeared as the surprise star of an international press conference at the Moscow offices of the Soviet Women's National Committee, gripping her prepared remarks with both hands in an unsuccessful effort to keep them from shaking.

And thirty-two hours later, across the globe in Princeton, New Jersey, Martha Horvath is well asleep by the time that *Nightline*—the late-night news program on which video footage of this "historic Soviet news event" first airs in America—comes on. The television in our house is located in the "family room" on the ground floor; and it is in there alone, with a drink in his hand, that Peter Horvath struggles to absorb the reality of what the woman he loves is saying, and what, in fact, she has gone and done.

The Kremlin has provided its prized propaganda trophy with an official translator—a poor, cowed woman in a female-comrade necktie is visible at the right of the screen—the better to control the Party's Cold War message. Svetlana, however, has apparently decided to stage-manage her self-destruction in her own fashion. And so she delivers her remarks first in Russian, and then, in a strangely forced and emotionally unstable voice that seesaws between defiance and uncertainty, as if she both despises the lies she's spouting and dares the world to call her on them, she reads them aloud herself in English:

"I, Svetlana Alliluyeva, and my son Yakov Evans, voluntarily renounce our American citizenship in order to live permanently in the Union of Soviet Socialist Republics. We are doing this in order to rejoin my two older children to live, finally, as a unified family, all my children together, as we should, free from corrupt influences of lawyers, businessmen, publishers, politicians, and intelligence agents who, during my unhappy and regretful years in the West, attempted to turn my name and the name of my father into nothing more than a sensational commodity. My children need me, and now I am here."

The experience of watching this scene unfold (only vaguely aware that it took place yesterday and is already history) is such a shock to my system that even after downing the rest of my drink, I find I am able to understand what's happening on the television screen only in discrete units of perception. First is Svetlana's physical appearance, so changed from the woman I made love to just weeks ago in her drafty bedroom in Cambridge that for several moments my brain refuses to accept that this is the same person. But it *is* the same person—that is a fact. The transformation begins with her hair, which, while still mostly rusty red, is chopped mannishly short and worn now parted to the side in the manner of the good Party soldier she is warring with herself to be. An effect deepened by a new pair of wide-framed steel eyeglasses of a distinctly sexless, Politburo style, and a heavy, brown wool suit. Her feet aren't visible to the camera—she is seated behind a table on a dais, flanked by the unused translator and an unidentified Party member—but it is no difficulty to imagine her sporting a pair of thick-soled Soviet clunkers. Her face too (or perhaps this owes more to the Communist decor and institutional lighting) is paler and fleshier than I remember, with a rote, mechanical quality to her expression that seems to willfully deny the vitality, intelligence, and passion of the complex woman I believed I knew.

Is the Kremlin treating her like a celebrity? Or a puppet?

Both, of course.

Does she realize this herself?

From such great distance, helpless and stupid as I am, there is no honest way—other than the faintly trembling actor's script in her hands and the artificial eddies of her voice—to tell.

Because for all that is said at this charade of a press event, it's what she doesn't say that will keep me awake this night and others, and that more than once in the latest, darkest hours will send me back to the kitchen for another dose of alcohol.

She and Yasha had actually arrived in the USSR two weeks earlier. (Dick Thompson confirmed this for me.) Yes, two profoundly awful, Kremlin-authored, sequestered weeks spent in the Hotel Sovietsky in Moscow. Enough time, certainly, to realize that her entire maternal re-defection dream was a terrible mistake.

She would have felt it from the plane window as they circled Sheremetyevo before landing: snow suffocating the land. In no homecoming fantasy she'd ever had, had it ever been winter. But it was winter now, what they call a Russian autumn. Fur-collared overcoats on the officials waiting for her by the terminal's VIP entrance. Bouquet handed to her by the female comrade ("Welcome home!" without a smile, as if smiles cost rubles), the flowers already wilting under the invisible weight of ice crystals in the air. The route into the city, kilometer after kilometer of apartment blocks like hideous, gargantuan prisons built by Khrushchev and the others. She did not recognize any of it—yet she did (*Lubyanka Lubyanka Lubyanka*). The recognition lay in her heart, which at this much-anticipated moment of historic reentry felt nothing at all, and which only now did she understand she had confused with some different, untreatable longing in herself.

Still, she refused to give up hope for a better beginning. She'd told Josef not to meet her at the airport—too much pressure and publicity—but she was certain that he and his family would be waiting for them at the hotel.

In the back of the Chaika limousine, heat blasting over her knees, she glanced at Yasha. He was staring out the window at the unwinding line of massive, identical "fortresses of the people" and concrete plazas blanketed with soiled snow.

"Josef and his family will be waiting to greet us," she said, as much to soothe herself as to reassure him.

He ignored her.

"You have been assigned a luxury two-bedroom suite," said the official perched tensely on the jump seat across from her. "Hotel Sovietsky is the finest, most expensive hotel in Moscow."

He was speaking Russian, which Yasha would not be able to understand. And the American teenager who was her son did not turn his head, or seem to have any interest in what he could not understand. As if all that lay behind, rather than ahead of him. As if he were not in this Chaika limo in real time, but still on the incoming Aeroflot jet, circling and circling over white empty fields of a foreign country that he'd never wanted to see, never given a shit about, in the first place.

And that was when it hit her, his mother, with a certainty that left her breathless: now that they were here, they would never be allowed to leave.

(I am speculating, I know; how very unlawyer-like of me. But please, if you will, allow me this moment—just this once—to go now where I could not go then.)

The lobby of the Hotel Sovietsky was constructed entirely of white marble. Even the potted trees were albino. Svetlana had seen an American TV program once about a man dressed as God— well, it must have been a joke because he was playing the Almighty wearing a white jumpsuit and white disco shoes and lightly tinted aviator sunglasses, jumping around and lip-synching to a song called "You Make Me Feel Like Dancing"—but not even that Disco Jehovah had been as sad and shocking to her as the sight, in the grand white lobby of the Sovietsky, of this bald, pouchy, drained-looking, thirty-nine-year-old man staring at her from across the room.

The last time she'd seen Josef was eighteen years ago in the departures lounge at Sheremetyevo. Slim as a poet then, and still with the possibility of a smile behind his eyes. Calm enough in his heart because he'd believed he would be seeing his mother again in two weeks. She would spread Brajesh Singh's ashes, visit with his people, and then return to her own children, bringing them presents from India.

Josef was not waving now. Katya had never got her hand-dyed sari, nor he his miraculously preserved black mamba. It had all been a ruse of the most obscene cruelty. Added to her elder son's frozen aspect in the grand lobby, his mother observed with a shiver of her own, was his visible mortification that whatever she should be after all these years of abandonment, however she should appear on this day of all days, it must not be like this. Fifty-eight? How could she be fifty-eight? And foreign? Why wasn't she dead? No. It was against propriety; a final broken promise.

1984-1985: MOSCOW/TBILISI

19 November 1984
Hotel Sovietsky

Katya's response to my letter asking if I might see her:

> *If I call you a traitor to the Motherland, this is not a figure of*
> *speech. I mean the words as they were designed.*
>
> > *Understand me clearly: The moment you left the Mother-*
> *land eighteen years ago, I became an orphan. The Motherland*
> *adopted me. I do her bidding now, as a daughter would, if I do*
> *anyone's.*
>
> > *Do not contact me again.*
>
> > *I do not forgive you for what you did. I will never forgive you.*
> *And under no circumstances will I allow you to see your grand-*
> *daughter.*

This in its entirety, written in scientifically compacted handwriting on a stained postcard (Siberian postage stamp) showing a

mud yurt with a funny bear-shaped weather vane sticking out of its roof. Location: somewhere at the end of the earth.

I try to place the daughter I used to have in this extreme, anti-human landscape, but fail. And fail again. Sound of the oven door groaning. Her sniffles as she cried in my arms the day she accidentally tore the cover of the notebook I'd just bought her at GUM.

Her husband, the former son-in-law I never met, I have been informed by people who know, died the other year of a self-inflicted rifle shot. A fatality officially registered as an accident.

I look now at Josef, my eldest, where he sits on an overstuffed hotel chair with gold-leaf arms, Katya's postcard on the glass table between us. Only his third visit since our arrival, none of them pleasant. If we were to listen together at this moment, we might overhear Yasha and his government-provided tutor engaging in their Russian language lessons in the other room. But Josef, I can see, could care less about his little brother, whom he has completely ignored since our arrival. Nor does he seem at all occupied with his sister's categorical rejection of her blood family. Rather, he shifts on his chair and sighs harshly, wishing to signal as yet unspoken grievances on his own account (though many have already been spoken, beginning with outrage over the *Greek trinkets*, as he dismissed them, that Yasha and I brought him and his family from our stopover in Athens), yes, grievances he has stored up across the years, while preparing me for never-ending acts of maternal recompense to come. In the spiked grating of his sigh I hear the second wife, Lyuda's ventriloquist efforts. Perhaps Josef does as well, because he picks up the vodka bottle that he charged to the hotel suite without asking, pours himself a drink, and swallows it down. Not his first. It is eleven in the morning. His eyes have a yellowed tint, the skin beneath them waxy and darkened from fatigue and a liver under perpetual assault. By comparison, I am almost a good bet for longevity. A thought that sickens me, because I am his mother, and it was I who stole their youth from these two children and crippled their futures.

23 November 1984

My dear nurse found me crying one day because I'd just finished reading Pushkin's *The Tale of the Dead Princess and the Seven Knights* and had loved it so much I could not stand to believe it was over. This was the first true heartbreak I can recall before losing my mother.

Alexandra Andreevna dried my eyes with the hem of her apron. Then she picked up the beautifully illustrated picture book, which in my anguish and disappointment I had thrown on the floor, placed it back in my hands, and said, *Now, silly, there's no reason for tears. Don't you know that a good book never ends? It just runs out of pages.*

You see, my nurse imagined that all the characters in the books she loved were real people who had actually done and experienced all the things she'd read about. The author too, she believed, was a real person posing as a character, someone simply telling a true if perhaps miraculous adventure that had actually happened, a storyteller like the storytellers of old, before there were books or paper or implements to write with, when all we had to be known in the world were our voices and our memories.

Yesterday, I went to see my beloved nurse's grave in Novodevichy Cemetery, where, after her death at the age of seventy in 1956, I had her buried beside my mother.

I brought Yasha, irritable and oppressed by the hours of Russian study with the tutor who he complains is so much stricter than the Quakers, and by the harrying persistence of the reporters who'd pursued us from hotel to cemetery and were now spying on us through their Soviet cameras at a distance. From our special cordoned-off section of the graveyard the snow had been cleared, leaving a damp, freezing chessboard of white and brown, on which we were the only foreign pieces. Yasha stood off by himself, kicking angrily at a mound of gray ice with the toe of his British hiking boot. He does not like Russia. And it was clear that the two women buried here—the two most important women of my life—were no more real to him than characters in a story, decidedly not for children, that he had not chosen to read himself but rather was forced to listen to by me. He does not possess my nurse's unshakable rustic faith in the literal verities of the myths that we choose to comfort ourselves with because, without them, we know that we are naked before the cruelties of fate. My son, in other words, is American. Where I am not. And yet, whatever I am, whatever I was, whatever I may have come from, is no longer to be found here, buried in this graveyard under mud and ice.

25 November 1984

This morning, because I cannot seem to get enough of this masochism show the Americans love to call *memory lane*, I go to see Fyodor V, whom I recall, at least until today's visit, as an eminent physicist, intellectual, and true friend in the years after my father's death. There were not many such people, and among them Fyodor stood apart for his human understanding that what I had come from was perhaps not all that I was. Late one night over dinner at my apartment, after the other guests had gone, he took my hand and said, *My dear, if you ever choose to write about this history you were born into and must now grow out of, I hope you will do me the honor of writing it to me. That way you can remain as private as you need to, and protect your children, and at the same time you may feel that there is a friend sitting across the table from you, late at night and just like this, listening with compassion.*

I did not forget. It was to Fyodor, however unnamed, that I wrote the twenty "letters" of my memoir, describing in that intimate epistolary form aspects of my relationship with my family and upbringing that no contemporary had cared to understand. I wrote about my father as only I knew him and believed he was; my mother to what degree I could remember; my brothers, Yakov and Vasily; my aunts, uncles, grandparents, so many of them gone.

And then, in the summer of 1963, I finished that book of letters (*Don't you know that a good book never ends? It just runs out of pages.*) and never showed it to Fyodor, never showed it to anyone, and three years later, never quite comprehending what I was doing, took it with me in my luggage, packed beside the ashes of Brajesh Singh, to India.

Fyodor does not care about any of this now. He does not wish to know. Sick and dying, his wife gone, his once abundant hair in shreds across a sun-pocked scalp, with matted gray beard smelling of week-old borscht, he greets me at the door to his apartment with the resentful question, *Why have you returned?* He means, as he wishes to elaborate at bitter length over tea, that I have allowed myself to become a tool for state propaganda, nothing more. *For what purpose? To save your children? You delude yourself. They do not need this kind of saving, it only brings them trouble and pain. Now you are truly powerless, a stupid puppet acting out the role written for you.*

Not tea, then, but a bloodletting. My cup still undrunk, I get to my feet and thank him ironically for his former friendship. *Did you know, Fyodor,* I can't resist adding, *that book—you remember, those letters to you that you encouraged me to write—turned into a million-dollar blockbuster in America? Every word became a dollar that I spent. And all thanks to you.*

I leave the great man sunken in his chair. He won't last till spring. And later, after a bath salted with my own regret, I sit in one of these two luxury rooms paid for by the State, my American son in the other repeating God knows what phrases in Russian, with my semi-reconstituted name (my father once again the military genius who won the war and saved the nation), writing these words with the irrefutable knowledge that my soul is in peril. Yes, my very soul. Who am I to speak? To have left my children unprotected, not once but countless times—this not even my father did to me, only my mother, and only after putting a bullet in her heart.

I may not be able to leave this country again. But some way—any way, God forgive me—I must get Yasha out of this loveless prison of a city before it is too late.

5 December 1984
Tbilisi

And so, mirabile dictu, it turns out that little *Housekeeper* still has it in her to write a certain kind of letter to a certain rank of Soviet official. Who would've guessed? Though not so wondrous, perhaps: the fact is they don't want me here, any more than I want to be here. All I needed to say was that it was of the utmost urgency that my son and I be removed from these *ceaseless attacks by the Western Press*, so destabilizing to our resettlement process in Moscow. That I still hold *fondest memories* of occasional visits with my father to Georgia, where Yasha and I have relatives . . . Perhaps Tbilisi, then, might be a place where we could live in peace and quiet? Because to *lie low* is all that I wish at this stage of my life, now that I am *home* again. Of course, once in Georgia, I would communicate regularly with the local authorities while steering clear of the foreign press . . .

The response was astonishingly swift: our relocation was permissible. In fact, it was a good deal more than that. Everyone knows the government is less than stable these days. One feels tectonic cracks in the streets and food lines. And how many old men, dare one ask, can lead the Party in a row, literally dying at their desks, without the inevitable necrosis of the whole animal? Nor, indeed, am I turning out to be the high-end political product they thought they'd purchased at international auction, in this land where *buyer's remorse* insurance policies do not exist.

And so, within a week, very quietly, Yasha and I were extricated from the Hotel Sovietsky and put on a plane to Tbilisi.

Never in my life had I seen snow in Georgia. Palm trees yes, but not snow. On the few trips my father ever invited me on, however chilled the company, the southern climate was always temperate and balmy, even, once, as late as November. But it was December now, and looking down through the tiny windows as the plane passed high over the Caucasus Mountains, Yasha and I were struck nearly blind by a fierce white glare, like a massive, disorienting lake of fluorescent milk, reflecting off the snowy peaks and troughs of the land, until, finally, we had to shade our eyes and look away.

11 December 1984

Our driver's name is Jora. He knows Tbilisi—all Georgia, he claims, probably truthfully—with the exaggerated passion of a lover rather than a husband. Yasha says Jora is *awesome, Mom* (the faux-Cockney accent seemingly gone overnight, I'm relieved to find), while I appreciate our driver's sometimes poetic powers of description, if not his discretion. For there is no doubt that Jora, with his full Georgian lips and powerful sloping shoulders, is the mighty Shevardnadze's pocket man, reporting on our every whim and sneeze. Just as it can be no coincidence that the modern-style apartment complex in which the State is housing us, luxurious though it is, is located not in the beautiful, teeming center of the old capital, but on its less populated outskirts, where it is easier, as Dick Thompson might have said, to more closely monitor our individual needs.

The apartment complex is as over-the-top in its way as the Hotel Sovietsky, all marble and glass, and as stuffed with visiting dignitaries and Party members on their regional tours. Yasha immediately began calling it, with apparent sincerity, the *palace*, and I have not had the heart to point out to him that *palace* and *prison* both begin with the same letter of the alphabet.

There is only one thing here that soothes me. On the grounds of the complex is a reindeer farm. We have been in Tbilisi nine days, and on every one I have been to see the reindeer, none of whom have ever heard of Stalin, or the *vozhd*, or Koba, or Soso, or Soselo, or Ivanov, or any of his other names. I make my visits alone, since Yasha, with his thirteen-year-old's erratic hormones and quick fuse, won't be bothered. Because it is a working farm and not a zoo, there are no plaques offering information about these large antlered mammals who never seem to do very much except stand and eat and shit and, oh so subtly, comfort lost women like myself. So it is only by my own memory that I recall, as Peter told me one December afternoon when we were in the Lord & Taylor department store shopping for a Christmas blouse for me and "Rudolph the Red-Nosed Reindeer" began playing over the loudspeakers, that in North America reindeer are sometimes called caribou. A silly, pointless fact which nonetheless makes me miss Peter so much at this moment that I can hardly bear to write his name.

22 December 1984

Comrade A, curator of the Stalin museum, phones today to tell me how much she regrets that I declined to attend yesterday's ceremony for the 106th anniversary of my father's birth. It was unquestionably a triumph, she says. Did I know that over one million people visited the exhibitions this year alone?

The people, the comrade concludes proudly, almost hysterically, *cannot get enough.*

I make no comment with regard to who and what might be enough. Instead, I spontaneously decide to tell her the little anecdote that amused my father more than any other.

Do you happen to know, I say to the curator, *what my grandmother's last words were to my father, her son, before she died?*

Last words? The curator's tone initially skeptical, now fading into hesitancy, as if sensing a trick. *No, I . . .*

She said to him, "But what a pity you never became a priest."

What? Impossible!

Not at all. My father loved it. No story I ever heard him tell made him laugh so hard.

2 February 1985

I have been to Gori and seen the monstrous, three-ring hagiography they have manufactured there after his death. The Greek-columned shrine enveloping the two-room hovel where a boy named Josef Dzhugashvili and his family slept like miserable farm animals, a single pot on a *karasinka* their only way to cook what little food they had. And nearby, the marbled entrance and monumental staircase that leads one into the museum bearing his later surname of Stalin. Inside, enough statues and likenesses of the *vozhd* to fill the Parthenon. A room displaying a dozen copies of his death mask. A glass case containing his military greatcoat, boots, cap. On and on.

One object alone evokes genuine emotion: a fragile pair of spectacles that belonged to his mother.

10 February 1985

Today, as most Sundays, I make Yasha go with me to Sioni Cathedral, standing high above the Mtkvari River. We listen to the choir intoning the Georgian Orthodox liturgy (allowed by the State) and singing hymns, raising its voice as one to the true power under which no individual of any name stands different or apart. In this embrace, for entire stretches of timeless time I feel the peaceful beauty of being no one and nothing in a land where this has never been, never will be, possible. At some point as we sing (from his relentless tutoring, Yasha's Russian has improved, and even his Georgian is coming along surprisingly well), I reach out and take my younger son's hand. Horrified with teenage embarrassment, he pulls it back. But I take it again, forcefully pressing it between my own so he might feel the fury of my love at this moment, not just for him but for the infinite universe of which we are but the smallest particles, the simplest words in a story that has no ending.

Then it's over. Believers rise to their feet and begin to file out. Crosses everywhere one looks: Tbilisi a city of crosses. I sense eyes on me again from all quarters and know that if we linger even a minute inside this holy house, inhibitions will be discharged and people will start approaching, driven by their obsessions with that other Him, the *vozhd*, compelled to tell us how he was the greatest of all men, the one, the only, the true, for he was Georgian was he not, yes from Georgia he sprang fully formed (and robbed and killed, one might add, and then left). Though he spoke perfect Russian, he kept his Tbilisi accent all his life! Embraces will follow—kisses, hugs, invitations to feasts.

But it is a fleeting, thorny love: for if Yasha and I do not rush to add superlatives of our own to their burning pyre of horseshit, there and then will we be called traitors to our own blood.

26 February 1985

I have not heard from Josef since we left Moscow, and all my letters to Katya have come back unopened.

I met with the church Patriarch, a private audience he granted me because of my name. He told me that I must write *only words of love to your children, for they have forgotten what is love and forgiveness.*

2 March 1985

Terrible fight with Yasha. Terrible. My hands still shaking.

> *I hate this place!*
> *Why the fuck did you bring me here? Do you even know?*
> *You'll be sorry when I run away!*
> *I'll find Dad and live with him!*
> *You'll never fucking see me again!*
> *Maybe then you'll be happy!*
> *I hate you!*
> *You're the worst mother in the world!*

6 March 1985

Jora steers the Lada slowly through the village of Akhalsopeli. A village that looks much like any other in the vicinity of Tbilisi. He pulls up in front of a ramshackle gate decorated with a little gold bust of my father.

> *I'll come in with you.*
> *No, thank you, Jora.*
> *You know this guy?*
> *A friend of my cousin's. He's spent years building an "homage" to my father, and has asked me to do him the honor of visiting. It will offend my cousin if I don't go. I won't be long.*
> *He could be a nutjob.*
> *We're all nutjobs, Jora.*

Jora smiles. Because even though I know he's spying on me, we both occasionally appreciate the absurdity of this pervasive madness that has made even once-familiar absurdities surprising.

Just inside the gate, I am met effusively by a bearded Georgian with deep-set dark eyes and a nose that would not be out of place on a Romanian count. His first words to me, in Georgian-accented Russian: *I love Stalin!*

Whatever he is building, single-handedly by the look of it (I notice a smattering of paint on the sleeve of his coat), it will clearly take years, decades to complete. Everywhere around the premises of the sprawling property are buckets of plaster, bags of cement, heaps of colored glass shards to be used in constructing further mosaics, busts, statues, effigies, mausoleums, dreamscapes in honor of *our hero, the greatest man ever to come from our great country of Georgia, to say nothing of the world!* He apologizes that the *museum space* itself is not ready; he's still in the process of gathering necessary materials. There are also to be a *Stalin fountain* and an *electric dawn-to-dusk Stalin mechanical elaboration*, along with *three secret Stalin gardens*, though none of these exhibits, unfortunately, along with so much else, is anywhere near ready for viewing.

One display, however, has already been finished. This took five years to achieve. Into it he poured all the love he has for my father, the pride in his existence. Would I care to see it?

A bit annoyed now, wishing I had brought Jora with me, I tell this maniac that I would be happy to see whatever he has to show me, though my driver is waiting and I really don't have much time.

He bows formally. *Please, follow me.*

Through unkempt hedges with openings hacked into them, and little *Stalin grottoes* in nascent rough-hewn form, we make our way down through an overgrown garden to an entrance covered by a moldy blanket of earth-colored felt. My host holds aside this rotting cloth, switches on an old flashlight, and points its watery yellow beam into the darkness beyond.

This is what you will wish to see.

I enter the cave. The light extends along the floor until, a meter in front of me, it unexpectedly reveals a wall thickly textured with some dark substance that gives off its own waxy glow.

I shy back, trembling uncontrollably. For what he has brought me to see, I understand, is a ghoulish effigy of my dead father.

The *vozhd*'s face distorted and ruined as it had been at the very moment of death. His mouth lipsticked, his mustache dusted with obscene cosmetics. His once-powerful body trapped forever in the hell of an open coffin. His sunken chest piled with filthy plastic flowers.

What have you done? I whisper in horror.

Isn't it wonderful? my host says proudly. *Now he will truly live forever.*

18 March 1985

Chernenko is dead. So Gorbachev will take his turn. They say he's liberal; we will see. A cunning look to his face, this one, with the enigmatic punctuation on his bare scalp. He is convinced that the USSR has become a retrograde nation of raging alcoholics, and promises that his first act will be a massive crackdown on vodka. Perhaps he's smarter than I gave him credit for. Or perhaps they will kill him for trying.

I will write and ask his permission for us to leave. Beg him if I have to. Prostrate myself, kiss his cunning feet. Somehow I must extricate Yasha from this calamity I have made, that is all I know.

This is no place for a child. It never was.

EDITOR'S NOTE

"Pete, I thought you should know," Dick Thompson began as soon as our drinks had been served in the Irish bar near Penn Station that we used to frequent and that now, under new management, appeared to have a Spanish theme, "that yesterday 11:17 A.M. Moscow time, our Russian friend was taken into custody by the Soviets outside the American Embassy."

"What? I thought she and Yasha were in Tbilisi."

It was almost exactly a year after Svetlana had written in her journal about Gorbachev and his "cunning feet"—though of course I had no knowledge of such a personal record at the time. I had not heard from her in eighteen months.

"They took her to the Kremlin," Dick said. "Our sources report a meeting with Foreign Ministry officials. Best guess is that the sit-down was her goal all along, since she would have known that as a Soviet citizen—which she is again—she'd be barred from all foreign embassies."

"So what do you think she's trying to do?"

"Get her and her kid the hell out of the USSR. She's been

hounding Gorbachev with letters to that effect all this past year. Poor Gorby's smack in the middle of his first Party Conference as General Secretary, and ten to one, he's ready to let her leave the country without a fight."

"Where are she and Yasha now?"

Dick paused. "That's another thing I wanted to tell you personally, Pete, so you wouldn't hear it from somebody else. It seems that hours after leaving the Kremlin, Svetlana suffered some kind of cardiac incident."

"You mean a heart attack?"

"She's alive—we would've heard if she wasn't. But she's in Kremlin Hospital right now."

"You saw Dick Thompson today."

Martha and I were in the kitchen of our house that evening, finishing what, until now, had been an uneventful dinner of broiled salmon and potatoes. I had removed my tie and suit jacket; Martha was wearing her gray cashmere cardigan and her mother's pearls; she always took pains to look nice at home, even when it was just the two of us.

When I refused to take the bait, Martha confirmed my suspicion about her source: "Beverly told me."

"Beverly should know to keep her mouth shut about things that don't concern her."

"What did Dick have to say? We both know he never appears unless he's got news of some kind. Usually about your 'Russian friend.'"

I stared hard at my wife. "Svetlana had a heart attack."

My announcement had its desired effect: briefly stunned, Martha sat back in her chair, perfectly still. "Is she dead?"

"No, she's not dead. She's in a hospital in Moscow."

"Well, I hope she has another heart attack and this time it kills her."

My wife took a moment to compose herself, and then she began to clear the dishes.

1986

5 *April*
Kremlin Hospital

I should be gone by now, or dead. Where I should not be is this high-security prison run by apparatchiks where the nurses are iron maidens and the doctors all spies. A guard attempting not to look like a guard stands outside my door day and night. Not the state of my heart they are worried about, but my death-defying name and the loudness of my voice.

Visiting hours come and go. Yasha brings me the Akhmatova book I asked for, sits by my bed holding my hand for a quarter of an hour. I tell him that physically I will be fine, he must believe me, I just need to get the hell out of this hellhole.

Mom, he says in a small voice just past cracking, *you really scared me this time.*

Then I must have fallen asleep under these Gulag lights, because when I next open my eyes Yasha is gone and it is my other son sitting in a chair a meter away. Josef, whom I have not seen in some fifteen months, appears even older and more unhealthy than last time.

We stare at each other.

I should have come back for you and your sister, I tell him. *I'm sorry.*

I have spoken with your doctors and looked at your chart myself, my older son addresses me in the voice of a state-appointed medical functionary. *What you suffered was not technically cardiac arrest, rather a cardiovascular spasm caused by extreme stress. It didn't kill you this time, but you must find a way to calm down or it will kill you soon.*

You wish I was dead, I can't stop myself from accusing him.

I did not come here to fight with you, Mother.

Then why come at all, if you despise me so much?

His furious, pained, defeated eyes boring into mine, my son rises to his feet.

I am here, he says, *because you gave birth to me. I am here because to not come would be to make more of a statement about you than I care to make. I am here because soon you'll get your wish and be gone again and I will still be left wondering what I ever did to you, what any of us ever did to you, to make you treat us, your own flesh and blood, like your most hated enemies.*

Oh, Bunny, please don't . . .

No, Mother. It's too late to act as if you never did what you did. It's way too late.

13 April
Hotel Sovietsky

A week out of hospital. Yasha and I still waiting for decisions about our future to find their way from Gorbachev to Ligachev and the Central Committee to the embassies and various shadows on the ground. Gatekeepers and gates. Waiting for passports and passage. Yasha's term at the Friends' School begins in a week, so perhaps they will let him leave first.

If I could give him anything I would give him this: let him go free not only from this country of poisoned families and broken manifestos but from me. Let him, for once, live his own mistakes instead of his mother's.

I have been the ruin of too many children already.

A minute ago, I heard him stirring with unhappy restlessness in the maid's cot on the other side of our room. I went and stood by him, tugging the edge of the blanket to cover his exposed feet.

Telling myself: *He is not a man yet, thank God. There are things he cannot understand. My time on this earth may be measured now only in memories, but he is still the unwritten future.*

Mom?

His eyes have opened and found me standing over him like a watchdog.

My darling.

What if they never let us leave?

Don't be silly. Go back to sleep.

But what if they don't?

Listen to me, my love. Are you listening? If I have to, I will call George Kennan, the CIA, the New York Fucking Times, Gorbachev and Gorbachev's mother—I will call everyone there is on the planet, and I will make such a scene that in the end they will beg, beg us to leave their miserable country and never come back. Do you believe me?

Yasha's smile is slow and sleepy. *I believe you, Mom.*

Good. Now go back to sleep. When you wake up, we'll be in another country.

LETTER

16 April 1986
Zurich → London

Dear Peter,

I write you today like a god, ten thousand meters in the sky, flying at a speed that would make gods weep. But if I'm a god this incarnation is a tragic absurdity, for I am traveling backwards, not forwards, in my life; blind, not all-seeing; humbled, not proud.

Any hour now—with datelines and deadlines I have lost track—Yasha, five feet, seven inches tall and a month before his fifteenth birthday, will arrive at his beloved Friends' School in Saffron Walden, which has offered its former student a very generous scholarship for the remainder of his studies there. It was insisted by the Soviets that he travel ahead of me, bearing his brand-new American passport and exit visa procured at the U.S. Embassy following my meeting with Comrade Ligachev of the Central Committee. ("The Motherland will survive without you," he told me. "The question is: Will you survive without the Motherland?")

I am going to live in London this time. My old Cambridge neighbor Fiona Driscoll, lover of Irish breakfast tea and action films, has kindly arranged for me to stay in a North Kensington charity home for "distressed gentlefolk and indigent people," where I will have a single room and shared kitchen and also a shared bathroom with other distressed and indigent residents. Furniture will come from a charity truck, not the biggest humiliation of my life. This English society, funded by a nice man with a "Sir" to his name, will pay sixty pounds a week to cover my lodging, food, and so on. Fiona cheerily reports, with her ability to smell roses in winter, that my fellow boarders include "a Chinese cook, a reformed alcoholic, and a gay man of twenty-four."

I will meet them all. I am not afraid. But it is all a black mirror somehow, what is happening. This stopover in Zurich. This Swiss plane. This long look down, once again, through a small window.

And here, just in time to keep away catastrophic depression, comes the pretty Swiss Air stewardess with extrafine stockings, asking would I like another vodka martini?

You bet I would.

Where are you now, Mr. Staehelin? What have I done to you? Mrs. Staehelin toasts you anyway. You and I were here before, remember? It was you who brought me across this ocean. You spread your proverbial jacket over the water so I could make the crossing like a lady. I was no lady, but I enjoyed every moment of the journey.

Your loving

Svetlana

EDITOR'S NOTE

The teashop doorbell tinkles softly, and a squat, heavy-set old woman, with rheumy eyes and broken red veins ribboning her cheeks, peers suspiciously inside. It is a crisp winter morning in a remote West Country seaside village, and the place is deserted. Even so, she pulls down her black beret, raises the collar of her camel overcoat, and requests a table in the most conspiratorial corner. Svetlana Evans (née Stalin)—her voice a strange mixture of drawing-room English and East European idioms—says, "Tell me please, how did you find me here?"

—*Daily Mail*, 15 February 1996

LETTER

8 April 1996
Cornwall, England

Dear Peter,
You were with me just a few short days ago—such surprise, and so strange to write it now—so perhaps this letter reaches Princeton before you. Would you give my hugs to your Jean, who has not been little for many years? She will not remember crazy "Aunt Lana" from long ago, but I will never forget my first American summer with your family on Block Island. Such stories in the sands of Time.

I must apologize for not allowing you to see the flat where I was living. No matter, for I have again moved house just since you were here—another charity-run flat in another Cornish village, which are all much the same, some closer to the sea than others. Closer preferably, for salt air does my mind good even if cold and damp make my joints creak and my nose run. Yasha says I have "thrown in the towel" by living unknown and poor in this boring West Country England of soggy tea parlors and sagging boats. He doesn't enjoy visiting me in these surroundings compared with his London life with girlfriend and art classes. So when you talk about your Jean I understand. You and I have reached ages when silences we have known in life have finally taught us that words alone are not always the answer. Sitting across from you in the pub under that stuffed one-eyed bird neither of us could identify, I took your hand and held it, which you let me do with the same shy courtesy I remember from our first hours together on our very first journey.

And yet, my love, do not become too quiet to yourself in your late years. This idea you still carry that despite noble exertions you have not lived some better version of yourself—or rather, that you have lived too well some lesser version you believe you were handed down by your wounded father—this does not do you justice. Your loyalty to Martha (to say nothing of your profession) stands for more than this. Choices you made and must now try to understand while there is time, the strength of the man you are who made these choices and what he means to you. I too have made choices and have a contradictory strength, which sometimes frightens these Cornish villagers, who have no real idea who I am. Perhaps, in my case, this is merely the natural product of permanent exile: such stateless state in which my dear aunt and uncle and all the disappeared members of the Alliluyev family lived, but which I have earned most of all through my failure, ever since the loss of my mother and my father's turning against me, to feel at peace anywhere in this world.

Dear Peter, I confess there are times now when my mind feels like a fist clenching (you taught me this word, remember?) itself too tightly, so that thoughts are pressed one against another and all the air, all the _freedom_, gets squeezed out and I realize to my dismay that in the end I am holding nothing. The result is what you found on your visit. How my words not in Russian cannot manage to express to an urgent enough degree what it is like inside this fist of my being. I could not describe to you how our time that afternoon turned so short. Like winter light, you were gone before the day was finished. But first you walked me out of the pub and across the road. People who saw us must have thought you were helping some bag lady, but you didn't mind. Arm in arm we crossed the green with its ancient stone well—dry now— and continued all the way to the edge of town and the river that has flowed through here since the beginning of time, and I said, "If this is the last we ever see each other—" And you cut off my words saying, "It won't be. We will see each other again." And you sounded so certain that all the rest of that day and evening, after you left me there by the river, I believed you.

Have you ever read Nabokov's autobiography: "The years are passing, my dear, and presently nobody will know what you and I know."

My love always,

Svetlana

I didn't want to leave her standing alone by the river. I didn't want to leave her at all. I wanted to walk her back to her flat as the sky began to fade and the chill came down; to see her safe inside, where she would stay; someplace where I would be able to find her again.

Because I would find her. I always would, somehow, no matter how much time passed between us. I believed this.

But she would not let me walk her back to her flat. And I had a plane to catch; a wife to return to. And so, in the end, I left her there: an old woman, facing away across a river in a foreign town, staring at ghosts.

It was the last time I ever saw her.

LETTER

12 November 2010
Spring Green, Wisconsin

My dearest Peter,
What can I say to comfort you after such sad loss of your Mar-
tha? I am not the person she would have chosen to give such
comfort, this we both know. And yet one way and another, how-
ever unlikely, my life and hers did cross and a kind of intimacy
discovered us where we were hiding.

Do not punish yourself. This is what I wish to say: anyone
who has never committed mistakes of the heart has never com-
mitted himself bravely enough to life. So yes, you perhaps had
more courage than either of you expected. Did she have as much
as you? I don't know. But I know that you did not leave her. You
accompanied her until the end. This is much more than I have
ever done for another.

There is something else I know and wish to tell you. You have
always been a far stronger and braver man than you ever be-

lieved, with a capacity for love that is not an accident of your experience, but rather its reward.

And you have left your mark on me.

So, my love, do not be lonely in this new solitude that has come to you. An old lady in Wisconsin holds you close in her thoughts. She herself is almost across the bridge of this life, stopping here and there to record the view while there is still light. And, with all her heart, to remember how it truly was.
My love always,
Svetlana

CODA

On November 22, 2011, Svetlana Iosifovna Alliluyeva, the only daughter of Joseph Stalin, died from complications due to advanced cancer in the hospital at Pine Valley assisted living facility in Richland Center, Wisconsin. She was eighty-five years old and had always believed she would die in November, the same month as her mother's suicide. Officially she was an American citizen, though as she claimed to a local journalist—the last she would ever speak to—a year before her passing, she was "not American, not Russian, neither this thing or that thing but always now <u>between</u> these things, which is the tragedy of my life."

According to his website, Jacob "Yasha" Evans is a "video artist and professional digital archivist" living in Seattle, Washington, with his wife and son, whose names are not given. His photograph shows a lean, handsome man in early middle age with strong cheekbones, light-streaked brown eyes, and his mother's (and grandfather's) thick reddish hair.

I do hereby authorize and demand that following my death my body be cremated to ashes and spread by considerate person or persons into the Atlantic Ocean, where the waves touch the shore of the beautiful Block Island, USA.

—Lana Evans, Last Will and Testament

And so she was.

AUTHOR'S NOTE

In the spring of 1967, a young New York lawyer named Alan U. Schwartz traveled to Switzerland under CIA cover to meet a Russian woman and escort her secretly into the United States. The woman, Svetlana Alliluyeva, was the only daughter and surviving child of Joseph Stalin, ruler of the Soviet Union from the mid-1920s until his death in 1953 and unquestionably among the most lethal, ruthless, and monstrous dictators the world has ever known. The young lawyer was my father.

On the wall of our house while I was growing up was a photograph of him standing beside Svetlana on the tarmac of John F. Kennedy Airport facing a forest of microphones. Svetlana spent most of that August (when I was two) with my family—the first of numerous such visits over the next several years. Then, after this relatively brief period, she fell out of our lives and my thoughts until the day in late November 2011 when I read about her death—and her haunted, nomadic, improbable life—on the front page of *The New York Times*. All of which is to say that, though the character of Peter Horvath could not be more different from my father in countless ways, and—for the record—my father and Svetlana never to any degree fell in love or had an affair, the roots of my interest in this story date back to my childhood.

My father could not have been more generous to me in my years of research. He opened his expansive "Svetlana" file to me, which included fascinating original material not only from her first few years in America, when he was her legal representative, friend, and trusted adviser but from the decades afterward, when occasionally she would write to him in her stridently emotional and (as she aged) increasingly aggrieved English about various problems of her life and heart. And he patiently answered my questions about his involvement in her defection and in her first turbulent, dislocating years in America. It was with no small amount of surprise that I learned, for example, that he had been Svetlana's only representative at her sudden marriage to Frank Lloyd Wright's son-in-law in 1970; had, in fact, given away the bride.

My love and thanks to my father, then, for his help with this book that has meant so much to me. The fact that he did so while harboring some understandable ambivalence about my literary project—a nagging feeling (perhaps not uncommon among the close relatives and friends of novelists) that I might be leaving colonizing footprints on aspects of his own personal narrative—only increases my sense of gratitude and admiration for his assistance.

Twenty Letters to a Friend—the manuscript that Svetlana Alliluyeva carried with her during her defection, and that was first published, in English, in 1967—was not her only memoir, but it was certainly her best. One can question the author's perceptions about her life, times, and especially about her murderous father, with whom by most accounts she shared a loving and tender relationship until she was sixteen, but the book as a whole still rings true at its emotional core and in its very Russian expressiveness. *Twenty Letters*, however, takes Svetlana only up to 1963; it gives no hint of the seismic break with her past that she would enact only a few short years later. Her second memoir, *Only One Year*, published in 1968, was intended for that purpose. Yet where the first book was written in unhurried privacy in her home country, surrounded by her children and her living memories, the second book too often shows the stress cracks of rushed ruminations and the unsettled, confusing environment of American semi-celebrity in which she now found herself. Her final attempt at memoir, *The Faraway Music*, written in English not long before her disastrous decision to re-defect to the Soviet Union in 1982, and never published anywhere but in India, stands mostly as a long, fractious letter of disenchantment with the West at a particularly unhappy time in her life.

In addition to these three books, no current bibliography about Svetlana would be complete without Rosemary Sullivan's very good 2015 biography, *Stalin's Daughter: The Extraordinary and Tumultuous Life of Svetlana Alliluyeva*. Ms. Sullivan's exhaustive research, smart use of primary sources, and the overall empathy she displayed toward her challenging subject's contradictory nature and emotionally irreconcilable personal history all acted as a nurturing tributary to my own endeavor, while at the same time underscoring for me the fundamental differences between my novelistic intentions and those of a historian or biographer.

With such differences in mind, I think it bears repeating that *The Red Daughter* is a work of fiction. Its portrayals—from Svetlana and Peter Horvath on down—are products of my imagination. Within this fictional frame, however, I have in certain places used actual letters, or parts of them, between Svetlana and her parents and children; certain news items that were published at the time; and a section of the actual psychological profile of Svetlana done by the CIA at the American Embassy in Delhi in the days following her initial defection. The "private journals of Svetlana Alliluyeva 1967–2011" depicted in these pages are my own invention—to my knowledge, there were no such journals—as is the voice in which they are written.

There were other works too, to varying degrees and in various ways, which helped light my passage through the years of research: Simon Sebag Montefiore's pair of vivid histories, *Young Stalin* and *Stalin: The Court of the Red Tsar;* Wendell Steavenson's evocative and perspicacious book about her time living in Georgia, *Stories I Stole;* Harold Zellman and Roger Friedland's tell-all account, *The*

Fellowship: The Untold Story of Frank Lloyd Wright and the Taliesin Fellowship; Priscilla J. Henken's far quieter *Taliesin Diary: A Year with Frank Lloyd Wright;* Adam Hochschild's *The Unquiet Ghost: Russians Remember Stalin;* Francis Spufford's historical novel *Red Plenty;* the great Belarussian investigative journalist and nonfiction prose writer Svetlana Alexievich's *Secondhand Time: The Last of the Soviets;* and Nicholas Thompson's March 2014 *New Yorker* article, "My Friend, Stalin's Daughter."

My thanks to all, and many more. One writes alone but never in a vacuum: my wife, Aleksandra, and son, Garrick (and my dog, Griffin, too) are my constant guarantors of this truth, for which I am forever grateful. Onward, with love.

J.B.S.
Brooklyn, New York

ACKNOWLEDGMENTS

One day in the spring of my last year of college, I took the train down from Boston to meet the literary agent Binky Urban in New York for the first time. Binky had read a hundred pages of fiction I'd written about a young man living in Japan and had sent me an encouraging note. I very much doubt that she expected me to arrive at her office in person later that week. But arrive I did. And she has been by my side, and had my back, ever since. She has my profound gratitude and deepest affection.

My extraordinary editor, Susanna Porter, arrived in my life when I most needed her, just as I was finishing the first draft of *The Red Daughter,* and with patient wisdom and miraculous grace guided me through the many further drafts that it required. Susanna is that rare thing: a teller of hard truths whom one always looks forward to hearing from. I was, and am, so excited and thankful to be working with her.

My thanks also to David Ebershoff, whose comments about *The Red Daughter* in its early stages showed the fine perceptiveness mixed with clear-eyed literary ruthlessness that have made him not only a wonderful editor but the excellent novelist that he is.

Finally, a team of very talented people at Random House took my final draft of this novel and turned it into the published book it is today: Emily Hartley in editorial; Carrie Neill, Melissa Sanford, and Katie Tull in publicity and marketing; Paolo Pepe, who designed such a stirring cover; Debbie Glasserman, Kelly Chian, and Susan Brown, who added their skills in text design, production editorial, and copyediting respectively; and, in the publisher's office, Avideh Bashirrad, Susan Kamil, and Andy Ward. My sincere thanks to all.